PI
D. HAF

THE KAFKA EFFEKT

"Reading *The Kafka Effekt* is like riding a rollercoaster that runs entirely through a kaleidoscopic tunnel."
—Ace Boggess, *The Adirondack Review*

"In *The Kafka Effekt*, D. Harlan Wilson shows himself to be a Dr. Suess for adults. He is clearly encouraging us to push to new levels of thought and imagination—only in his case the Hat is in the Cat."
—G. Wells Taylor, *The Wildclown Chronicle*

"Throw out any preconceived concepts or notions you may have about your perception of this reality and all of its trappings, and be in awe as a new one stretches out before you in *The Kafka Effekt*. From the opening word of the first story, all the way through to the last period of the last tale, you will laugh, ponder, and cringe at the words on the pages as they form meanings different than the way you ever knew them to exist."
—Diana Bennet, *Dream Forge Magazine*

"If you're open to the gleeful tweaking of literary conventions, *The Kafka Effekt* should satisfy you like literary candy."
—James Michael White, *SF Reader*

"This is without a doubt the most peculiar and surprising set of short stories I have ever had the pleasure to read. Demanding that you revise your opinion of reality, this collection is truly following in Kafka's footsteps."
—Eva Almeida, *E-Book Reviews Weekly*

STRANGER
ON THE
LOOSE

STORIES BY

D. HARLAN WILSON

ERASERHEAD PRESS

Acknowledgement is made to the following publications in which these stories first appeared:

"Restaurant": *3 A.M. Magazine*, 2002. "The Groundhog that Didn't Know He Was a Man": *Eclectica*, 2001. "Cops and Bodybuilders": *3 A.M. Magazine*, 2002. "Glacier": *Redsine* (Australia), 2002. "Yak on a Hot Tin Roof": *The Dream People*, 2002. "Digging for Adults": *Bewildering Stories*, 2002. "Before the Board of Directors": *The Dream People*, 2002. "Deer in the City": *Word Riot*, 2002. "Community": *Driver's Side Airbag*, 2001. "The Impulsive Man": *Word Riot*, 2002. "The Voiceover Man": *Word Riot*, 2002. "Professor Dyspeptical's Parrot": *Wildclown Chronicle*, 2002. "Pityriasis Park": *Locus Novus*, 2002. "My Barbarian": *Eclectica*, 2001. "When a Man Walks into a Room": *McKenzie Magazine*, 2002. "Ten Flâneurs": *Muse Apprentice Guild*, 2003. "The Ostensibly Immortal Piece of Bread": *Muse Apprentice Guild*, 2003. "Stranger on the Loose": *Samsara*, 2002. "Shriek": *Diagram*, 2001. "Evolution and Its Vicissitudes": *Riverbabble*, 2002. "Disney Reanimated": *Thunder Sandwich*, 2002. "On Filmnoirmaking": *Expressions*, 2002. "A Barber's Tale": *Another Realm*, 2002. "Avalanche of My Self": *Jack Magazine*, 2003.

Eraserhead Press
16455 E. Fairlynn Dr.
Fountain Hills, AZ 85268
email: ehpress@aol.com
website: www.eraserheadpress.com

ISBN 0-9729598-3-1

"We are so accustomed to disguising ourselves to others that we wind up disguised to ourselves."

> —François de la Rochefoucauld

"In nonsense is strength."

> —Kurt Vonnegut

CONTENTS

Restaurant ... 7

The Groundhog that Didn't Know He Was a Man ... 13

Cops & Bodybuilders ... 16

Glacier ... 18

Yak on a Hot Tin Roof ... 27

Digging for Adults ... 30

Before the Board of Directors ... 35

Deer in the City ... 49

Community ... 50

The Impulsive Man ... 58

The Voiceover Man ... 69

Professor Dyspeptical's Parrot ... 82

Pityriasis Park ... 86

My Barbarian ... 91

When a Man Walks into a Room ... 94

Elephant Invasion ... 112

Ten Flâneurs ... 121

The Ostensibly Immortal Piece of Bread ... 125

Stranger on the Loose ... 140

Shriek ... 149

Evolution and Its Vicissitudes ... 150

Disney Reanimated ... 152

"Fie," Said Her Knight in Shining Armor ... 158

On Filmnoirmaking ... 166

The Back of the Man's Hand ... 175

A Barber's Tale ... 179

Avalanche of My Self ... 181

Igsnay Bürdd the Animal Trainer ... 187

RESTAURANT

I ordered a ground beef sandwich with mozzarella cheese, pickles, onions and psychedelic mushrooms. The waiter was a thin, olive-skinned man with a platinum handlebar mustache. After scribbling down my order, he bowed and goose-stepped away, his long rubbery legs flying out in front of him like liquid slingshots.

While I waited for my meal, I smoked a cigarette and eavesdropped on the silence being publicized by a couple that had nothing to say to one another. They sat bolt upright in their chairs, the woman staring at the man's chin, the man staring at the woman's cleavage.

The waiter returned. "Voila, monsieur," he said, and placed a large round plate in front of me. "Be careful s'il vous plait. That is hot!"

The plate was artfully garnished with parsley, fruit slices, and precise droppings of colorful, unknown sauces. A nice thing to look at, this decor. What wasn't so nice to look at was the object positioned in the middle of the plate.

It was a human tongue.

The thing looked like it had just been yanked out of somebody's mouth a few moments ago; blood was still oozing out of its truncated backside. It had also clearly been nibbled on in places, possibly by one of the cooks that prepared it.

Concerned, I began to chew on my lower lip. "This piece of food has been nibbled on by somebody," I explained, eyeing the waiter. "And it's still bleeding." I leaned over and sniffed the tongue. It smelled like a dirty earthworm. I eyed the waiter again. "On top of all these things, I didn't even order

7

this piece of food. Take it away."

The waiter stared at me. I couldn't tell what he was thinking.

The waiter casually lifted his hand over his head and slapped me across the face with all of his might. Now I had a good idea what he was thinking.

"How dare you antagonize me with such impudence," he remarked in a perfectly cool, perfectly smart-assed voice. "You have no right to speak to me in that fashion, mon ennemi. Whether or not this piece of food is inadequate is totally irrelevant. What is relevant here is your reaction to that which is irrelevant!"

Wide-eyed with determinacy, the waiter placed his fists akimbo on his hips and waited for my response. His powerful slap has caused my face immense pain. I could feel the bright red imprint of his hand on my throbbing cheek, and my eyes were watering uncontrollably. I wasn't crying; the slap had simply turned my tear ducts on like faucets and I was having difficulty turning them off.

"Take your time, vous âne," the waiter said, sensing my struggle. "I will wait here patiently until you feel decent enough to equip me with the apology that is my due."

His audacity gave me the strength I needed to dry up. I threw my chair out from under me and stood erect in one explosive motion. The couple I had been eavesdropping on took their eyes off of one another momentarily. However, unlike most of the other diners in the restaurant, they didn't look in my direction.

Without a word I lifted my hand over head, held it there for a second or two, and returned what the waiter had given to me. I slapped him so hard his handlebar mustache flew off his face and struck a diner sitting on the far end of the restaurant in the eye. The diner cursed loudly as he toppled backwards out of his chair.

I said, "There's your apology, you smug sack of bullshit.

8

There's your apology." Nodding in triumph, I picked the tongue up off of my plate, delicately, using my thumb and index finger, as if the tongue might be a dead tarantula I was going to throw in the garbage. Then I dropped the tongue on the floor and stomped on it, as if it might be a live tarantula I wanted to kill. "That's what I think of you," I added.

The waiter showed little sign of being in pain. His facial expression was calm and sedate, and his posture was casual. His cheek, on the other hand, was grotesquely stained by a bright red hand mark, and his overlip looked naked and ill at ease without its mustache to cover and comfort it. I knew he was stewing inside.

"I get the impression that the monsieur is dissatisfied in some way," said the waiter.

"Stop calling me monsieur," I replied. "Stop using French words altogether. You don't even have a French accent. You have a crummy Midwestern accent and you sound like a moron. Knock it off."

"And if I don't?"

"Then you don't. The point is, you're a douche bag."

People started to whisper amongst themselves now, placing gentlemen's bets on who would win the battle that was about to unfold. It happened all the time in the restaurant and that's why nobody bet for money; if they did, nobody would be able to afford to eat there. So they picked their man, grasped hands and exchanged sportsmanlike nods.

"Do you challenge me?" said the waiter.

"I challenge you," I said.

"Are you prepared to taste my wrath?"

"I'm prepared to beat the living Christ out of you."

"Whatever will be will be."

The waiter took two paces backwards. He flung his arms out so that they were parallel with the floor. He tilted back his head, opened his mouth and made a loud birdcall. Immediately a furious herd of waiters and bus boys flowed out

9

of the kitchen and lined up at his side. There were about twenty of them in all. Most were hunch-backed, fierce-looking, plated in armor constructed out of the hides of giant Egor beetles, and drooling and growling like mad dogs.

The waiter allowed his arms to fall to his side. He cracked his neck. Pursed his lips. Held his breath, puffed out his cheeks . . . and the same mustache I had slapped off of his face popped back onto his face. "You see the piece of trouble you've gotten yourself into, oui?" he sneered, twirling one of the new mustache's handlebars around a fingertip. "Let me tell you something: it's about to get worse."

I was not afraid. Little did this prima donna know that, being a man of society, a man of the crowd as it were, I had my resources, too. Rather than fling my arms out, I cupped my hands to my mouth and sounded off a hogcall so shrill and raging it splintered one of the restaurant's windows and shattered more than a few of the restaurant's thin-stemmed martini and wine glasses. Diners and would-be aggressors alike grabbed their ears as the insanity roared out of my lungs.

Afterwards there was a silence.

"Impressive," said the waiter, blinking. He glanced around the restaurant vigilantly, expectantly . . . then smirked and shrugged. "But ultimately ineffective, I'm afraid. And now I shall beat and torment you until you are completely deranged. Mes frères—attack!"

The waiter and his entourage fell on me.

I was not beneath them when they landed. I had backflipped onto a tabletop, the one that belonged to the couple that had nothing to say to one another. I promptly called each of them an obscene word, kicked in their faces with my steel-toed boots and knocked them onto the floor (once a battle in the restaurant starts, anything goes and you can let anybody know what you really think of them, whether they threaten you with their mouths and fists or, in the case of these two degenerates, with their ennui-ridden existences).

A few seconds later the boy bands responded to my hogcall. As always, they responded late. But not too late. Never too late.

I don't particularly care for the music produced and promulgated by boy bands. But I make a point of having the members of the bands at my beck and hogcall at all hours of the day and night. You never know when you might need a helping hand, after all, and who better to lend you that helping hand than a spunky bunch of full-grown short men impersonating horny young boys.

The waiter and his cronies were still on the floor. They thought I was beneath them and their arms and legs were moving up and down like the pistons of an engine in an attempt to smash and deliver me into oblivion. They quickly realized their mistake, however, and got to their feet just in time to watch the boys bands, dressed in uniforms that were a cross between glittery disco outfits and SS Nazi fatigues, repel into the restaurant from the ceiling: ropes fell to the floor and legions of men-boys slid down them, hollering like lunatics and singing bits of loud-mouthed, cheesy song lyrics. I didn't have to do a thing after that. All I did was point at the waiter and say, "I'll show *you* ineffective."

And the boy bands attacked.

Having no sense of discretion, they attacked waiters and bus boys as well as diners and even the bartenders and cooks in the back—everybody in the place except me. Some of them used throwing stars and numchucks to do their dirty work, some used Tommy guns and Indiana Jones whips, some just used their impeccably manicured bare hands, and as they proceeded to beat and maim everyone in sight, they paused now and again to hit high notes and do breakdance moves.

It was over very quickly. In less than two minutes the boy bands had cleaned house. Saluting me each in their own special way, they moonwalked one after the other out the front door and were gone. I had calmly observed the entire battle from the tabletop onto which I had backflipped. The restaurant was demolished. Body parts of chairs and tables were scattered everywhere. Body parts of people were scattered everywhere, too.

The waiter that had accosted me lay on the floor. He wasn't dead, but he had been beaten badly. He moaned like a sick cow.

I crossed my arms over my chest and told the waiter that he shouldn't pick fights with monsters. Then I told him to get up and fetch me my ground beef sandwich, but he was too dazed and defeated to hear me, let alone stand up.

Sighing, I hopped off the table and picked the human tongue I had stomped on off the floor. It wasn't the prettiest piece of food I had ever seen, and it wasn't a piece of food I would consciously seek out for consumption. But it was edible, it was perfectly edible, so I dusted the tongue off and began to nibble on it as I made my way out of the restaurant into the city night.

THE GROUNDHOG THAT DIDN'T KNOW HE WAS A MAN

There was a groundhog that didn't know he was a man. I stuck my mouth in his hole and tried to tell him what he didn't know, but he wouldn't listen. "Go away," he mumbled.

"Fine," I replied.

I ran into a nearby hotel and stole a mirror off the wall. A bellhop saw me out of the corner of his eye and started chasing me. During the chase, the groundhog that didn't know he was a man stuck his head out of his hole. He sniffed the air with his sharp aquiline nose and looked around with his wide blue eyes. People clapped. Some people threw their hands up in the air and said, "Alleluia!" It wasn't Groundhog Day, but people were out and about anyway.

The bellhop got caught in a revolving door that, the moment he stepped into it, accelerated to 75 mph and wouldn't let him out. I shook a finger at him as I blustered through a normal door, the big mirror awkwardly tucked beneath my armpit.

Outside the hotel, the groundhog that didn't know he was a man was peacock-prancing around his hole in a perfect circle, his chest thrust out, his arms akimbo, his knees gracefully jabbing at the sky. After his third revolution people started to pass out, they were so happy. I said, "Stop encouraging him." The people that had passed out woke up and shook their heads no at me. Puckering up my lips at them, I dislodged the mirror from my armpit and held it out in front of the groundhog that didn't know he was a man.

He saw his reflection and stopped peacock-prancing.

13

"Oh my," he said. He began to touch his naked body all over the place. He touched his nose and chin, he touched his nipples and love handles, he touched his elbows, he touched his belly button ("It's an outie!" he hollered), he touched his genitals, he touched his thighs and his ankles and all ten of his toes, one at a time . . .

"See?" I said. The groundhog that didn't know he was a man nodded, then turned to his hole and swan dove into it. When he emerged again he was wearing a giant groundhog suit that looked more like a stuffed animal groundhog than a real one. Now he began to poodle-prance around his hole in a jaded elliptical shape. People cheered. Some people removed sandwiches from picnic baskets and stuffed them into their delirious grins . . .

strike a
pose

COPS & BODYBUILDERS

A bodybuilder in a purple spandex G-string snuck into my home and started to pose. His tan seemed to have been painted onto his skin, and his muscles seemed to twitch and flex of their own volition. His grin was as white as the image of God.

I reached underneath the couch cushion I was sitting on. Pulled out a crowbar. "I'll teach you to invade a man's privacy," I exclaimed, and made like I was going to swing at him. He didn't flinch. He went on posing, turning his broad back to me and tightening up his gluteus maximus.

Impressed, I couldn't help making a comment. "Nice gluts," I said. The bodybuilder thanked me, straightened out one of his arms and exhibited a sublime tricep muscle. I made a frog face. "That's pretty nice, too. But could you leave please? My wife will be home soon and if she sees us here together she might get suspicious. And anyway you're breaking the law. You can't just sneak into somebody's house, start posing and expect everything to be all right. Please go."

The bodybuilder shook his head. "I'm sorry but I can't do that. Once I start posing, there's no stopping me." He placed a foot out in front of him and mockingly jiggled his profound thigh muscles back and forth. "I may take five now and then to shoot up an anabolic cocktail and fix myself a protein shake, but otherwise, you're stuck with me. You're stuck with me for a long, long time."

I called the bodybuilder an asshole. Then I called 911. "You're going to jail for what you've done," I snorted. The body-builder shrugged. The shrug was as much a pose as it was a gesture of indifference.

16

In light of the severity of the crime I had reported on the phone, the police didn't bother knocking on my door when they arrived. They simply crashed through my door like a stampede of psychotic oxen. There were three of them, each equipped with a bushy handlebar mustache, each wearing two articles of clothing: a ten-gallon police hat and a purple spandex G-string. Their tans seemed to have been painted onto their skin, and their muscles seemed to twitch and flex of their own volition. Their grins were as white as the image of God.

"What seems to be the problem here, sir?" asked the cop in charge, and struck a pose. It was an impressive Front Double Bicep pose. Following his lead, the rest of the cops also struck it.

I said, "This bodybuilder is an intruder. Take him away."

"We weren't talking to you," replied the cop in charge. He and his colleagues synchronously shifted into an equally impressive Side Chest pose. "We were talking to the bodybuilder."

Confused, I glanced at the bodybuilder. He nodded at me. "This man is inhospitable," he said. "Take him away."

The cops made belittling, sniggering comments about my less than rock hard body as they frisked me, cuffed me, and led me out to the squad car . . .

GLACIER

One morning Rakehell Bartleberry walked outside of his house to retrieve the paper that was sitting at the bottom of his driveway. As he shuffled down the driveway in his slippers and robe, he noticed that the sun was abnormally bright. He didn't take the time to pause and scrutinize the sun, though, and it wasn't until he actually bent over to pick up the paper that he realized it wasn't the sun's fault everything was so bright—it was the fault of the glacier laying in his front yard. The glacier was very big and very white and was reflecting the sun's rays all over the place. The glacier itself, which might have been as large as the Hawaiian island Molokai, was all over the place, too.

Rakehell walked over to the foot of the glacier and frowned at it. "Where'd you come from?" he asked. The glacier didn't reply. Annoyed, he kicked it a little with his toes. "Get outta here," he told it.

The glacier didn't move a muscle. Its broad frontal lip lay there on top of his grass and the rest of its body lay there on top of the vast suburb that surrounded his grass. It wasn't melting either. A cloudless 75 degrees out today and the glacier, as far as Rakehell could tell, hadn't even broken a sweat. It worried him. If the glacier didn't melt, there was a good chance it would continue to make its way across his front yard and erode and ruin the whole damn thing. Rakehell spent a lot of time doing yard work. He couldn't allow any of his neighbors to have a better-looking yard than his, and he liked how mowing the grass and trimming the hedges and pulling the weeds built up his muscles. He was also an incorrigible neat freak and had a tendency to pass out when things fell out of place. Whether

18

these things happened to be runaway hairs on his meticulously combed head or runaway glaciers on his suburb and front lawn made no difference.

Rakehell kicked the glacier one more time before passing out. When he woke up, his face was sunburnt and the lip of the glacier was laying on top of his foot. "It's moving!" he yelled. A few seconds later he had a panic attack. The glacier had a firm grip on his foot and he didn't think he had the strength to pull it loose. But the panic attack lent him the necessary strength, and after he retrieved the foot he got up and ran inside his house.

"Mrs. Bartleberry!" he screamed. "Mrs. Bartleberry! Grab the prepubescents and pack our bags. We're leaving this place!" Mrs. Bartleberry was Rakehell's wife. Her first name was Gwendolynne but he preferred to call her by her marital title. She would have liked him to call her Gwen, or better yet honey or darling, but she would rather have him call her Mrs. Bartleberry and be happy than call her something else and be sad.

Mrs. Bartleberry peeked her head out of the kitchen. "What's that, dear?"

Rakehell stomped his foot on the wooden tiles of the foyer. One of the tiles broke. "I said let's go! LET'S *GOOOO* . . ." He passed out again. When he woke up, Mrs. Bartleberry and their six prepubescents, Furter, Ianesco, Sublimina, Bartleberry, Gregious and Yicfung, were all looking down on him with puzzled expressions. Sublimina's puzzled expression had a hint of disgust in it. But not as much disgust as Rakehell had in his own expression.

"Jesus H. Christ," he griped. "Can't I stay conscious for two seconds?"

The prepubescents looked at each other. Mrs. Bartleberry said, "What happened?"

Rakehell clumsily got to his feet. He stumbled around the living room for a few seconds in a daze. His family watched him with voyeuristic intensity.

19

Rakehell steadied himself. He turned to his family and said, "There's a glacier in the front yard. I don't know where it came from and I don't know why it's here, but it's laying out there like a dead cow in the road and it won't go away. Not only that—*it's moving*. Not very fast, but it's moving all right, and it's headed right in our direction. We have to leave. Do you understand?"

The puzzled expression returned to Mrs. Bartleberry's face. The prepubescents, in contrast, all sprouted masks of fear. "Are we going to die?" bleated Ianesco.

"I don't know," replied Rakehell. "Maybe."

"You're scaring the prepubescents, dear," said Mrs. Bartleberry.

"Sorry," said Rakehell.

Mrs. Bartleberry cocked her head. "Are you?"

"Honestly? No. But at least I'm not lying to you people. Now listen, I want everybody and everything packed up in the SUV lickety-split. We may or may not have much time. That glacier's a slow mover but for all we know it could speed up and be going 80 miles per hour in the next few seconds, and I don't wanna be underneath that big bastard when it's hauling ass like that. So let's get a move on!"

The Bartleberrys scattered like a cluster of ants that some-body spit on. Twenty minutes later they were all inside the SUV. Rakehell and Mrs. Bartleberry sat in the front seats with plenty of room to stretch out. The kids sat behind them, balled up in between the nooks and crannies of the furniture, appli-ances, clothing, toys, sporting equipment, booze and canned goods that had been crammed back there. Being balled up like that was very painful. All six of the prepubescents were crying, but they made sure to cry softly so that their father didn't get upset and pass out. The prepubescents were abnormally aware of and attentive to their parents' emotions, especially their father's, who, since he lacked the psychological capacity to internalize anything, externalized everything.

20

Rakehell placed the SUV in reverse and backed out of the garage and driveway. He hit the breaks. He placed the SUV in drive and drove forward . . . and ran into the glacier. "Shit," he said. He placed the car in reverse and backed into the driveway, hit the breaks, placed the car in drive and drove forward, this time in the other direction. But the other direction consisted of a cul-de-sac encircled by square yellow houses with square green yards in front of them, and after Rakehell rounded it he ran into the glacier again. "We're trapped!" he exclaimed, and passed out. The prepubescents took the opportunity to cry louder than they've ever cried before, even louder than when they emerged from Mrs. Bartleberry's womb. Mrs. Bartleberry said, "There there, little ones," then popped a hot tamale in her mouth and blew on Rakehell's face until he woke up and the prepubescents toned down.

"Where am I, Mrs. Bartleberry?" asked Rakehell.

"You're right here," she replied.

"Oh."

"Oh?"

"Yes. Oh."

"Daddy," said a purple-faced Yicfung. He was on the brink of suffocation and unable to stand it any longer. "I think I'm g-g-gonna die."

Rakehell looked over his shoulder. "Behave yourself." He backed the car up a little, told his wife and prepubescents to stay put, and got out.

The sky had yet to be tarnished by a cloud and the sun was much hotter now. But the glacier still wasn't melting. Rakehell strode over to it. He kneeled down in front of it, blinked at it . . . Nope, no wetness on the thing, no wetness at all; it was as milky and frosty and lackluster as any old Antarctic glacier. "You should be gleaming with moisture," whispered Rakehell, shaking his head. "*Gleaming*, I'm telling you."

Rakehell got to his feet. He was disturbed, but not so disturbed that he was going to pass out again. Not yet at least.

21

Except for the cul-de-sac, and the houses and yards surrounding the cul-de-sac, and his own house and yard (well, most of his yard), the glacier lay on top of everything, in every direction. It was as if, the night before, somebody had dropped a small, bright white mountain range on his suburb. But that was impossible. The thing had to have crawled over here. But from where? The nearest glacier was something like 1000 miles away. Was he supposed to believe that it had crawled 1000 miles in one night, in eight (give or take) hours? That means it must have been going 125 (give or take) miles per hour! No way, Rakehell told himself, although he couldn't help smirking at the prospect of a gigantic hunk of ice going that fast. The only other explanation he could think of was that the glacier had been hiding underground, underneath his suburb, and, for some reason, decided to come up last night. But how would it have come up? Unless there was a manhole the size of a mountain range somewhere nearby, forget about it.

"I despise you," Rakehell told the glacier. As he turned to the SUV he thought he heard the glacier reply, but he was too full of hate to turn back around and confront it again.

"I think Yicfung's dead," said Mrs. Bartleberry as Rakehell hopped back into the driver's seat and passed out. His wife didn't blow on him this time, but he woke up almost immediately, grumbling, "I thought I told you to mind your manners back there." He drove the SUV into the garage, closed the garage, considered cracking open all the windows and locking all the doors and keeping the SUV running, rejected the consideration, then ordered everybody to unload and unpack everything while he calmly retired to the wine cellar to get drunk. He unpacked his vast store of wine from the SUV himself.

In virtual darkness, Rakehell Bartleberry sat on a downy patch of cobwebs and guzzled bottle after bottle of his favorite wine until he passed out. He stayed passed out for a while and had a nightmare about the glacier. It was extremely hypertense and gory, this nightmare, but his head was pounding so hard

22

when he woke up he couldn't remember it. He could barely remember his name.

He went upstairs and swallowed a handful of aspirin and a two-liter of spring water. While he drank the spring water he walked around his house, making sure the prepubescents and Mrs. Bartleberry had unloaded the SUV and put everything back where it was supposed to be. Along the way he stubbed his toe on the corpse of Yicfung. No doubt his wife had purposely left the corpse in the hallway for him to stub his toe on. "Ouch!" he yelped, dropping the spring water. The glass butt of the bottle landed on Yicfung's anemic, bug-eyed face and left a little dent in his forehead.

Mrs. Bartleberry stepped out of the closet she had been hiding in. "I hope you're proud of yourself," she said. She adjusted the tight plaid apron that accentuated her tight hourglass figure, a figure she maintained without regular exercise despite how many times she had given birth. "That's another prepubescent down the drain. Now pick that dead thing up and take it out back. While you're digging a hole, I'll go upstairs and round up the other prepubescents. The ones that are *alive.*"

The Bartleberry's back yard was a cemetery in which twenty-two of their prepubescents had, after untimely deaths, been planted. All of them were killed by freak accidents that usually involved something (a suitcase, an anvil, a safe, a wild turkey, a hostage, etc.) being thrown out of an airplane passing overhead and falling on them; the rest had died of either heart disease or tuberculosis. Twenty-two little gravestones stuck straight out of the cemetery's green, handsomely groomed grass in four rows of five and one row of two, and as Rakehell dug a hole for Yicfung, he twitched and spit and muttered obscenities, partly because Yicfung was gone, partly because he wasn't in the mood for manual labor, partly because he was hung over— mostly because he was angry at the glacier.

Once Rakehell had finished digging, he cradled Yicfung's

body with one of his feet and swept it into the hole. Mrs. Bartleberry and the prepubescents were standing around the hole in a half circle. They were all straight-faced except for Gregious and Furter, whose faces fidgeted impatiently. "This never would've happened if that damned glacier hadn't come along," panted Rakehell. "I'm gonna teach that damned thing a lesson, me. I'm not kidding."

Rakehell caught Mrs. Bartleberry rolling her eyes. "You dare doubt me?" he spat, pointing an index finger at his wife when he said "You" and a thumb at himself when he said "me". In response Mrs. Bartleberry puffed out her lips. The prepubescents, seeing their mother's lips, copied her.

Infuriated, Rakehell accused his family of hating him and told them to go inside. Everyone obeyed except for Gregious and Furter: the two youngsters wanted to play hide-and-seek in the cemetery. But when Rakehell growled at them they obeyed, too. Alone with his thoughts, he passed out, woke up, buried Yicfung, erected a gravestone, and laid a piece of fresh sod down on the newly unearthed patch of dirt in front of it.

After saying a little prayer in Yicfung's name, Rakehell speedwalked to his garage and got an axe.

He ran across his front yard towards the glacier like an Indian running into battle, the axe poised over his head, a war cry ripping out of the gash that was his mouth . . . He fell on the glacier. He hacked and hacked and hacked on it, his war cry evolving into a series of guttural squawks that sounded something like a heated conversation between two Neanderthals.

The glacier wouldn't break. It wouldn't even chip. But Rakehell was determined to make his mark and he continued to hack away until the head of the axe broke off, flew through his front window and slammed blade-first into the forehead of Bartleberry Bartleberry, the youngest of the prepubescents and by far Rakehell's favorite. Rakehell passed out when the axe head came off, when he found out Bartleberry was dead, and when he was burying Bartleberry in the back yard.

After saying a little prayer in Bartleberry's name, Rakehell speedwalked to his garage and, this time, got a pile driver.

"I'll teach you not to gleam with moisture on a hot day!" Rakehell shouted, fumbling with the pile driver's controls. He imagined the thrill of reducing the glacier to a bunch of ice cubes, the whole damned glacier, which was about to get a little taste of his wrath . . . if only he could figure out how to start the pile driver. But there was no start button on the thing. No ripcord either. And it had been so long since he had used the pile driver . . . When *was* the last time he used it? Had he ever used it? Why the hell did he own a pile driver anyway? He couldn't remember. Was the pile driver even his? Maybe he borrowed it from one of the neighbors. But whoever it belonged to, he couldn't get the sonuvabitch going, so he bench pressed all 150 lbs. of it over his head—he was a runty thing and only weighed 150 lbs. himself, but there was so much adrenaline pumping through his system he threw it up over his head like a ragdoll—and then, with a barbaric yawp, he slammed it down right in the middle of the piece of the glacier that was laying on his yard.

The pile driver shattered into a million pieces of steel. A few of the larger pieces lodged themselves in Rakehell's flesh and his eyes immediately watered up. He staggered to and fro, punching at the air and making dog noises, and as he staggered-punched-barked, he noticed his next door neighbor, Humidor Humphrey . . .

Humidor was busy trimming his already perfectly sculpted hedges—compared to Rakehell's not imperfectly (but not perfectly) sculpted hedges—with a toenail clippers, but he had been watching Rakehell's battle with the glacier out of his eye corners all along. When Rakehell saw him he tried his best to pretend that he didn't see him. Humidor saw that he saw him, though, and Rakehell saw that Humidor saw that he saw him, so he pretended like he hadn't been pretending not to see him and like there wasn't a glacier in his yard and he wasn't bleeding from multiple wounds and in more pain than Mrs. Bartleberry when she gave birth to their first, late child, Giddyap Bartleberry.

Rakehell said, "Hello."

"Hello there, Rakehell," tweeted Humidor with a pinky finger salute. "Nice day today, dontcha think?" Then, nodding at the glacier: "I like what you've done with your yard."

The subsequent huff from Humidor's nose and shit-eating grin on Humidor's face prompted Rakehell's eyes to roll back into his head and his knees to buckle. A few seconds later he was curled up like a fetus on the ground, bleeding, unconscious, and sucking on his thumb. He remained this way for a long time, his dreamworld oscillating back and forth between a spacetime subject to the glacier's tyranny and a spacetime that had never known the glacier at all.

Rakehell woke up. The glacier was laying on his legs, waist and halfway up his chest. His arms were loose but no matter how hard he pushed on the glacier he couldn't get it off him. He called to Mrs. Bartleberry and the prepubescents, even to his neighbors, but nobody heard him: they were all taking naps and dreaming about flying like trapeze artists over the heads of giant, cheering crowds.

YAK ON A HOT TIN ROOF

A group of firemen suddenly grew bored with the sound of the siren on their fire engine. They decided to replace the siren with a small yak, which they kidnaped from a shelter that houses hobos and animals that are not indigenous to metropolitan domains.

The firemen removed the siren and superglued the yak's hooves to the roof of the fire engine. They stared at each other and waited for a fire to start somewhere in the city.

No fire started.

Annoyed, the firemen disguised themselves as arsonists, snuck a few blocks down the street and set a building on fire. Then they ran back to the fire station, took off their disguises, put on their big red hats and uniforms, and piled into the fire engine.

"Scream!" the fireman behind the steering wheel said to the yak as the garage door creaked open and they pulled onto the street. His head was sticking out the window and he was looking up and glaring hatefully at the yak. "I said scream, you!"

The yak didn't respond. It didn't even look down at the driver and blink.

The driver told the fireman in the passenger's seat to get up there on the roof and make that yak scream. The fireman hesitated at first but then he climbed up on the roof, adopted the stance and voice of a drill sergeant, and screamed in the yak's ear. "Scream you sonuvabitch! Scream you sick motherfucker!" he screamed.

The yak made a noise that sounded like a baby burping.

"We need a new yak!" the fireman blurted. The yak nudged him in the belly with its shoulder and sent him flying off the fire engine and through the front window of a haberdasher's shop. Bowlers and fedoras spilled onto the sidewalk and street in an hysterical mudslide.

Irate, the driver told a fireman in the back seat to go make the yak scream. The fireman said he was scared of heights. The driver swore at him and told him that acrophobic fireman are oxymoronic and can't possibly exist. Reluctantly the fireman agreed. He clambered onto the roof and tried his best to scare the yak into screaming submission, but the yak nudged him off the fire engine and he flew through the front window of a haberdasher's shop, too. This time it was tandos and ten-gallon hats that flooded the sidewalk and street.

(Having a special penchant for ten-gallon hats, the driver peered at his rear view mirror in envy of the pedestrians that fell on the hats like sharks on bleeding carcasses.)

The same thing kept happening after that. One by one the firemen were ordered to climb up on the roof and so they did it and screamed at the yak and were nudged off of the fire engine into a haberdasher's shop until the only fireman left was the driver, who promptly abandoned the wheel, crawled out of his window and onto the roof. He crossed his arms over his chest and frowned at the yak. The fire engine was out of control. Cars, people and pets were leaping out of its way as it soundlessly, recklessly swerved down the street.

The fireman grabbed the yak by the neck and nearly stuck his whole face into its ear. "What's your problem!" he hollered. "We're almost at the fire and you haven't made a peep yet! You're embarrassing me! How are people supposed to know we're coming?"

The yak shrugged—not in response to the question that had been posed to it but in a fruitless attempt to free its glued hooves from the roof—before throwing its shoulder into the fireman's rib cage.

28

"Sound off!" said the fireman in a last-gasp effort to activate the yak as he sailed through the air towards that window full of hats. The effort, of course, was in vain. The fire engine rambled past the burning building and it was not until much later, when the vehicle had left the city in its dust, that the yak broke its silence.

Cruising across fields of deep empty green, the animal opened its mouth and discharged a noise loud enough to shatter reality . . .

DIGGING FOR ADULTS

A little boy was clicking his jaw. He was doing it to annoy a little girl. He was in love with her. She had pretty red hair, nice skin, and the freckles on her nose . . . well, he wanted to lick them off her face. He sensed the perverse nature of this desire, but he was too young and unfamiliar with the character of his impulses to think twice about the desire: one time was enough, and then the thought was gone . . .

As he continued to click his jaw, he could almost taste those freckles. He had to have them in his mouth right now! But he couldn't just walk up to his love and start lapping at her nose like an excited puppy. He had to get her to fall in love with him first. And the best way for a little boy to get a little girl to fall in love with him is to make her hate him by annoying the crap out of her.

Click! went his jaw. *Click! Click! Click!* His mouth opened wider and wider each time he did it, and drool began to flow down his chin.

The little girl pretended he didn't exist.

The little boy pretended that she wasn't pretending he didn't exist, and went on clicking and drooling.

Crouched down on their knees, the two children were digging for adults in the soil of the neighborhood playground. The adults in the neighborhood had disappeared a few days ago; sick of always having to take care of the children, they made a communal decision to bury themselves underground in hopes that, after a while, the children would get the hint that nobody liked them and go away. So far the endeavor was ineffective. Not only were the children not going away, they persisted in

30

trying to find the adults and dig them out of the ground. It was frustrating for the adults. But they had promised themselves to stay where they were for at least a week, dreaming of and praying for a neighborhood that was not subject to the cries and whines and whimpers and demands and threats and maligns and freakery and demonism and pathology of Young Life.

The ground beneath them was very soft and brown. They had dug up over two feet of earth a piece, but they hadn't uncovered any adults yet. They would dig for a little while longer and then move to another spot.

Click! Click! Click! Click! Click!

Eventually the little girl was forced to say something to the little boy. She didn't want to say something to him, but his jaw was driving her up the wall.

"Stop doing that," she said. "It bothers me very much. You're a very bothersome person, do you know that?"

"What?" replied the little boy, playing dumb. He clicked his jaw especially loud, so loud the group of children digging for adults on the other side of the merry-go-round heard it. They stopped digging and looked in his direction with dazed and curious expressions, as if they had just woken up from being knocked unconscious.

The little girl looked at him with an embittered expression, as if somebody had just dunked her head in a pot of garlic water. She sat back on her knees and put her tiny fists on her hipless hips. "Stop that, I said. Stop making that noise with your mouth. It's distracting me. I'm trying to concentrate. I'm trying to find my mom and dad so I can ask them if I can stay up past my bedtime. How am I supposed to do that with you doing what you're doing? You're drooling all over the place, too. You're gross. You're ugly. Go somewhere else. I was here first."

"I was here second," the little boy responded matter-of-factly, not looking up at her, continuing to dig, drool and click.

"What's that supposed to mean?"

"Nothing."

31

"It means something. Nothing means nothing."

"Except nothing."

"What?"

"Nothing. It means I was here second and you were here first and it doesn't matter one way or the other, okay?"

"I don't get it. I don't get what that means."

"That's because you're a girl and girls don't get anything. Dig your hole, whyncha?" *Click!*

"Oh!" said the little girl. "Oh! Oh! Oh!" She wanted to say something clever to the little boy, something that would make him feel as retarded as she felt right now, but she couldn't find the words. So she said "Oh!" one more time.

"Stop saying 'Oh'," said the little boy. "It's really starting to bug me and I'd appreciate it if you'd shut up. Thank you."

A deranged, wide-eyed glare overcame the little girl's face. How dare that creep! Her lips began to twitch with rage. They got to twitching so intensely that the little boy could actually hear them.

"You're lips are making a funny sound," he said. "Tell them to knock it off."

The lips pinched together as if a clothespin had been applied to them. A long, tense pause followed . . . Then the little girl calmly leaned over, as if she was going to whisper a friendly secret into the little boy's ear, and yelled, "I HATE YOUR GUTS, FREAK!!!" When she yelled, the kids over by the merry-go-round glanced at her. She cast an evil glance back at them and said, "MIND YOUR OWN BUSINESS, NERDS!!!"

Being nerds, the kids obeyed.

The little boy smiled. The little girl had told him she hated him—*that* meant she loved him. He may have been young and idiotic, but he wasn't young and idiotic enough to not know that saying you love somebody and saying you hate them means the same thing. His plan had worked. He could now lick her

32

freckles without feeling guilty about it. Just a few more louder-than-hell clicks to make sure his lover genuinely hated him, and wasn't just saying that to make him behave . . .

The little girl stood up and threw her fists down at her sides. "I'm going over there. You stay here. Don't follow me, or I'll scream. I hope you die!" She waited for a response. Didn't get one. She stomped away.

Proud of himself, the little boy snickered under his breath. He would give the little girl a minute or two before disobeying her command and allowing true love to run its course. He scooped another handful of dirt out of his hole.

And exposed the face of an adult. The face was pretending to be asleep, but he knew otherwise: it was the face of his mother and she was always pretending to be asleep. Ever since his father left them and moved to Gary, Indiana . . .

"I know you're faking it," he said. There was no reply.

He clicked his jaw once . . . twice . . . a third time . . .

The eyes of his mother opened. They were red, worn, sickly eyes that looked like they had been crying for years. "Keep it up young man," she said, "and your jaw will fall off. It'll fall right off of your face. Then what the hell will you do?"

The little boy shrugged.

"Don't shrug at me. Listen to me. I want you to stop acting up and mind your goddamn manners. Do you understand?"

The little boy shook his head no.

"Yes you do. You understand me perfectly. Now be a good boy and bury me. Bury me, and don't ever try to dig me up again. Pack a bag and move to a different country, too."

The little boy blinked at his mother. She blinked back at him.

Then: *Click!*

Maddened, his mother ordered him to go to his room. He refused. She told him to get a handkerchief and wipe the drool off of his face. He refused. She called him a bastard. He called her a bitch. They continued to bicker until a ball of dirt fell in her mouth and she choked on it. Her face convulsed, and her eyes rolled back into her head.

The little boy knocked on his mother's forehead as if it was a door. "Anybody home?" he asked. But he knew the answer to that question.

He pushed all of the dirt he had dug up back into the hole, then stood and patted it down with his feet. When he was finished, he stared down at the grave and worried, for a fleeting moment, about his own mortality. But then the moment was gone . . .

The dizziness of freedom washed over the little boy as he quietly slunk towards the little girl, who was digging another hole, this one beneath the colorful bulk of a tall spiral slide.

BEFORE THE BOARD
OF DIRECTORS

I had my tear ducts sewn shut. The doctors used very tiny strands of razorwire to do the job. They could have used very tiny strands of dental floss or platypus hair, but that's not what I wanted. And I always get what I want.

To tell the truth, that's not true. The truth is I rarely get what I want. But I want to get what I want all the time, and sometimes this want of mine is so strong I deceive myself into thinking that I'm getting what I want all the time.

I can remember a number of occasions when I wasn't deceiving myself, and when I wasn't getting what I wanted. On one of these occasions, what I wanted was to get away from The House On Anti-Avenue Avenue. No matter how fast I drove, no matter what direction I drove in, I always ended up where I started: the parking lot that was The House On Anti-Avenue Avenue's front yard. It didn't make any sense. I was in motion but I wasn't going anywhere. It was a breach of the laws of physics, my inability to get away. And yet I couldn't get away.

A Stick Style house, The House On Anti-Avenue Avenue was a High Victorian elaboration of the Gothic Revival style, which harkened back to medieval castles and cathedrals. It was tall and gray and distinguished by its three needle-sharp rooftops and its long, distorted windows. The windows resembled the frozen, screaming mouths of cartoon characters. If you stared at the structure for too long, you got the uncanny impression that it was not only staring back at you, but taking notes on you, judging you, maybe even plotting against you.

Then again, if you stared at anything for too long, ani-

35

mate or inanimate, you got the same uncanny impression.

Finally I gave up trying to get away from The House On Anti-Avenue Avenue and parked in the best-looking parking spot I could find. All of the parking spots looked more or less the same, so in order to gauge which spot was the best-looking, I deployed what might be called intuitive logic.

I got out of my car.

The moment I closed my door and turned my back on my car, it was immediately stolen. I didn't see or hear who stole it. I didn't even see or hear it get driven away. But I knew that the car had been driven away, because when I glanced over my shoulder to see if I had remembered to lock the doors, it wasn't there anymore.

My car was just an everyday ordinary SUV with four doors, a sun roof, a cracked rear view mirror and chrome bumpers, but I had grown close to it over the years and the prospect of never seeing it again frightened and infuriated me.

There were eleven other cars in the parking lot: eight Model-T Fords, all of them in excellent shape; one Volvo station wagon, which was in crummy shape (rust and mud were caked all over it); and a souped-up hearse with monster truck tires, shotgun exhaust pipes and the head of a shiny silver engine peeking out of a hole in its broad black hood. All of the cars were empty except for one of the Model-Ts. Inside it, two teenage albinos were making out.

Since I couldn't swear at the person who stole my car, I decided to swear at the albinos.

I stomped over to the Model-T, rapped my knuckles against the window, and waited impatiently for the couple to stop making out and roll the window down.

"Sunzabitches," I seethed.

Their pink eyes blinked at me. I noticed that they were both wearing lipstick. There was lipstick, in fact, smeared all over each of their crooked, ovular faces from the top of their foreheads to the tips of their chins. I wanted to call them a couple of goddamn weirdos. But that would be overkill: sunzabitches would suffice for now.

I turned and marched to the front door of The House On Anti-Avenue Avenue. I tried to open the door. It was locked. I knocked on the door. Nobody answered. I rang the doorbell. There was no ringing noise.

I walked back to the albinos in the Model-T. They were now naked and having sex. The one who had been in the driver's seat was straddling the other one. Both of them were staring down at the social interaction of their genitals with the fascinated scrutiny of an entomologist studying a newly evolved species of bug through an electron microscope. I rapped on the window again. The couple didn't stop having sex or looking at their genitals, but they did roll down the window. I apologized for being intrusive, apologized for calling them sunzabitches a minute ago, explained that somebody had ripped off my car, explained that I needed to get inside The House On Anti-Avenue Avenue and use the telephone to call the police, told them that the door to The House On Anti-Avenue Avenue was locked and nobody was answering it, assured them that I was very upset, and at last asked if they had an axe in their trunk. Luckily, they did. I asked them if I could borrow it.

The soft growl of a mellow orgasm seeped out of the car as the trunk popped open and the window rolled back up.

I tested the axe to see if it would be sharp enough to do the job I needed it to do, first by running my thumb over its blade, then my tongue. Both extremities were cut open. I was bleeding all over the place.

The axe would do just fine.

I waited patiently for the blood to coagulate and seal my wounds. It took a long time, but I had nowhere to go.

Screaming like an insane Indian, I charged towards the front door of the house, waving the axe above my head. Sound and spittle flew out of my rip tide mouth like buckshot.

It was not long before the door was in pieces and I was

standing in the foyer of The House On Anti-Avenue Avenue, loosening the burgundy tie of my whitenoise-colored suit and using a handkerchief to clean all of the saliva off of my chin and cheeks.

I'm very interested in the details of things. As a matter of fact, the details of things interest me more than things themselves. It's the details of things, after all, that give meaning and character to things, which, in the absence of details, would cease to be things. Before I had a chance to take note of the details of the inside of the house, however, I was accosted by a man and forced to take note of the details of him instead. The man immediately reminded me of another man I used to know, not because he looked so much like him, but because he looked so much unlike him. The man I used to know might be described as bald, thin and religious. This man right here, in contrast, was the opposite of that one: the hair on his head was thick, profuse, and resembled a lion's mane; he had the body of a bull standing on its hind legs; and his belief system, if I was reading the shit-eating gleam in his eyes correctly, was clearly not informed by hopes of, let alone faith in, the prospect of an afterlife. I had chopped down the front door of The House On Anti-Avenue Avenue, I had invaded The House On Anti-Avenue Avenue— and so this big bastard clobbered me on the head with a hard, meaty fist. He didn't knock me out, but I was dazed and help-less to defend myself when he picked me up by the head with his giant hand and stuffed me into an itchy burlap bag.

He mumbled inarticulately as he dragged me down twenty flights of stairs. The stairs were made of granite. By the time we had reached the basement, my body was a morass of welts and bruises.

Had my tear ducts not been sewn shut, I may have begun to leak . . .

My bound body was tossed through the air. I struck a wall and went, "Ouch!" I fell on the floor and went, "Fuuuck!" More curse words came out of my mouth as I wriggled out of the bag like a crippled worm trying to wriggle out of a hole that's too small for it.

Disturbed and disoriented, I got to my feet and began to stagger around. My head was spinning. My eyeballs were each moving in different directions and I couldn't see two feet in front of my face.

My legs collapsed beneath me. I fell on my ass, burped, coughed . . . and puked up my breakfast (steak and eggs with a side of blueberry pancakes and six cups of coffee).

After that it was fuzzy. I think I may have passed out for a while. Or maybe not. The next thing I remembered, I was feeling surprisingly refreshed and my vision had returned to me.

The room that confined me was a basement with a smooth concrete floor and walls and a ceiling caked in spider webs. There were no windows. Swinging from a short chain on the ceiling was a big flickering light bulb that chirped and clicked like a half-conscious cricket. The only major article of furniture in the basement was a long wooden table that stretched from one side of the room to the other.

Sitting behind this table was the board of directors. I knew they were the board of directors because somebody had used a manure stick to draw a line of graffiti onto the wall behind and above them. The graffiti was printed in neat, diligent lettering and looked like this:

board of directors

Despite the poor lighting in the basement, I could see them fairly clearly. There were one, two, three, four . . . nine of them in all. They all had tight business suits on like me, albeit their suits were black instead of whitenoise in color, and they all had artichoke-tinted skin and pencil-faced heads. Thin horn-rimmed pince-nez were perched on the tips of each of their sharp noses, except for the man in the very middle, who wore thick black-rimmed spectacles.

They sat in their seats like petrified plants.

Two of the nine board of directors were large-breasted women. Like the men, they had scraggly black beards. I couldn't tell if their beards were strap-ons or if some genetic defect had effectuated the production of too much testosterone in their systems. Perhaps they even administered regular testosterone injections to themselves in order to maintain their beards. I wanted to walk over to one of them and tug on their facial hair, to see if it would come off. But that would have been too aggressive a thing to do: strangers don't tug on the facial hair of other strangers, no matter how outrageous and inexcusable the circumstances of their coming together.

I stood before the board of directors, staring at them. The board of directors sat before me, staring back at me. In their eyes was the cold understanding of people who think they have certain affiliations with Destiny. In my eyes was the curious regalement of a person who thinks that people who think they have certain affiliations with Destiny are dipshits.

We regarded each other for an indefinite amount of time in complete silence before I noticed that my now crumpled up suit was stained in places with vomit. I had been observing the board of directors one at a time in a methodical, calculated manner, but I took my eyes off of them when I pulled out my handkerchief, wet it with spit and began to wipe away the vomit.

A few moments after my gaze strayed from the gaze of the board of directors, the man in the thick black spectacles pounded his fist against the table and stood up.

"Indeed," said the director sitting on the man in the thick black spectacles' immediate right, and glanced up at him. At first I thought the utterance signified that he was in concordance with his colleague. By saying what he said, I thought he meant, "I support your decision to get angry, comrade."

It wasn't what he meant. Indeed was the man in the thick black spectacles' name.

40

"How dare you address me by my surname and my surname alone," said Indeed, staring down at the man with profound enmity in his eyes. "Do that again and I will have you banished from this hellhole, do you understand me? I say do you understand me?"

The director penitently bowed his head. "Yes, Dr. Indeed," he said, and then added, "Yes indeed."

Dr. Indeed stared at the top of the out-of-order director's bowed head for a few more seconds, as if he was trying to burn a hole through his bald spot with his eyes. "It *irks* me," he kept repeating under his breath. I couldn't tell if he was referring to the man's bald spot or his impudent conduct.

The rest of the directors coughed, cleared their throats, and made subtle, obscene gestures with their lips.

I wondered what kind of doctor Dr. Indeed was. He looked like a history professor—all of the directors looked like history professors—but for all I knew he was a herpetologist. I could have asked him what he was, but frankly I didn't care enough about it. Not now anyway. Now there were more pressing matters to get to the bottom of.

"It *irks* me. It *irks* me. It *irks* me," Dr. Indeed bitched. It was as if I had disappeared.

I said, "Is somebody going to tell me what's the matter here? Is this about the front door? Sorry I chopped it down. But you're the ones who locked it and didn't answer it when I knocked on it. What did you expect? Well, it's just a door. You can get another one. They sell doors all over the place."

Dr. Indeed's aquiline head slowly turned in my direction. His eyes were on the verge of popping out of his skull and smashing through the lenses of his thick black spectacles.

"Who do you think you are, sir!" he shouted at the top of his voice.

I frowned. "What do you mean? I don't understand. Could you rephrase yourself, possibly?"

Agitated by my response, the doctor exclaimed, "What

41

a burden!" He began to vibrate with rage. To stop himself from vibrating, he slapped himself across his own face. For good measure he also slapped the director who had mouthed off to him. Then, to me, he spat, "I shall ask the questions in this realm of existence! Am I making myself clear! Am I!"

"Actually you're the most unclear person I think I've ever met in my life," was my calm, calm response. "Look, I just want to use the phone. Some dickhead stole my car and I need to report it. Where's the phone? Does anybody have a cell on them?"

Two irate veins inflated on either side of Dr. Indeed's high forehead. The other directors took stupid glimpses of one another.

Placing his fists on the table before him, Dr. Indeed leaned closer to me. He blinked at me. He nodded at me. And in a low, malevolent whisper, he said, "*Kneel before the board of directors.*" His colleagues tilted back their heads, pursed their lips, sucked in their cheeks and raised their eyebrows, awaiting my reply.

My reply was a mask of confusion.

The mask was not well-received. In response to it, one of the female directors stood up, turned her back on me, angled over and dismissed a long, loud fart. The sound and the fury of the fart prompted all of the other directors except Dr. Indeed to nod in grave affirmation and tap the table with the thorny tips of their index fingers. It prompted me, on the other hand, to transform my mask of confusion into a mask of disgust.

"*Kneel before the board of directors,*" the doctor repeated.

I kept my mouth shut and made another face. What were these people trying to accomplish? More importantly— *what were these people?*

The doctor repeated himself again. And again. And again. His determined eyes were penetrating me like knives.

I had a feeling that anything but obeying the command would ignite a tedious dialogue between Dr. Indeed and I, and

I wasn't in the mood for a tedious dialogue. All I wanted to do was call the cops and try to get my car back. At the same time, I wasn't in the mood to obey Dr. Indeed's command and give him the upper hand in the power-relation that had been established between us. I may not have known what the board of directors was trying to prove, but it was clear that they were attempting to dominate me.

I'm not a big fan of being dominated. I opted for the tedious dialogue.

"*Kneel before the—*"

"I heard you the first twenty-three times," I snapped.

Dr. Indeed raised an eyebrow. "Then submit. Submit, I say."

"Why?" I said.

He groaned as if I had kidney-punched him. "I thought I told you that I, not *you*, shall act as the inquisitor here. What about what I told you did you fail to understand?"

"I understood you. I simply chose not to mind you. I made that choice."

"I can respect that. I can also denounce it. I can do anything I want to do."

"Of course you can. You're a powerful man, aren't you."

"Indeed," said Dr. Indeed, and the corners of his lips curled up.

"Very funny. Now listen to me. Where's the phone? I have to go. Can you tell me where the phone is?" I gesticulated at him impatiently.

The doctor's smirk persisted. "I can tell you. But I won't."

"Why not?"

"Because of your disgraceful insistence on defying my authority. Disgraceful—yet by the same token, delicious. I like a man who resists bending over and taking one in the yahoo at the drop of a hat. But I hate him more than I like him. *Much* more."

I shook my head. "I'm not going to kneel down. No, I'm not going to do that. There's no point in it and nothing will be accomplished by it. What is this, elementary school? You're an idiot, you jackass."

"So you say."

"Knock it off."

"Silence!" Dr. Indeed made a maestro-like cutting motion through the air with the blade of his palm as he squawked the word.

I smirked. "No."

He sneered. "Be quiet!"

I intensified my smirk. "No."

He intensified his sneer. "Do as I say!"

I allowed my smirk to fall off my face. It hit the ground like a potato. "No."

Dr. Indeed's sneer, in contrast, leapt off his face and drifted up to the ceiling like campfire smoke. "Why not?"

Both of our faces were empty now. I considered filling up the emptiness with something, then decided against it. I said, "Because it doesn't make any sense."

Dr. Indeed flexed his jaw. "That's because you're not applying the correct logic to this situation."

"What's the correct logic?" I returned the flexing jaw gesture with a widening nostril gesture.

It was countered by a wiggling of the ears gesture. "That's for me to know and for you to try and fail to figure out."

"Asshole," I said.

"Silence!" Dr. Indeed said.

And so on. We continued to argue in this way for another five minutes. By the time we tired out, all of the other directors had nodded off; heads slumped onto their shoulders, they were snoring a strident warthog symphony.

I suddenly became aware of the fact that the basement smelled like a latrine. I attributed my not becoming aware of this earlier to one of two possible things: 1) I was so

44

discombobulated by being dragged down the stairs and thrown against the wall that my olfactory senses had not been working properly; 2) the basement had not smelled like a latrine before, it smelled like a basement, until one or more of the directors took it upon themselves, for whatever reason, to urinate in their pants a few seconds ago.

In any case, I was ready to go. My body hurt. I was bored out of my mind, too.

"I'm leaving," I said. "I'm going to see if there's a phone upstairs. If there is, I'm going to use it. If there's not, I'm going to raid your refrigerator. I'm hungry. Goodbye." Favoring my half-sprained left foot, I walked towards the stairs.

Dr. Indeed pointed at me with the resolve of somebody fingering a criminal in a lineup. He looked like he wanted to leap over the table and tackle me, but something was prohibiting him from doing it. It was as if an invisible containment field was keeping him and the others at bay behind the table and beneath the graffiti that told people like me who they were dealing with. "Not so fast!" he carped, jarring his colleagues awake. In one communal motion they jumped out of their seats into a soldier's ten-hut position, thrust their left fists over their heads and bleated, "Leben lang die Direktion!" Their hypnogogic eyes were glazed donut holes.

I stopped at the foot of the stairway and turned to the board of directors one last time.

The doctor eyeballed me, shook his finger at me. He lifted up his bearded chin and flashed his teeth at me. His visage looked demonic in the flickering light of the basement.

"Indeed," I intoned . . . and that was all I intoned. To call him by his name like that, I had an inkling, would incite something unpleasant in him.

I was right. Incensed, Dr. Indeed's demonic expression became more acute. He also started to vibrate again. He had no choice but to slap himself as hard as he had slapped himself a little while ago, only this time he used the back of his hand.

Maintaining their rigid stances, the other directors answered the slap by repeating the phrase, "Leben lang die Direktion!"

It was fascinating. The conduct of Dr. Indeed and his entourage reified my belief in the idiocy, the utter lunacy of the human condition. I said his name again. "Indeed."

Another backhand flew across his cheek. This one smacked his thick black spectacles clear off his face.

"Leben lang die Direktion!" said the board of directors.

I closed my eyes, nodded, and started up the stairs. After I had taken a few steps I looked over my shoulder and cried, "Indeed!"

Slap.

"Leben lang die Direktion!"

"Indeed!"

Slap.

"Leben lang die Direktion!"

"Indeed! Indeed!"

Slap. Slap.

"Leben lang die Direktion! Leben lang die Direktion!"

I kept saying Dr. Indeed's name until I reached the third flight of stairs, at which point I figured my voice would no longer carry. I climbed up the remaining seventeen flights in vigilant silence. At every corner I expected the Neanderthal that was responsible for putting me in this position to jump me, but he never did. Not even when I emerged from the staircase back into The House On Anti-Avenue Avenue. The godless freak was nowhere to be seen, nowhere to be found.

Maybe he was outside smoking a cigarette? Maybe he was in the bathroom taking a crap?

Maybe he never existed in the first place.

I decided to ask. I cupped my hands around my mouth and shouted, "Hey shitface, I'm back! Do you exist?"

My answer was an echo. The echo sounded so sad I could have cried. But I couldn't cry, of course, so I shrugged and proceeded down a long dark hallway towards what I thought might be the kitchen, where I would either find a phone and report my misfortune, or rid the refrigerator of its finest, tastiest booty.

DEER IN THE CITY

A canary grinned at me. The bird has lived in my apartment for over two years and it's never grinned at me before. Its teeth looked like Jack Nicholson's. Straight and white as the keys of a piano.

Unnerved, I stumbled out into the street and tripped over a fire hydrant somebody had capped with a derby hat to pass off as a short person. I fell face first on a manhole and was run over by a deer. "Well," I said. "That happened."

"There's a deer in the city!" hollered a flâneur, pointing . . . Everybody pulled out their handguns and started to chase it. The deer glanced over its shoulder, shrieked in terror and accelerated. It leapt over cars, newspaper stands and snoring bums with the grace of an Olympic gymnast.

After the deer was gunned down and stripped of its hide and meat, which was divided evenly amongst its pursuants, I hurried back inside to see if the canary was still grinning. It was. "So it's true," I said. The canary nodded.

I stumbled back out into the street. This time somebody had capped the fire hydrant with a pair of antlers. I tripped over it, fell face first onto a manhole and was run over by the fire hyrdant.

"There's a deer in the city!" hollered the flâneur, pointing . . .

COMMUNITY

Derillict Hagadorn's Achilles' tendons are made of spidersteel. He wasn't born with spidersteel Achilles' tendons, he was born with steel ones, and when he was an infant a spider snuck into his crib, slit open his heels and spun its silk all over the aberrations. Over time the silk was assimilated. Not only did it reinforce the strength of his steel tendons, it made them pliant and nimble, just like all of the other neighborhood children's Achilles' tendons. The only thing is, all of the other neighborhood children's Achilles tendons, which are made of a wet, feeble substance reminiscent of the stems of lily pads, are always snapping, without warning, and usually without the slightest provocation. Since the last thing Derillict's impervious tendons are about to do is snap, all of the neighborhood children (and their parents, whose Achilles' tendons are always snapping, too) despise Derillict and wish him ill. Nothing would give the neighborhood more pleasure than to hear two of those guitar string-breaking sounds ringing out of Derillict's heels, and then to watch him topple over and land on his face. But that's just not going to happen. Not by natural causes anyway.

"You stuck up dickhead!" yells Bobby Van Futon as he crawls by Derillict on the sidewalk. His left Achilles' tendon just gave out on him. That's the third time the tendon gave out this week and he's on his way to the hospital to have it stitched up again. Like Derillict, Bobby's only eight years old and his parents should probably be driving him to the hospital. But they're both already at the hospital getting their own Achilles' tendons stitched back up.

It was Saturday morning and Derillict was on his way to

his imaginary friend Sanders' house to play. They had a big day planned, he and Sanders, and he was excited to get over there. When he ran in to Bobby, however, he stopped and asked him if he needed some help. That's when Bobby said, "You stuck up dickhead!"

Derillict ignores the insult and tries to hoist the boy onto his back. "Don't worry, Bobby," he says, "I'll save you."

"Save yourself, asshole," growls Bobby, shaking himself free of Derillict's hold. Overcome with jealously, he impulsively bites Derillict on the heel as hard as he can, hoping to even out the score. But he only succeeds in breaking all of his teeth.

"Are you okay?" asks a wide-eyed Derillict. A teary-eyed Bobby mumbles something hateful out of his damaged mouth before he turns and crawls away, a sloppy trail of blood marking his wake.

Later that afternoon, as Derillict and Sanders are playing a game of ghost-in-the-graveyard even though the sun is out—playing ghost-in-the-graveyard any time besides nighttime is kind of sacrilegious, but Sanders says it's healthy to be sacrilegious and anything Sanders says is healthy is, in Derillict's eyes, healthy—there is a neighborhood meeting called by Mr. and Mrs. Van Futon shortly after they are discharged from the hospital. They were outraged to find that their son's teeth had been, in Mrs. Van Futon's words, "wrongfully attacked by that little maniac's Achilles' tendon" and are demanding that the neighborhood take some kind of collective action.

Mrs. Van Futon is standing behind a podium. The podium is her short, balding, battered husband Victor. His back is turned to her and his head is bent, and he's situated on the axis of a merry-go-round in Hamstring Park. All of the neighborhood residents and their offspring surround the merry-go-round—except, of course, for the ones that are at the hospital having their Achilles' tendons operated on.

The merry-go-round is spinning very slowly so that everybody can catch an ample glimpse of Mrs. Van Futon's enraged, ranting visage. Beneath this visage is a trashy velour jumpsuit littered with sweat patches. Above this visage is a nest of ratty brown hair.

"Derillict Hagadorn is a nuisance, a freak, and a menace!" she spits. "His existence places all of our lives in jeopardy! Are we going to sit here and allow this monstrosity to continue to antagonize us? Jesus Christ!" Her madness exacerbated by the sudden, unexpected bite of an elephant mosquito on her thigh, Mrs. Van Futon bangs her gavel smack against her husband's bald spot. Without a word Victor Van Futon crumbles to the bright multicolored platform of the merry-go-round like a Jenga tower. His wife points the gavel at his soggy-looking body and growls, "Get up you crossbreed or I'll beat you twice as hard as when we get home! I said get up!"

It takes a few seconds, but eventually his body stiffens with consciousness and Victor Van Futon manages to push himself back up into a standing, bent-headed, eyes-on-his-toes position.

Mrs. Van Futon nails him on the bald spot again, hard but not as hard as before, and dares him to pass out. He takes the dare without putting up much of a struggle.

Most of the neighborhood listens to and stares at the Van Futons with indifference. A few mothers are breast-feeding naked infants and don't pay attention to them at all.

"Well?" says Mrs. Van Futon, kicking her husband in the ribs. He moans like a man with a toothache. "I'd like to hear some of your thoughts on this matter. I assume everybody here today feels the same way I do, but I could be wrong."

The adults look up at the sky or down at the ground and pucker their brows, pretending they see something odd. Mr. and Mrs. Dippleskim's son Boris opens his fat mouth and unleashes a giant belch. All of the children explode with laughter. Saginaw Tripp and Larry Hamitup laugh so hard and with so much gusto their Achilles' tendons break and they have to be escorted to the hospital by their parents.

Eventually the laughter subsides. Hungry for more acclaim, Boris Dippleskim tries to belch again. He is saddened to discover that his first effort totally expended his store of resources.

The neighbors stare at each other, unsure of what to say, what to do. A small cumulonimbus cloud passes over Hamstring Park and blots out the sun for a moment.

Mrs. Van Futon throws up her arms in surprise. "None of you dumbasses has anything to say? I find that difficult to believe. C'mon! Say something."

Nobody says anything.

Annoyed, Mrs. Van Futon massages her forehead. She says, "I mean, the reason we call Achilles' tendons Achilles' tendons is because of Achilles, right? And what kind of Achilles' tendons did Achilles have? Weak ones. Not strong ones. For the most part Achilles was a strong person, yes, I'm not suggesting that he was anything less than a strong, strong person. But as we all know his strength was not inborn, not genetic, it was a result of his loving mother Thetis dipping him in the infernal River Styx, which immortalized every inch of his body except, obviously, his Achilles' tendons—Thetis was hanging on to those when she dipped him. Now why she didn't make sure his Achilles' tendons got wet is a mystery to me, so don't ask me about it. Maybe she was in a hurry or something. What am I, a historian? The point is, Achilles' worthless tendons are the foundation upon which this community is set, and Derillict Hagadorn's Achilles' tendons are the very antithesis of this foundation! I won't endure it a moment longer. Neither will Victor. We're going to put an end to that young fiend's tyranny once and for all."

"What is it you intend to do?" says Mr. Hagadorn, pushing his way to the front of the crowd. Mrs. Hagadorn, the equivalent of Mr. Van Futon in terms of physical and emotional bent-headedness, cowers at her husband's side, twitching like an insect. A sterling silver choke chain hangs from her pencilneck.

"Oh dear," says Mrs. Van Futon and touches her chest. She's been having an affair with Mr. Hagadorn for two years now. She spends more time with him than with her husband, but still, every time she sees him, she gets butterflies in her stomach.

The merry-go-round comes to rest just as Mr. Hagadorn bursts onto the scene. Rather than order her husband to get up and start it spinning again, Mrs. Van Futon turns and faces the tall, barrel-chested drink of water that is her lover.

"Hello Buck," she intones in a deep, seductive voice.

"Hello Veronica," Mr. Hagadorn replies and smirks as the image of an illegal sexual position the two of them accomplished this morning materializes on his mind's screen. "We're willing to help, the wife and I. We've been reticent to do so in the past, Derillict being our son and all. But enough is enough. Truth is, we really don't care much for the boy. He'd be better off dead than be raised by a couple of people who don't like him. Isn't that right honey?" Mr. Hagadorn grabs Mrs. Hagadorn's choke chain and tightens it. "That's right," she squeaks. Her squeak is an earnest one but he continues to choke her until her face turns purple and she faints.

The neighborhood blinks.

Fed up with the neighborhood, Mrs. Van Futon ignores them. "Well done," she mouths to Mr. Hagadorn in silence. Mr. Hagadorn nods and mouths, "Thank you," back at her. They continue to mouth things at each other without actually speaking. These things are all in reference to the actions that will be taken against Derillict Hagadorn. Everybody else watches the mute conversation like a tennis match, trying to read the two players' lips, but nobody is an adept enough lip reader to figure out what's being communicated. Boredom sets in like a forest fire and the congregation quickly disperses, leaving the Hagadorns and the Van Futons to their scheming . . .

Elsewhere Derillict is giving his imaginary friend an imaginary hug goodbye. "I had fun today, Sanders," says the boy. "See you again tomorrow?"

Sanders replies, "Sure thing." And implodes.

As always Derillict begins bawling, mourning the loss of his best friend even though he knows he will be reunited with him tomorrow. But a lot can happen between the present moment and tomorrow. A whole lot.

As Derillict meanders home, he thinks about all of the things that might happen to him. He thinks about them so pointedly that he doesn't even notice when Mrs. Van Futon crawls out of a nearby bush and begins to tail him. In her firm grasp is a supersized pair of stainless steel garden shears off of which the sunlight glints and occasionally gets in her eyes, stinging them. She curses the shears under her breath for being so shiny, then hikes up the overstretched elastic waistband of her jumpsuit and bends over, determined to cut Derillict's Achilles' tendons in half. It's difficult to get at them, however, when they're both in motion; time after time she snips at the air, missing the tendons by mere millimeters. She begins swearing louder and more regularly until she trips on a crack in the sidewalk and her newly mended Achilles' tendon snaps loose. She awkwardly topples onto her face. Her left elbow lands on one of the shears' razorsharp blades and is sliced off.

Derillict doesn't so much as glance over his shoulder. He sees and hears nothing but what the future may have in store for him . . .

Mr. Van Futon crawls out of a bush next to the one his wife had been hiding in and comes to her assistance. He uses a handkerchief to apply pressure to her wound, which is gushing with blood. She yells at him for applying too much pressure, then too little pressure, then too much pressure, then too little pressure . . . Once the blood stops flowing with such vehemence, she orders him to retrieve her elbow.

"I d-d-dunno where it went," he stutters.

His wife shouts, "Horseshit! You find that elbow or I'll have your ass!"

Nodding his bruised, lumpy head, Mr. Van Futon begins to scrutinize the sidewalk.

At the same time Mrs. Hagadorn is in the process of emerging from a manhole that her son has just passed by. She's holding a freshly sharpened hatchet. Beneath her, underneath the road in the sewer water, is her husband. Mr. Hagadorn pushes her skinny hide all the way out of the manhole, sticks up his head and whispers, "Don't let me down, woman. You hack those Achilles' tendons in two and let that brat bleed to death, okay? Listen to me now. Otherwise I'll divorce your ass!"

Heat lightning swims up and down Mrs. Hagadorn's spine at the thought of life without Mr. Hagadorn by her side. She hates him, she fears him more than God . . . *she needs him.* Who, after all, will she hate and fear if he were to leave her? Derillict certainly isn't up to the challenge, not at his age. She would rather kill her loving son than be deserted by her hated husband, in which case she would kill herself, so she assures Mr. Hagadorn that the deed will be done at all costs. (Little does she know the sewage her husband is immersed in contains a mycotoxin that is at this moment infusing his body with a rare strain of Methusula's syndrome, which will age and kill him in under a month.)

Mrs. Hagadorn tiptoes behind the oblivious Derillict for a block and a half before working up the courage to lean over and take a swing at him. She misses. The hatchet nails the sidewalk and sends a flurry of sparks into her face. The sparks are piping hot and burn tiny craters into her paper-thin skin. She stifles a yelp of agony . . . and swings again. Another miss, another faceful of sparks, another stifled yelp. On her third try she finally makes contact with her son's left Achilles' tendon. It's a beautiful shot, right on target. She couldn't have hit her mark more squarely.

Too bad her mark treated the hatchet like Bobby Van Futon's teeth.

Thinking a mosquito is biting him on the ankle, Derillict

56

Hagadorn comes to an abrupt stop, lifts his ankle out in front of him and slaps it. He stands there a moment. In the distance a few snapping Achilles' tendons followed by a few loud curses can be heard. Derillict hears nothing—nothing but the voices inside his head. He walks on, wondering if, in the next few minutes, he will die . . .

Mrs. Hagadorn watches him go. She's sitting on the sidewalk like a propped-up ventriloquist doll, her eyes glazed, her cheeks steaming . . . A few feet behind her, a cluster of ants is hoisting an elbow onto their backs . . .

THE IMPULSIVE MAN

"My passions are extremely strong, and while I am under
their sway nothing can equal my impetuosity. I am ame-
nable to no restraint, respect, fear, or decorum. I am
cynical, bold, violent, and daring. No shame can stop
me, no fear of danger alarm me. Except for the one object in my mind the universe for me is non-existent. But
all this lasts only a moment; and the next moment plunges
me into complete annihilation."
—Rousseau, *The Confessions*

A recent study has shown that on average everybody acts impulsively, without thinking things through in sufficient depth, at
least twenty-six times a day. The study is not race, gender or
class conscious, and it is attentive to all impulsive acts, however
minute or seemingly insignificant. A man out for a Sunday
drive in the Hollywood hills who for no reason at all suddenly
decides to jerk the steering wheel of his convertible a little to the
left and drive over a mile-high cliff screaming his head off, and
a man intent on eating a bowl of cereal for breakfast who for no
reason at all suddenly decides to fry up three or four eggs along-
side three or four strips of bacon and a piece of rye toast with a
thin film of strawberry jam spread across it—in this study, both
acts are considered equal and together account for one-thirteenth
of the day's rash behavior.

Dr. Leopold Noteboom, senior professor of noology at
The Bosshog Institute of Technology and clinical research coor-
dinator of the study, was quoted as saying, "This number may
come as a surprise to the man who likes to think he has emotional autonomy over his own existence. What surprises me,
however, is that the number isn't ten times greater! But my

team and I were very thorough and meticulous, and in any case twelve instances of unbridled impulsiveness a day is still immense. The frequency of such conduct is symptomatic of the implosive nature of contemporary blip culture and the soundtrack of white noise that ceaselessly accompanies it. I'm afraid Baudrillard isn't the hack that so many humanities professors have made him out to be . . ."

Of course, everybody doesn't act on impulse twenty-six times a day. Most people don't. Of the 1,052 subjects that were scrutinized by Dr. Noteboom and his team for ten straight months, 825 of them acted on impulse roughly eleven times a day, whereas the remaining 227 averaged out at a staggering fifty-four times a day. "Some subjects are simply more susceptible and responsive to white noise than others," the doctor concluded. "Nevertheless they are clearly not the dominant faction."

Fair enough. But there are well over six billion potential subjects in this world. Can we really pass judgement on who is dominant (and who, *a fortiori*, is marginalized) based on a study of 0.00002% of those subjects, despite the care and particularity with which they were selected?

In light of the existence of potential subjects like Holmberg Finn, the answer, in this critic's view, is a screaming no. Had this miserable man (and others like him, although nobody is quite like him) been subjected to Dr. Noteboom's probes, no doubt the doctor's findings would prove much more tenuous and out-of-whack.

Holmberg Finn is an impulsive man in the most literal sense of the phrase "an impulsive man." Everything he does, everything he thinks, everything he *is* is effectuated by a perpetual fit of spontaneity. The man can't plan. He tries to plan. He tries to prepare in advance to do something, anything, but when the time comes for the thing to be done another thing is done, spur of the moment. He goes to bed at night, for instance, and tells himself, "Tomorrow morning I will get up at 8

59

a.m. and go to the bathroom," but when 8 a.m. rolls around and his eyes pop open he finds himself laying in bed for another hour or two and then getting up and going to the kitchen. His love life is the same way. More than once he has told women that he loves them but the moment those three words come out of his mouth he realizes they are a total scam and, with the springboard gusto of Gilles de la Tourette himself, immediately blurts, "I hate you!" But these words aren't true either. Nothing is true for Holmberg Finn. How can anything be true for a man who is compelled to live life like a material, fleshy incarnation of Chaos theory? Truth requires that the man who acknowledges Truth possesses the capacity to ground himself in something. Holmberg Finn lacks the capacity to ground himself in anything.

Actually, that's not altogether accurate. There is one thing Holmberg does that is not a product of sheer impulse and might be called (or at least equated with) Truth: every night at 10 p.m., no matter where his impulse takes him when the sun is shining, he returns to the grand piano that he calls home.

The piano is located in the great room of a mansion in the Hollywood hills. The mansion is tall, majestic-looking, supported by a plethora of whitewashed pillars, and owned by one Mr. Lawrence Hecklebake, a round-shouldered, somewhat homely, but always well-dressed gentleman who has a fetish for instant coffee and a wife named Cynthia. Cynthia does not enjoy having sex. A repressed traumatic childhood experience prohibits her from gleaning any pleasure at all out of being penetrated by her husband; over the course of their twenty-two year marriage, the Hecklebake's have only engaged in sexual relations on a handful of occasions. One of these occasions produced a girl named Narnia, who was named after the writer C. S. Lewis's renowned fantasy land (C. S. Lewis is Mrs. Hecklebake's favorite author). Being a teenager, Narnia has immeasurable problems, especially in light of her affliction with dysfunctional family syndrome.

In addition to this family of three that occupies the mansion, there are fifteen butlers, thirty-three maids, six cooks, twenty window washers, three hairdressers, nine gardeners, one golf pro and two haberdashers that also occupy it. All eighty-nine of them know a stranger is living in the piano. None of them have ever thought to ask him why he lives there, nor have they asked him to leave. Everybody's usually very busy and has too much on their minds to go out of their way and start asking questions.

Sometimes Holmberg tries to remember how he came to live in the piano, but his memory always fails him. He doesn't remember anything. Every time he tries to remember one thing impulse kicks in and prompts him to remember another thing instead, and then that other thing, once it is remembered, is immediately forgotten, supplanted by yet another thing, which is in turn forgotten and supplanted with another memory, and another memory, and another one, and on and on like a TV whose channels are being changed at a random, rapid-fire pace until Holmberg can only swear at the top of his lungs and stop trying to remember things like how he came to live in the damn piano! But this is hyperbole. Holmberg could remember things if he really wanted to. It would just take an immensely painstaking effort on his part. In order to invoke the past, it would require that he *concentrate* on the past with all of his cerebral might. It wasn't impossible, no. He could do it, yes. He just didn't want to do it. He wasn't an abnormally lazy or halfass person. But when it came to something like overcoming his impulses, well, he just couldn't be bothered with it.

Since it's such a chore to exercise his memory, Holmberg prefers to simply exist in the present and stays as far away from his memory as possible (albeit, for some reason, he has no problem remembering the piano). As a result, he suffers socially and financially. He's always forgetting who his friends and acquaintances are and where he works, so he's always making new friends and acquaintances and getting new jobs. Not having any intimate relationships or a solid, steady income can be very frustrating for him. There are times when he wishes he was a normal person with normal problems. But at least he has a place to sleep.

For the most part, the Hecklebakes and their entourage leave the eccentric lodger alone, except when they are entertaining guests and need to use the piano, in which case they have a butler kindly escort him to the wine cellar. Holmberg doesn't mind. He taste-tests the cellar's vast inventory to his heart's content . . .

Once or twice a week a small flock of maids will advance on the piano while Holmberg is in it. Each of their petite, calloused hands are clutching feather-dusters that vibrate like the wings of so many hummingbirds and when they fall on it the piano rattles and shakes like an earthquake and Holmberg awakens with a curt shriek. His first impulse is to leap out of the piano and attack the maids for disturbing his sleep, but just as he is about to act on this impulse, he gets the impulse to *not* act on it and resolves to ride out the rest of the earthquake in silence. The lid of the piano opens up and a few vibrating feather-dusters are thrust inside. Holmberg tries to stay out of the way of them as they buzz to and fro, but he's never quick enough, and he doesn't have much room to move around anyway; by the time the feather-dusters are through sanitizing the interior of the piano, Holmberg is routinely a giggling, purple-faced mess. Part of him likes being made to giggle so hard. He wishes it was because somebody told him something funny, though.

The only other contact Holmberg really has with the Hecklebakes is when Narnia sneaks out of her room at night and comes to visit him. Narnia is an attractive little sixteen-year-old despite her figure, a borderline anorexic figure attributable to the daily neglect paid to her by her parents, namely her father, who spends most of his time at golf courses and brothels and is rarely home (her mother, in turn, locks herself in her closet, drinks gin and reads the Narnia Chronicles all day and night). She has intense sapphire blue eyes and long flaxen hair, and her skin is the color of electricity. Holmberg likes her. She likes Holmberg, too. She's annoyed and disturbed by the fact that he never takes the time to remember her, even though he has explained his plight to her. But she never remains annoyed and disturbed for very long.

Narnia and Holmberg's late-night rendezvous are all fairly similar. Whenever they are confronted by one another, they tend to do the same things, act the same way, and talk about the same subjects.

Here is what one of these rendezvous looks like:

INT. HECKLEBAKE ESTATE. GREAT ROOM. NIGHT

Narnia is wearing a white, somewhat revealing satin gown that seems to flow of its own volition as she pads barefoot across the cold hardwood floor. Very little furniture in this room, but there are a number of bronze sculptures. The sculptures are of extremely tall, skinny people with no faces or genitalia. They appear to have dried out in the sun—their limbs resemble oblong bones wrapped tightly in waxed paper bags. Narnia weaves through these sculptures like a ghost in a graveyard towards the grand piano that sits in a corner on the far side of the room.

Finally she reaches the piano, an enormous obsidian black Bösendorfer Imperial. Its lid is closed. Narnia arranges herself on a long padded bench and taps on the lid with an index finger. No response. She whispers the name Holmberg and knocks on the lid, softly, until it creaks open.

A man's puffy-eyed head pops into view and begins scrutinizing Narnia like a dog might scrutinize a suspicious-smelling bowl of dog chow, unsure of whether or not it is dog chow.

The man is Holmberg. The first thing we notice about him is that he is balding; the pizza slice of hair that defines his sizable widow's peaks is so thin and craggy it looks more like a long dead cockroach than a pizza slice. He is forty-something years old. He has baggy eyes and a four-day beard, and his teeth, while straight, are stained yellow and brown. His face is the shape of his skull. Not a pretty sight, but we sense that at one point Holmberg might have been an attractive man. Narnia shows no fear or consternation at all in his presence. In fact, her expression is completely blank.

HOLMBERG (*testily*): Who are you? Where do you come from?

NARNIA (*calmly*): I'm Narnia, for the eight thousandth time. I live here, for the eight thousandth time.

HOLMBERG: That's not what I meant.

NARNIA: Oh? What did you mean?

HOLMBERG (*confused*): I don't know. I mean . . . well, that's what I mean.

NARNIA: What's what you mean?

HOLMBERG: Go away.

NARNIA: Where to?

HOLMBERG: I don't know. Back where you came from.

NARNIA (*thinks about Holmberg's reply for a second, then shakes her head*): No. I don't want to.

HOLMBERG (*thinks about Narnia's reply for a second, then shrugs*): Okay.

A long pause here that would be awkward if Holmberg and Narnia's faces weren't wearing such disinterested expressions. Then a hint of interest suddenly takes shape in Holmberg's eyes. He pushes open the lid of the piano all the way and locks it into place. We see that he doesn't have a shirt on and is wearing only a pair of paper-thin boxer shorts. Tangled, dirty-looking hair covers his flaccid chest and beer belly. It's a wonder he can fit into the piano.

Narnia is unmoved by the spectacle of Holmberg's degraded body, which is now in Buddha's Indian-style sitting position, and which resembles the body of Buddha sheathed in the skin of a baboon. Narnia continues to regard him indifferently.

HOLMBERG (*testily*): I love you. I love you madly.

NARNIA (*calmly*): You don't even know me.

HOLMBERG: That's not true.

NARNIA: That's true.

HOLMBERG (*confused*): Huh? . . . Okay, it's true. Kind of. But what does me knowing or not knowing you have to do with me loving you?

NARNIA: Do I have to answer that question?

HOLMBERG: Unless you want me to hate you, yes.

NARNIA: You might as well hate me then. Do you want to hate me?

HOLMBERG: I don't know. Can I think about it for a while?

NARNIA (*thinks about Holmberg's reply for a second, then shakes*

65

her head): No.

HOLMBERG: (*thinks about Narnia's reply for a second, then shrugs*): Okay.

Footsteps pass overhead. They are loud and unsteady and sound like the footsteps of a drunk Clydesdale. Holmberg and Narnia look up at the ceiling and stare at it. While they are staring, Narnia reaches into the piano and takes Holmberg by the hand. Holmberg flinches. He yelps, yanks his hand away. Unlocks the lid of the piano . . . which slams shut on top of him.

Startled, Narnia flinches and yelps herself. She scurries underneath the piano bench and hides there as a trio of butlers enter the great room and survey it with the vigilance of hungry velociraptors looking for prey. After they leave, Narnia seats herself on the bench again and taps on the piano lid. No answer. Very softly, she plays a rudimentary version of Beethoven's "Ode to Joy" on the piano's moonlit keys.

A few muffled curse words from Holmberg. Narnia stops playing. The piano lid opens a crack, just enough for us to see two beady eyes.

HOLMBERG (*testily*): That hurts me when you play. I can feel the notes all over my body. Stop it.

NARNIA (*calmly*): I did stop it.

HOLMBERG: Oh.

NARNIA: I'm going to bed. Goodnight.

HOLMBERG (*confused*): Goodnight? (*Throws the piano lid all the way open.*)

NARNIA: I'll see you later.

HOLMBERG: Don't leave. I'm lonely. I need somebody to talk to.

NARNIA: About what?

HOLMBERG: I don't know. Whatever pops into my head.

NARNIA (*thinks about Holmberg's reply for a second, then shakes her head*): Okay.

HOLMBERG: (*thinks about Narnia's reply for a second, then shrugs*): Okay.

Fade out to black as Holmberg attempts to articulate the impulsive goings-on of his mental universe . . .

Since Holmberg Finn's existence is hopelessly defined by impulsiveness, it is difficult to even approximate how many acts of impulsiveness he commits per day. If one was held at gunpoint, however, and forced to approximate it—or rather, if one was forced to produce an approximation of an approximation of it—the figure 850,050 would not be all that far from the real. Imagine how this man would have disrupted Dr. Noteboom's study! The figure that signifies his behavior amounts to far more than the figures that signify all 1,052 of the doctor's test subjects combined, and he would have rendered the study altogether ineffectual—especially in that his affliction has absolutely nothing to do with white noise.

Coincidentally, Narnia Hecklebake was a test subject in Dr. Noteboom's study. It was determined that impulse overpowers the girl only four times a day on average, which makes her the least impulsive subject of them all. The doctor attributed this anomaly to the fact that Narnia doesn't watch TV or the news on a regular basis and hardly ever goes to the movies. "She exists just beyond the event horizon of the black hole that is our sociocultural matrix," he opined in one newscaster's microphone at a recent press conference. "In other words, whether we are here or there or anywhere, we all pick up white noise, and the white noise her sensorium picks up is distilled by distance, by virtual absence."

THE VOICEOVER MAN

The patient lays on the hospital bed. He is naked and unconscious, and his quiet snore is the sound of a fingernail running back and forth across a piece of sandpaper.

The apprentice doctors surround the patient in a half-hearted football huddle, whispering dirty jokes and poking one another in the ribs with their thumbs. Surrounding them is a massive body of medical students situated in the cheap seats of the panoramic loft that circumscribes the assembly hall. Most of the medical students are whispering dirty jokes and ribbing one another, too, but their jokes aren't as funny as their superiors', and when they thrust their thumbs into one another's ribs, it is accomplished with much more hostility and angst . . .

A door in the whitewall slides open and Dr. Ickling strides onto the main floor of the assembly hall. The apprentice doctors and medical students abruptly clam up and bury their thumbs in their armpits, and the patient, even though he is unconscious, somehow senses the doctor's presence and stops snoring.

Dr. Ickling nods at the apprentice doctors that kiss his ass on a regular basis while he adjusts his mask and snaps on latex gloves. He squints at an EEG screen. He checks to make sure his operating utensils are in order. He cracks his knuckles one at a time and begins to pet and stroke the flesh of the patient's chest. Everybody observes these actions with silent, simulated vigilance.

"Say," the doctor remarks in a voice loud enough for the medical student sitting farthest away from him to hear him, "did you hear the one about the bulldog, the Mexican, and the dried-up asshole?" Everybody smiles and shakes their heads. As the doctor tells the joke, he continues to fondle the patient's flesh, rummaging his hands across the patient's stomach and then up to his neck with that soporific fluidity and grace only a full-fledged doctor's hands possess. When he delivers the punch line of the joke, a battery of simulated hysterics erupt from his audience like water from a whale's blowhole.

"Where did you come up with *that* one?" giggles an apprentice doctor, whose hysterics are too conspicuously simulated—and who, for that matter, is not one of Dr. Ickling's pets. The doctor huffs and ignores the question. He clears his throat.

"Teufelsdröchk please."

Teufelsdröchk is the heroic, transcendental protagonist of Thomas Carlyle's novel-autobiography-essay *Sartor Resartus* (1833-34), a seminal Romantic narrative. It is also a pseudonym for Dr. Ickling's scalpel. The doctor could care less about Romanticism or the signification effectuated by the act of referring to his scalpel as Teufelsdröchk: he just likes the sound of the word, it's goofy yet compelling and dynamic, and it makes him in-snigger with pleasure every time the word skips out of his lips.

Dr. Ickling sizes up the portion of the patient's flesh that is about to be filleted. He holds out his open palm. The long stainless steel handle of Teufelsdröchk is gently placed inside of it. "Alright then," he announces. "Here we go, people." A commotion rings out across the assembly hall like a stormy gust of wind blustering through the leaves of a maple tree as the medical students pull note pads, writing instruments and candy bars out of their briefcases.

Dr. Ickling carefully places the sharp, gleaming tip of Teufelsdröchk onto the patient's chest at the point where his impeccably sculpted pectoral muscles bifurcate and arch away from one another. His tongue and inner cheeks have suddenly turned into cotton fields. He dry-swallows in discomfort.

"I hate this shit," he mumbles under his breath.

A few of the apprentice doctors glance at him sideways but they don't say anything. Dr. Ickling sighs. He licks his lips and sighs again . . . and slices the patient open, skillfully moving Teufelsdröchk down and around his navel. While he is making the incision, the bitter, disgusted expression on his face becomes more and more pronounced. Nobody can see this expression, of course, thanks to the doctor's mask. But they hear him loud and clear when, the incision finished, he peels back the patient's skin, exposing a little garbage heap of slimy internal organs, and says, "Gross. That is *sooooo* gross."

The apprentice doctors scratch their masks and blink at each other. One of them says, "Doctor Ickler? Are you all right sir?"

"The name's Ickling, you evil retard," gripes Dr. Ickling, stifling the vomit that is fighting its way up his throat. He feels woozy.

The apprentice doctor cocks his head. "What's that, sir? I'm sorry, I didn't hear you. Could you repeat that for me please? Sir? You okay there?"

Overhead the medical students are eating their candy bars and drawing tormented-looking stick figures on their notepads. A few of them are writing sentences that read "Blah blah blah blah blah blah."

"Right!" blurts Dr. Ickling and returns Teufelsdröchk to the hand that fed it to him. He pulls off his mask, nervously removes his blood-stained rubber gloves. He raises his chin and intones to the assembly hall: "Well, that's how it's done folks. If you'll excuse me now, I'm going outside to smoke a pack of cigarettes." Then, to the medical student who had called him Ickler: "Would you be so kind as to finish up the procedure please? Remember, this man will die if you yank his liver out of him too enthusiastically, so yank it out gently. Then soak it in this ointment"—points at a cereal bowl full of green slush that resembles decayed algae—"for ten minutes and while it's soaking present a short lecture on the vicissitudes of autoimmune hepatitis, tyrosemia and, for good measure, primary sclerosing cholangitis. Then rinse off the liver, return it to the patient's abdomen and sew the patient up. Can you handle that? Don't fuck up. If you fuck this shit up, I'll see to it that you're booed out of this industry like a bad comedian. Now if you'll excuse me, I need nicotine. The sight and smell of all of those innards is freaking me out." Dr. Ickling bows, salutes his pets and marches out of the assembly hall.

Outside in the cool evening air he sits down on a curb and fumbles a Lucky out of its pack. He lights it, takes a deep drag. "Ahh," he says to the bum whose residence is the portion of the curb on which he has sat. "Nothing like that first post-operation puff. Nothing like it in the whole world. Know what I mean, Dr. Plott?"

Dr. Plott, the bum, and Dr. Ickling's therapist, coughs up a little squall and rolls over. He is a grimy man with a grimy beard and two glazed, beady eyes. His soiled trench coat smells like it has been soaked in a tank full of liquid b.o. for a few days.

A ball of dusty tumbleweed dribbles across the street. Dr. Plott mistakes it for a movie- star-in-real-life and shouts out for its autograph. The tumbleweed doesn't respond. Dr. Plott swears at it, then sits up straight. He scootches behind Dr. Ickling on the sidewalk. He hugs his legs and asks for a smoke. Dr. Ickling lights one and flicks it over his shoulder. Dr. Plott smokes the whole thing in one great inhale. A profound head rush overwhelms him and he passes out, his chin sagging onto his chest.

Half a minute later Dr. Plott wakes up. He burps. He stretches his arms over his head. "Tell me all about it then," he yawns.

Dr. Ickling flicks his cigarette into the gutter and lights another one. As he externalizes himself, he continues to chainsmoke, staring across the empty street at the flickering, fizzing neon sign hanging over the entranceway of the hole-in-the-wall bar where most of the full-fledged doctors in the hospital prefer to get drunk. The sign says "———" but he does not see the word. All he sees is himself, standing there alone in the center of his mind's screen, a victim of his wildly ironic inability to stomach the interiors of human beings.

"See, the thing is," says Dr. Ickling, "I'm in the wrong line of work. I hate the insides of people! I've always hated them. I can't stand cutting people open and fooling around with their organs—especially when I'm teaching a class! You have no idea how difficult it is for me to keep my cool. Hangnails gross me out, for god's sake. Right now I'm staring at a hangnail on my finger and I'm telling you, I'm grossed out. Imagine how I feel when I'm confronted with a handful of grubby intestines or a cirrhotic liver that looks like a giant tequila worm with a bad case of dysentery. Holy cow! I despise viscera. I despise the entire human anatomy. The only reason I became a doctor in the first place was because I was the seventh son of a seventh son and all seventh sons of seventh sons are supposed to become doctors, preferably plastic surgeons. That's what my father said anyway."

Simulating curiosity, Dr. Plott raises an eyebrow. "You're father, you say? Hmm. Hmm. Hmm."

"Why did you just say 'Hmm' three times?"

"You know why. That's what therapists are supposed to do when words like 'father' are uttered by an analysand. Continue please."

"Right. Okay. What was I saying?"

"You were implying that your father coerced you into becoming what you are."

"Right. That's right. I shouldn't have become a plastic surgeon. I shouldn't have become a doctor of any kind."

"What do you think you should have become?"

"Good question. That's a good question." Dr. Ickling wrinkles up his lips and knits his brow. "I guess if I could have become anything, I would have become one of those guys who does voiceovers for movie trailers. Yeah. One of those voiceover

73

men."

Now Dr. Plott wrinkles up his lips and knits his brow. "I don't know what you're talking about. I don't go to the movies."

"You've never been to the movies before?"

"No. Why don't you explain what exactly these quote-unquote voiceover men do."

"Are you kidding me? You've never been to a movie before? Bull."

"Can I have a cigarette?"

Dr. Ickling peers over his shoulder at Dr. Plott and gives him a dirty look. Dr. Plott says, "Don't do that. How many times do I have to tell you not to do that? It's bad karma for an analysand to look his therapist in the eyes, particularly when the analysand is in the process of constructing his mental labyrinth with the bricks of language. Turn around please."

Grumbling, Dr. Ickling reluctantly obeys. He sticks two cigarettes in his mouth, lights them and throws one over his shoulder.

"Thank you," says Dr. Plott, picking the cigarette up off the sidewalk. Another doctor walks out of the hospital, lights a cigarette and confirms his appointment with Dr. Plott the next morning, at 8:30 a.m., on the curb. Dr. Plott politely tells him he's in no position to discuss his schedule as he is currently treating a patient. The doctor apologizes and heads across the street to get drunk.

Dr. Plott hawks up a hairball of phlegm, spits it out. He runs his eczema-plagued fingers through his dandruff-plagued hair. "Now then. You were saying something about voiceover men?"

"I can't believe you've never been to the movies before," says Dr. Ickling, smoke surging out of his nostrils in an irritated huff. "You're lying."

"Perhaps. But whether I'm lying or not is not the issue here. Just pretend I'm an uninformed yet intelligent listener who will not judge you under any circumstance. Of course, in reality I will be judging you through and through, but let's pretend we're not operating under the aegis of reality for a moment. Reality is for the birds anyway."

Dr. Ickling rolls his eyes. "Fine, I'll pretend you're a total jackass. Although to say I'm pretending you're a total jackass would be a lie, because that's what I really think of you. So you're just going to have to pretend I'm pretending."

"We're in an especially distasteful mood, aren't we?" replies Dr. Plott. "But I understand you're under a lot of pressure. I forgive you."

"You forgive me? You're not supposed to forgive me. You're supposed to be impartial. I'm supposed to be able to say anything I want to you and you're supposed to take what I dish out like a crash test dummy. What the hell is this?"

Dr. Plott removes one of his shoes. He looks inside of it, as if there might be a buried treasure in there. "Do I ever tell you how to do your job? Don't tell me how to do mine. I know what I'm doing."

"Do you? It doesn't seem like it. It seems like you're a douche bag."

Dr. Plott returns his shoe to his foot. "Maybe we ought to call it a day," he says, and threatens to roll over and go back to sleep.

Dr. Ickling flexes his jaw. "Voiceover men provide commentary for movie trailers," he blurts. "They have deep, powerful, smoke-scratched voices and they never fail to articulate every last syllable of every single word that comes out of their mouths. They speak dramatically, their voices are aflame with panache. As a selection of scene fragments from the movie that the movie trailer is advertising flash across the screen—that's what trailers do, advertise movies—the voiceover men flawlessly belt out punchy, cheesy bits of dialogue that are meant to entice audiences and that usually have something to do with the movie's plot and the trials and tribulations of the main characters."

"How many voiceover men provide commentary for a given trailer? Five? Twenty? That seems like a lot of voices talking at once. That sounds like a lot of verbal chaos to me."

Dr. Ickling closes his eyes and shakes his head. "You know goddamn well—" He cuts himself off before he has a chance to cut Dr. Plott down. "There's *one* voiceover man per trailer. Twenty voiceover men all talking at once? Come on. I don't even think there's that many voiceover men in the industry. Can't be more than a handful. I swear, every time I see a sequence of movie trailers it's the same guys talking to me."

"I see. And what attracts you to this line of work?"

Dr. Ickling lights a new cigarette with the ember of an old cigarette. "Well, for starters, I wouldn't have to cut anybody open."

"There are numerous professions that don't require you to cut anybody open. A shoe salesman, for instance. A graphic designer, too."

"Thanks for the examples," mutters Dr. Ickling.

Dr. Plott says, "Can you think of a reason why you might find the life of a voiceover man attractive in and of itself rather than in comparison with the life of a plastic surgeon?"

As the doctor is about to respond, an ambulance pulls up to the curb. A company of orderlies clumsily spill out of the back of it. They bluster into the hospital carrying a twitching, blood-soaked body. Dr. Ickling shudders and covers his eyes with his hands. He keeps his eyes covered until he hears the back doors of the hospital close and the ambulance cheerily beep its horn and drive away.

"I'm pathetic," sighs Dr. Ickling. "Pathetic! Can you believe I'm the doctor-in-chief at this hospital? But when I have to perform, I perform. I have that knack. Yes, despite my intolerable queasiness, despite my paradoxical phobia for the visual and olfactory nastiness of human innards, me and my Teufelsdröchk can go to work when we really have to. I may not like it. I may not like it one bit. But I can do it all right."

The doctor flicks another cigarette away and lights a fresh one. "Still, I'm a moron. I've dedicated my professional life to something that I loathe and dread. I should be a voiceover man. I should be shrouded in mystery, making the millions that I'm making now but living in total anonymity. Nobody knows who those assholes are! They go into some dark little studio on Hollywood Boulevard and talk their talk into a microphone and then they go home. Everybody hears their voices, but nobody sees who they are. They're one of the few classes of celebrities whose fame isn't established by means of their image. I mean, how often do you come across a famous person that's a total dog! Not too often. I'm not a dog, no, but I'm a famous person, in my profession anyway, and I wish I could just become a nobody and at the same time retain my notability. A famous nobody is what I want to be."

"Why do you feel the need to be, as you say, a famous nobody?" interjects Dr. Plott.

"Why do you feel the need to interrupt me when I'm trying to tell you something!" exclaims Dr. Ickling. "Jesus. You don't know the first goddamn thing about psychoanalysis. And you're degreed from Yale! Well, you claim to be. You're full of shit. You're a whole lot of bullshit."

"Curious invective. I think I know what you're problem is. I think you need to get laid."

"Get laid? Get laid my ass. I'm a doctor. I get laid all the time and you know it. What kind of advice is that? What are you, in high school?"

"All right, all right. Forget I brought it up. Let's get back to the matter at hand."

"Are you going to shut up and let me talk?"

Dr. Plott doesn't reply; another tumbleweed passes by and this time he calls it a few names without even asking for its autograph.

"That's not a movie star, you idiot," says Dr. Ickling.

"Can I bum another cigarette?"

77

Dr. Ickling closes his eyes and rubs them. For a short time he remains silent, wishing he could retain the services of another therapist. But all of the therapists that he knows in town—and he knows them *all*—are bums like Dr. Plott and, unlike Dr. Plott, most of them can barely string a coherent sentence together, they're always so drunk and strung out.

Eventually Dr. Ickling gives Dr. Plott a cigarette and continues to externalize himself. "Yeah, voiceover men have it made. Their names are unknown, their faces are unknown, but their voices bear the power of a steamroller at full throttle! I smoke enough cigarettes to be one. Clearly those men—and for obvious reasons they are invariably *men*—clearly they're chainsmoking fiends like me. I smoke one after the other and my voice resonates from the bottom of the abyss and you better believe that I know a thing or two about what it takes to articulate a syllable. Fact is, all these years I've secretly been waiting for a voiceover scout to discover me. Whenever I've been in public I've always made an effort to talk my ass off in the most sonorous and deep-seated manner imaginable. But I've never been solicited by a voiceover scout. If I had, trust me, I would have been picked up on the spot. Well, it's time to make my mark. It's time to actuate myself and fulfill my destiny. Sounds corny, I know, but corny or not it's my goddamn destiny to become a voiceover man. Tomorrow I'm quitting this place once and for all. I'm resigning as doctor-in-chief and I'm going to become a star with no name and no face!"

"But why do you want to be famous and to be a nobody at one and the same time?" Dr. Plott inquires, his cigarette crudely dangling from one corner of his mouth. "To place the word 'famous' in front of the word 'nobody' is to create a oxymoron. Why do you want to be an oxymoron?"

"I'm not sure. I just want to be. And I will. Soon."

Dr. Ickling, of course, is full of shit. He says more or less the same thing to Dr. Plott during every one of their bi-weekly psychiatric sessions and has no intention of quitting his job. If he were to quit, however, and if he were to pursue a career as a voiceover man, he would be disappointed.

There is only one voiceover man. A single, singular man does all of the voiceovers for all of the movie trailers and simply alters his voice now and then to give off the impression that he doesn't own and dominate the entire voiceover industry. But he does. He is a selfish, lonely, ugly, wicked man and the mere thought of anybody but him producing a voiceover for a movie trailer makes him nauseous. He is paid generously for what he does—he can't even remember how many Swiss bank accounts he has opened—yet he is a hopeless miser and lives in a cruddy, poorly furnished motel room somewhere in L.A., he's not sure where; having hired somebody to buy and deliver him groceries, he hasn't left the room in a good five years. He smokes approximately 100 cigarettes a day and only owns three articles of clothing: two beat-up flip-flops and a silk bathrobe that once belonged to his foster mother. Sometimes he wears these articles of clothing, but he usually prefers to wear nothing.

His skin is the color of television static. His body is dilapidated and deformed—it is as if somebody arranged a bunch of decayed, dried-up, moldy tree branches in a certain way and decided to call the arrangement a person. Despite the degraded physical condition of the voiceover man, however, he still manages to do his job. Every morning a new trailer and accompanying trailer script is waiting for him on his computer. He rolls out of bed, urinates, coughs up phlegm for half an hour, and exercises his vocal chords by uttering the following mantra seven times as fast as he can:

What a to-do to die today at a minute or two to two. A thing distinctly hard to say but harder still to do. For there'll be a tattoo at a minute or two, a ratatatatatatatatattoo, and the dragon will come when he hears the drum at a minute or two to two today at a minute or two to two.

79

This done, he chainsmokes a pack of cigarettes as he channel-surfs between talk shows, then sits down in front of his computer and goes to work. He works for about an hour every day, give or take. Around 1 p.m., including weekends, there is a knock on his door. He waits for one minute before quickly opening the door and gathering up the bag sitting in front of his feet. Inside the bag is a bottle of bourbon, a carton of cigarettes, two king-sized bags of Doritos and one regular-sized bag of Double Stuff Oreos. He spends the rest of the day and night drinking, and chainsmoking, and eating, and watching TV.

Then the voiceover man turns off the lights and crawls into bed. He falls asleep without too much difficulty, albeit as he drifts off he is harrowed by the nagging, chilling prospect of Death. And in his dreams, he is an agonized-looking stick figure being drawn on a notepad by a medical student in the middle of an act of simulation . . .

PROFESSOR
DYSPEPTICAL'S
PARROT

Professor Dyspeptical decided he would rather not teach his classes anymore. The lectures he had to write and present every day required an unreasonable amount of time and effort to prepare, not to mention that his students all despised him. He would much rather stay in bed all day, watching talk shows and soap operas while sipping mimosas from the glittery, high-heeled shoe of a drag queen. Then, in the evenings, he could dress up like a drag queen and carelessly prance up and down the sidewalks of his neighborhood instead of correcting papers and trying to figure out which of his students despised him with the most enthusiasm . . .

Determined to give up, the professor visited a pet store and bought a parrot. He took the bird home, fed it a piece of dry pound cake, and taught it how to talk and act like an intelligent human being.

The next day at 12:38 p.m., two minutes before his first class began, the professor was laying in bed, half-drunk, fully naked, a dipstick smile painted onto his rubicund face. On the television was an advertisement for a new brand of cereal that filled him with glee . . .

The door of the classroom creaked open at 12:39 p.m. There was a pause. During the pause, the students glanced and blinked at one another. The students glanced and blinked at one another with more vigor when the parrot fluttered into the classroom, the handle of a small leather briefcase clenched in its

82

sharp black beak. It was wearing miniature pince-nez and much of its colorful body was concealed by a little tailor-made tweed jacket.

The parrot landed on the podium. It removed a few tiny, crinkled papers from the briefcase with a mindful claw. It cracked its neck, stretched out its wings, cleared its throat.

"Good afternoon, class," said the bird. "Professor Dyspeptical has come down with a syndrome and will be out of commission for an indefinite length of time. Hence I will be teaching this class in his stead. Do not be offset by the fact that I do not hold a Ph.D. in this subject. The underlying content and structure of the lectures I will be presenting were conceived of by the aforementioned professor. True, I edited his lectures with extreme prejudice, but I nonetheless ask you to think of me as nothing more than a medium. Today I will be deliberating Freud's 'Notes Upon a Case of Obsessional Neurosis,' otherwise known as the 'Rat Man' case history. I am particularly interested in Freud's notion that the Rat Man is a victim of a persistent, if not rabid anal eroticism and the impact that this notion has on Freud's general psychoanalytic angle of incidence. I will begin by reading a passage from the case history that can be found on page fifty-two in your texts. That's page fifty-two. Five two. Hey, you there. Open your book and listen to what I'm saying to you, you ridiculous asshole . . ."

Professor Dyspeptical's parrot continued to preside over his classes for two weeks before his students retaliated. It began when a young frat boy visited a pet store and bought a parrot. He took the bird back to his fraternity house, fed it a pint of Mad Dog and a six pack of Natural Light, and taught it how to simulate interest in uninteresting things. For good measure, he also taught it how to talk dirty to sorority girls. Then he gave it his books, pointed in the direction of the building in which Professor Dyspeptical's classroom was located, and went to a bar to get drunk and laid.

The parrot that had taken over for Professor Dyspeptical evil-eyed the parrot that had taken over for the frat boy when it flapped into the classroom and drunkenly zigzagged over to the frat boy's seat. It's one thing for a professor to replace himself with a bird, the professor's parrot told itself, but it's quite another thing for a student to do the same thing. That's horseshit! Still, the professor's parrot didn't say anything. It merely continued to evil-eye the frat boy's parrot for a few more seconds before turning to the day's lecture.

A student's intelligence is only put to use when the possibility of avoiding the accumulation of knowledge (and consequently the amplification of intelligence) exposes itself. It wasn't long before all of Professor Dyspeptical's classes were populated by parrots. Like the students they represented, most of the parrots were drunk on cheap wine and beer and wore tattered pieces of clothing, and all of them were experts at simulating interest in information that authority figures communicated to them.

One night Professor Dyspeptical's parrot tried to tell Professor Dyspeptical that his students had followed his lead and were using talking animals to signify themselves. The parrot had been hesitant to bring it up before, knowing that the professor didn't want to be bothered with the social dynamics of his classes, but the whole fiasco was really starting to get on its nerves. The professor didn't care. In fact, he took a certain sadistic pleasure in his parrot's consternation. Lounging on his bed in blood red Victoria's Secret lingerie, he said, "It's a terrible thing, to be despised. Isn't it?"

"I don't feel despised," replied the parrot. "It has nothing to do with how I think your students' parrots perceive me. I just feel perturbed. I just feel weird."

"I'm sorry to hear that. Would you be a doll and go make me a martini please? Thank you, sir."

After that, Professor Dyspeptical's parrot never mentioned the issue again. There was no point in mentioning it. Word spread and soon all kinds of people, not just one insignificant professor and a bunch of his students, were retreating into the shadows and representing themselves with parrots. Businessmen, newscasters, computer technicians, janitors, lawyers, fry cooks, politicians, priests, even movie stars and television personalities had all "turned to the bird," as the saying went, so that they could pursue their true interests (usually something sexual) and be who they really waned to be (usually some kind of pervert).

Eventually everybody turned to the bird. What had come to be known as the Dyspeptical Gesture swept across the world like a new and improved sexually transmitted disease. Even homeless people and denizens of third-world countries managed to scrounge up enough spare change to purchase surrogate parrots from pet stores. On the streets of every city, in the fields of every countryside, on the televisions of every home, not a person was to be seen or heard. The goings-on of everyday life had been entirely given up to a parrot existence.

It wasn't long before Professor Dyspeptical's parrot decided it would rather not teach its classes anymore. The lectures it had to present every day required an unreasonable amount of time and effort to enunciate, not to mention that it was sick of dressing up all the time in miniature human clothes. It also came to believe that its stand-in students did in fact despise it.

Determined to give up, the parrot visited a pet store, bought a parrot, took the parrot home, fed it a clawful of bird seed and taught it how to talk like an intelligent parrot that has been taught how to talk like an intelligent human being.

The next day at 12:38 p.m. Professor Dyspeptical's parrot was laying on Professor Dyspeptical's big pink belly, half-drunk, fully naked, a dipstick smile carved into its crooked beak. On the television was an advertisement for a new brand of peanut butter that filled it with glee . . .

PITYRIASIS PARK

Back then I used to spend a lot of time at Pityriasis Park. They named the park after a skin condition called Pityriasis Rosea, a rash that develops on the chest and back and is often mistaken for ringworm. The cause of the rash is unknown. It is known, however, that the rash is not caused by a fungus or bacteria. Nor is it due to any type of allergy. Anyway, they named the park after a rash.

Pityriasis Park didn't have the features of a normal park. It had the features of a football field-sized plot of dirt that has just been rototilled. To make it look more park-like, people would come there and impersonate trees, bushes, benches, squirrels, picnic blankets, merry-go-rounds and so forth. I never took part in this exercise. I went to the park and impersonated a person taking a stroll through a park.

I distinctly remember the people that used to impersonate grass. Most of them were portly gentlemen with hairy backs. They would remove their shirts and lay down on their big stomachs all over the place so that the ground that constituted the park was more flesh than dirt. I always showed these people the courtesy of taking off my shoes before walking across them, albeit most of them would squeal like whoopie cushions when I stepped on their downy backs, my body being, like theirs, far tubbier than an average person's body. But I tried to move over them with a quick and delicate tread, as if I was traversing a vast bed of hot coals. I'm grateful for the pains they took to make my strolls through Pityriasis Park more like a stroll through a real park. To show my appreciation, sometimes I would go there with a satchel of silver dollars and bury one in the back hair of each of the grass-impersonators. It was an expensive undertaking. But I used to have more money than I knew what to do with.

The last time I visited Pityriasis Park, I ran into two people I knew. One was my father. Completely naked, he was impersonating a hound dog frolicking under a great weeping willow tree, which was being impersonated by a woman who I recognized as my ex-wife. She was also completely naked. I was surprised by how much weight she had gained since the last time I saw her two years ago; she used to be firm and toned, a fleshly work of art, but now her body was defined by clumps and rolls of fat. My father, in contrast, who I had not seen in almost a decade (I thought he was dead), was as thin, rickety and dusty as an old broom stick somebody had offhandedly thrown in a basement closet and forgotten about. But he managed to frolic with a certain amount of gusto, and when I held out my hand, he scurried over to me and lapped at it with a friendly tongue.

"That's a good boy," I said, massaging the corpulent grey scruff of his neck. He reminded me of what Walt Whitman looked like as an old man. Only this Walt Whitman, in light of his deathly frail frame, looked like he had been shooting up heroine for the better part of his life.

I massaged and petted my father for a minute or two, then allowed him to get back to his frolicking. I turned my attention to my ex-wife.

"Hello," I said.

My ex-wife didn't reply. She stood there rigidly, adamantly, her arms poised above her head, her in-motion fingers dangling from her cupped palms like strands of seaweed flowing underwater. Her mouth was opened into a obdurate O-shape that signified a knot in the trunk of her bulk, and her stout legs were firmly pressed together. She had even gone to the trouble of burying her feet in the earth.

Nobody was impersonating grass in her vicinity.

"Hello," I said again.

This time she replied. "Stop saying hello to me." After she spoke, her mouth immediately snapped back into an O-shape.

I shrugged. "Why? What's wrong with saying hello?"

My ex-wife spent a while fighting off the invidious frown that began to take control of her face. She put up a good fight but in the end the frown beat her to a pulp. Her mouth squeezed into a vicious sphincter. "There's nothing wrong with saying hello," she barked, "if you're saying hello to a regular person. I'm not a regular person. I'm a person who is impersonating a weeping willow tree. By saying hello to me you're pretending I am something that I am not. Since I am what I am, that's ludicrous. That's like asking a real weeping willow tree to weep."

"Don't be like that," I said.

She ignored me. "If you want some shelter from the sun, fine, recline under the shadow of the branches and leaves that my arms and fingers signify. Otherwise I can't help you. Otherwise—carry on with your walk."

For a moment I considered taking shelter in her shadow. It was a hot, cloudless day out and I could have used a little shade. But I didn't want to give my ex-wife that kind of satisfaction, so I nodded, turned, walked away. As I went I heard her snicker and shout out how the last two years had treated my hairline. "You'll be bald by year's end!" she blurted.

Now a frown tried to take control of my face. I didn't fight it; I let it overcome me like a cackle overcomes a hyena.

I stubbed my toe on a rock. I swore: a powerful "Shit!" erupted from my mouth and echoed into the distance. Hopping on one foot, I clutched my stubbed toe with my hands and massaged it through the worn leather of my shoe like I had massaged my father's neck just a moment ago. When the pain subsided, I glanced down at the rock and considered its potentiality. I wanted to pick it up and throw it at my ex-wife. But the rock was being impersonated by a young boy. He was face

88

down in the dirt, his knees flush against his chest, his arms wrapped around his knees, and I knew I lacked the strength to lift him, let alone wind up and fling him at my past.

MYBARBARIAN

MY BARBARIAN

The barbarian wasn't working out. It kept defecating all over the upholstery, and whenever the wife and I had company over, it insisted on tackling and molesting every last cleavage-toter it could get its bony, gritty fingers on. I decided to return it.

"You sure you wanna take that route?" said Harry Arboreal, general manager of The Barbarian Boutique. We were standing in the middle of the store. Surrounding us was an ersatz jungle laden with barbarians like mine. Most of the barbarians were swinging on vines or whaling on each other with femurs or logs. A few were masturbating. One was banging its face against a tree trunk. "I mean, I'd be happy to take your barbarian back, but maybe you're being a little bit hasty here," Harry added. "Maybe you should give your barbarian another chance. After all, it's your barbarian."

He had a point. I thanked him and greased his cold calloused palm with a fifty for the advice, then grabbed the barbarian by its leash and clicked my tongue.

On the way home, the barbarian gnawed through its leash and attacked a street mime. The street mime saw it coming and, thinking it was a dirty crazy person instead of a barbarian, tried to reason with it by gesturing at it in a certain way with his face and body parts. The barbarian paid no attention to the gestures; it leapt on and began strangling the mime. The mime didn't have a voice box—it was stolen and sold on the black market by his stepfather when he was a child, an awful thing in that he lacked the capacity to express himself by means of speech acts, but a good thing in that, had his voice box never been stolen and sold, he never would have become a mime, a profession he thoroughly enjoyed—so all he could do was mouth "Help! Help! Help!" in silence.

I felt sorry for the mime and said, "Leave that thing alone!" The barbarian didn't listen to me. I took what was left of the leash and gave it two quick, bloody lashes across the back. The barbarian squealed like a piglet and jumped off the mime. Urinating uncontrollably, it gamboled into traffic. Horns blasted, tires shrieked, cars crashed and exploded. I waited patiently for the smoke to clear . . . but when it did, the barbarian was gone.

I spent the rest of the day looking all over the city for it. I looked in dumpsters, I looked in manholes, I looked in every house of ill repute. No luck. I started knocking on people's doors and asking if they had seen it. Nobody had. Then, as I was leaning up against a lamppost catching my breath, I saw the barbarian running down the middle of the street. It ran right by me, saluting me with a curt fart as it passed.

I pushed myself off the lamppost. Flagged down and leapt into a taxi. "Follow that barbarian!" I pointed. The taxi driver refused. "It's against my religion to acknowledge the existence of barbarians," he said, "and if I follow that barbarian, well, that's precisely what I'll be doing, isn't it?"

"Not if you pretend that barbarian is a haberdasher," I said. The taxi driver grabbed his chin with the tips of his fingers and began fondling it. I waited patiently for the fondling to come to an end . . . but it never did. And by the time I leapt out of his taxi and flagged down and leapt into another one, the barbarian was long gone. After having a little fit, I told this taxi driver to take me to the police headquarters. I wanted to look around for the barbarian some more. I wanted to tell it that, even though it had been misbehaving, I was sorry for abusing it. But I was too tired and depressed. I filed a missing barbarian's report and went home, wondering how I was going to explain everything to the wife.

As it turned out, I didn't have to explain anything. I walked into my house and there was the barbarian, *my* barbarian, micturating on the couch. It was squatting on an arm rest and the wife was yelling at it, trying to convince it to go use the toilet. But the barbarian wouldn't budge. And when I nodded at it, it nodded back at me.

WHEN A MAN WALKS INTO A ROOM

When a man walks into a room, I ask myself two questions. The first questions is: Is he better looking than me? The second question is: Should I kill him?

I sat in my seat by the window and these two questions popped onto my mind's screen like subtitles in a foreign film. A smoking cigarillo was fixed between my lips and a determined, dominating expression was cemented onto my face. Outside of the window the blurs of flapping trench coats whizzed by in the neon fog of Pseudofolliculitis city.

Eventually I approached the man and asked him his name. The names of the men I approach are always something corny and pretentious, something socially invigorating, like Lonny Hoedown or Johnny Acerbic or Donny Clockworkorange. This man's name was no exception. But I complimented him on it anyway and asked if he'd like me to buy him a drink.

The man glanced nervously around the bar, as if he expected somebody to save him from me.

The bar was a representation of the inside of a human body. Its walls were slick soft surfaces; its tables and chairs were made of pelvises, humeruses, fibulas, ulnas and tibias; its glasses and ash trays were hollowed out internal organs; its vast store of booze was the color of blood. The clientele in the bar consisted of businessmen wearing business suits on their bodies and businesslike expressions on their faces. There were also a number of porn stars scattered here and there. All of them were hard-bodied females with monstrous plastic breasts that demanded an

94

excess of attentiveness. Other than the network of tribal tattoos that covered their bodies from head to toe, they didn't bother with the pretense of clothing.

Neither businessmen nor porn stars offered the man their voice and company when I accosted him.

"I'm meeting somebody," he lied. He was wearing a wrinkle-free vicuña suit with an alligator skin belt and snazzy wingtip shoes. His patternless tie was sapphire blue. He had a sharp physiognomy reminiscent of a bald-faced coyote with an aquiline human nose and chin. A good-looking fella, him. Slightly better-looking than me.

His name was Tommy Thingdoer.

"Yeah, I'm meeting somebody," he repeated with too much enthusiasm, staring at my mouth instead of my eyes.

"You lie," I said. I was wearing a wrinkle-free mohair suit with a snakeskin belt and sleek wingtip shoes. My pattern-less tie was ruby red. I had a sharp physiognomy reminiscent of a bald-faced fox with an aquiline human nose and chin. Not a bad-looking fella, me. But I'm sagacious enough to know when I've been one-upped.

My name is of no consequence.

Tommy flexed his jaw in consternation when I called him a liar. At that moment his desire to destroy me was as obvious and obnoxious as a Tourette's victim having a fit in church during a silent prayer. I stared coolly into his eyes, the corner of one side of my mouth curled up, and waited for him to address me. While I was waiting I took note of a well-known politician that traipsed into the bar and gravitated towards a group of porn stars who were in the middle of a subtlety executed but productive lesbian orgy. Unlike most politicians, this one wasn't ugly and hideous. He was bald, of course, but his head wasn't shaped like a pumpkin and his eyes weren't close-knit and beady. On the contrary, he had a head like a hawk and his eyes were strong, blue and in proportion with the features of his face. He was slender, too—I'd go so far as to say that his build was athletic. His hideous purple zoot suit, on the other hand, countered these merits in his character. By law all politicians are required to wear purple zoot suits—despite its unctuous appearance, the outfit is considered a sign of prestige—and the one this guy had on was an exaggeration of a zoot suit, which itself is an exaggeration of a real suit: the shoulders on it were far too puffed up, the tails on it were far too long and wispy, the gold chains hanging off of his chest were far too copious and shiny, and so forth. He wasn't even worth my time. And even if he *was* worth my time, I wouldn't have approached him. I don't approach famous people; in contrast to most non-famous people, I don't like to give the Other the satisfaction of thinking that I give a rat's ass about what it is they do that makes them famous, whether it be acting, writing, playing sports, inventing theories and machines, or, in the case of this famous person, making speeches and shaking hands and smiling ersatz smiles and accumulating as many mistresses as humanly possible. But more than that, the politician had already dropped his pants and began having sex with the porn stars. Once a man has laid down and administered a macdaddy, he has transcended my desire to plot against and kill him.

As I regarded and sized up the politician, I kept my eyes more or less fixed on Tommy Thingdoer's eyes, which remained more or less fixed on my mouth. This went on for a good half a minute. Then I allowed my little smirk to smooth out into a thin indifferent line. "I'm waiting patiently for you to respond to me," I said. "There's no hurry. I'm not itching to get anywhere or to do anything. But I want you to know that I'm waiting for you. I want you to know that."

Tommy made a face like a man who has just sniffed a skunk's ass. This face persisted for longer than I expected, but eventually it was overcome by an inquisitive, cynical smile. "You're a freak," he said. "You're a big freak, aren't you? Look, I'm not gay. I'm actually waiting for a woman. My girlfriend."

"You lie," I said again. "You don't have a girlfriend.

96

You're not gay, but you don't have a girlfriend. You've never had a girlfriend in your life."

The I-just-sniffed-a-skunk's-ass look returned to Tommy's face. "How do you know whether or not I've ever had a girlfriend? How do you know if I'm gay or not? Don't take this the wrong way, pal, but you're bugging the shit out of me. What is this noise?"

I shrugged. "Let me buy you a drink and we can talk about it."

"I just told you I don't want you to buy me a drink. I don't want anything from you other than for you to leave me alone."

I closed my eyes and softly shook my head from side to side. "You have no choice," I said. "Don't you understand that you have no choice? I'm buying you a drink and that's the end of it." I took Tommy by the elbow and squeezed it. Panicking, he tried to pull his elbow away. But my grip was too goddamn strong. I maintained the grip until Tommy, not wanting to make a scene, and realizing that he couldn't physically overpower me, stopped struggling. "Fine, buy me a drink," he said through clenched teeth. "Buy me whatever you want. Just let go of my elbow. Jesus. Let go of me. I—"

I let go of him. Tommy turned his eyes to the mirror behind the bar as he clutched and massaged his elbow. I turned my eyes to the mirror, too.

Was I staring into the reflection of Tommy's eyes? Of course.

Was Tommy staring into the reflection of my eyes? Of course not. He was staring at the reflection of his own mouth.

I said, "You're not meeting your girlfriend, are you."

He hesitated before responding. "No. No I'm not. But I have a girlfriend. Well, I've had girlfriends. Plenty of them."

"Bartender," I intoned.

The bartender looked in my direction. He flipped up his chin, snapped his fingers and winked at me. Some people

97

might have interpreted these gestures as signs of compliance. But they were signs of nothing: after making the gestures, the bartender went back to talking to the porn star that was sitting on a stool at the end of the bar. She was a dirty blonde with a nicotine-stained smile and cutesy dimples in her cheeks. Her waist was as skinny as my wrist and her ungodly breasts were laying on the bone-plated bar counter like two lazy groundhogs. Every now and then the bartender would reach out and introspectively poke one of the breasts, as if he might be testing its resilience. The bartender was not an attractive man. He had crappy brown hair and dire widow's peaks that were grossly asymmetrical. He also had a beer belly that hung over the cheap Naugahyde belt holding up the trousers of his suit. Like his hair, the suit was a crappy brown color. His face was so plain and forgetful it defied description; there's not much I could say about it other than it consisted of eyes, nose, mouth and chin. So I had nothing against the bartender other than his apparent reluctance to serve me and my recently acquired enemy a drink.

"Bartender," I intoned.

No response at all this time; he completely ignored me. I looked at Tommy Thingdoer and smiled pleasantly, calmly. Tommy looked at me and blinked. He was clearly distraught and wanted to leave, but I knew he knew that if he tried to leave I would make his leaving very difficult and unpleasant. To assure him I knew he knew this, I nodded at him darkly.

I excused myself and walked down to the end of the bar. By the time I got there the porn star's nipple had found its way into the deranged mouth of the bartender; bent over with his chin parked on the bar counter, he sucked and sucked on the nipple like a starving infant as the porn star broadcasted loud, fake moans for everybody to hear. And everybody heard. But nobody gave off the impression that they heard. In Pseudofolliculitis City, giving off impressions—whether these impressions are genuine or counterfeit or somewhere in between the two doesn't matter—is a faux pas in the public sector. That's why everything I do, everything I say, every move I make is firmly rooted in the soil of an impressionist ethic.

The bartender eyed me when I sidled up to the porn star but he didn't stop doing what he was doing. Frowning, I excused myself. Neither of the fornicators listened. Frowning with more resolve, I excused myself again. Neither of them listened again. Wiping the frown off my face, I continued to excuse myself until somebody acknowledged me. "Excuse me please," I said in a dull monotone, eight times, before the porn star's nipple was relinquished from the emphatic grip of the bartender's lips and the man stood up.

"Can I help you?" he said. A hot-and-bothered expression illuminated his boring face.

"I don't know, can you? I wonder if you can. I really do."

Something in my tone of voice must have struck a nerve in the porn star. Or it had nothing to do with my voice and she was insane. Probably the latter. Anyway, she threw back her mangy, dimple-faced head and began to cackle. Every cackle that came out of her mouth was like the crack of a lion tamer's thick black whip. Her electrocuted breasts jiggled and surged.

I lifted my hand to my head. I used my thumb to scratch one of my temples.

I backhanded the porn star as hard as I could.

She flew off her bar stool as if catapulted, sailed through the air in what seemed like slow motion, and smashed into a jukebox on the far side of the room. The jukebox was a giant skull cropped in neon with CDs spinning in its gaping eyes and mouth. When the porn star nailed it, the song that was playing, The Bee Gee's *You Should Be Dancing*, was displaced by Abba's *Summer Night City*.

The bartender's wide eyes stared dumbly at the knocked out porn star, who lay at the foot of the jukebox in a gawky pile. The eyes of a few of the bar's constituents also stared at her, but most of them were drunk on alcohol and sex and didn't even notice the spectacle.

The bartender slowly turned his gaze my way. "That's my wife," he said, enraged.

I closed my eyes, pushed out my lips, nodded. "Yeah, that's my wife, too." I gestured at some other porn stars at random. "They're all my wives, right? Now how about serving a couple of thirsty sonuvabitches something to drink? My man down there and I, why don't you fix us up a couple of godfathers. Know what's in a godfather?" I knew the bartender knew the answer to this question. So I told him the answer. "Scotch and amaretto, that's what. Okay then. I'll be down at the other end of the bar waiting for my drinks. Here's a twenty. Don't keep the change."

As I walked back towards Tommy Thingdoer, I kept an eye on the bartender. I was pretty sure that that porn star I had manhandled was in fact his wife. Part of me expected the bartender to retaliate against me in her name—which, incidentally, was Misty Colchester, also known as Lansakes Janet, and collectively referred to by critics as "The Harbinger of Anal Intrigue." At any rate, he didn't do anything. He made a constipated face and his white-knuckled fists began to vibrate. But then his face took a laxative and his fists opened up into normal, sane hands. He turned to make the drinks I'd ordered.

"Sometimes you have to be assertive with people," I said to Tommy as I sat down on a stool next to the one he had sat down on. "Otherwise people will not only walk all over you, they'll knock you out with ether and fuck you up the ass."

Tommy was still looking at his mouth in the mirror. His inability to look me in the eyes was as satisfying to me as it was inexcusable.

I said, "Look me in the eyes when I'm talking to you, Thingdoer. It's the least you can do. I just bought you a drink. The least you can do is look me in the eyes when I say something."

Tommy slowly turned his head and faced me. Just as

quickly as his eyes locked on mine, however, they fell down to my mouth.

"Not my mouth," I warned him. "My eyes. I know it's a difficult thing to do. People's eyes are full of meaning and it can be a pain in the ass to focus on all of that meaning, especially if you're talking and listening at the same time. But I demand it of you. I insist that you focus on my meaning when I address you. Is that clear?"

Tommy snorted in disgust. He struggled to lift his eyes from my mouth to my eyes with the resolution of a bodybuilder who's trying to lift ten times his weight over his head. He couldn't do it. So he said, "You're a total asshole. Do you have any idea how much of an asshole you are? I think you're the biggest asshole I've ever met in my life."

Showing no emotion whatsoever, I casually leaned over and whispered something into Tommy's ear.

"I'm going to kill you," I whispered.

The bartender placed two godfathers in front of Tommy and I in a less than friendly manner. He flicked a torn five and three crumpled ones at me.

"These drinks are six dollars a pop?" I said. "Bull."

The bartender sneered, "The drinks are five dollars each. I kept two dollars for a tip."

"I told you not to keep the change."

"You hit my wife. I'm keeping the change."

Tipping is for the weak and I never do it. People don't leave tips because they care about the economic welfare of their servers. They leave tips because they're afraid of their servers calling them cheapskates out loud and, in so doing, distributing a certain knowledge to the general public. People tip because they're selfish, because they're worried about what other people might think of them if they don't. Tipping is a matter of maintaining one's image in the eyes of society. Since I could care less about the way in which the eyes of society view me, I would cut off my nose before I left a tip for somebody—especially this

101

bartender.

"Give me the two dollars you owe me or else I'm going to do something very evil," I said. "I'm going to do a very evil thing to you if you don't give me my money right now."

"Fuck off," replied the bartender.

Without moving my head, I flipped my eyes to the ceiling. A vast web of thick palpitating veins covered its fleshy entirety. I observed a particularly energetic stretch of vein as I responded to the bartender. "Is that what you want to say to me? I don't think it is. No, I don't think so. Don't you want to say something else to me?" My eyes left the ceiling and found the bartender's eyes. I stared at him for a few seconds before speaking again. "Tell you what, keep the change. I'm allowing you to do that. But at some point in the near future I expect you to replace your crass directive with something, well, a little fresher, and a little less unappreciative. Tell you what—I think that's a fair trade. Don't you?"

The bartender didn't hesitate to call me a name before heading over to the jukebox and waking up his alleged wife with a handful of smelling salts.

I looked at Tommy and puckered up my lips, then looked at the drinks that had been served to us. The glasses into which the godfathers had been poured were petrified human livers that had been hollowed out like bread bowls. The liquid inside of the livers was the color and texture of blood, but it tasted like it was supposed to taste.

Behind me I heard the politician cum. I turned and watched him pull up and buckle the pants of his zoot suit, thank the porn stars, give each of them a thousand dollar bill, tilt his tando hat to one side, and stride out of the bar, lighting a fat expensive cigar along the way.

"The American people have spoken," I said, picking up the liver in front of me. I sniffed it and took a swig.

Tommy said, "What did you just say to me?" He was sitting rigidly on his stool, as if something uninvited had just been shoved up his ass.

"I said the American people have spoken. I was trying to be funny. Do I need to try harder?"

Tommy shook his head. "No, before that."

Now I shook my head. "Before that? I can't remember. I say a lot of things."

"You said you were going to kill me."

"Did I?"

"Yes."

"Are you sure?"

"Yes. I'm sure."

I took another sip of my godfather. "Well, I guess that's what I said. And I guess that's what I'm going to do."

The front door of the bar jingled open and two men walked in. Their names were Jimmy Wisecrack and Danny Deracination. Like me, they were regulars here and I'd spoken with them once or twice before, but never in a hostile manner: neither of the men were better-looking than me. They were both alright-looking people and had mildly aquiline physiognomies with relatively straight white teeth and tolerable suede business suits and patternless ties and lizardskin belts and shoes. They weren't bald either, although Wisecrack had a smooth patch on the top of his head, and they weren't overweight. But compared to Tommy Thingdoer and I they were hags.

Jimmy Wisecrack lifted up his chin at me when he saw me. Danny Deracination used a pinky finger to give me a half-ass salute. I smiled, then returned my attention to Tommy as the two men sauntered over to a dimly lit corner in which another gaggle of porn stars were quietly fingerbanging each other.

In the last few moments, Tommy seemed to have developed a case of confidence. Or fearlessness. But aren't confidence and fearlessness the same thing? No, confidence can be simulated; a man can give off the impression of being in control of his wits when in fact his wits are bouncing off the walls of his insides like coked-up teaheads in a crack factory. Fearlessness, on the other hand, is solely a matter of truth. There is no feigning the absence of fear—not in my universe.

In light of the way I had verbally and physically bullied Tommy up to this point, I concluded that his newly adopted demeanor was distinguished by confidence. But it was a superbly executed confidence. Unlike before, he now sat on his stool in a relaxed fashion, his shoulders slightly hunched over and one of his elbows resting comfortably on the bar counter. He even took a sip of his drink. I was dying to know what brought about this simulated change in his spirits. It was annoying.

"How are you, my friend?" I said in a happy (but not too happy) voice. "You seem well. Yes, you seem very well and refreshed. That's good. I like that." I didn't like it at all. When I intimidate a man, I expect him to stay intimidated. On the inside and on the outside.

"I've just been thinking." Tommy fixed his eyes on my chin as he spoke. He was doing it on purpose.

"What have you been thinking about?" No emotion at all in my voice now.

"About how you said you were going to kill me. When you said that to me, at first I was kind of anxious. I mean, it's not every day that a man threatens to kill you for no reason. But then I remembered that the man that threatened to kill me is a fucking retard, and suddenly I wasn't anxious anymore. I actually feel badly for you. I feel sorry for you. Obviously some kind of psychological trauma is making you act the way you act. Maybe your parents beat you up all the time. Or worse, maybe they didn't pay attention to you. Are you the product of neglect? I know a guy like that. He's a lot like you except he smokes a bag of pot every day so he's somewhat less intense. Anyway, I think you're full of shit. I think you're incredibly insecure. You're just this extraordinarily insecure shit talker and I think everything that comes out of your mouth is worthless and goddamn miserable."

"Interesting," I said calmly. I was telling the truth. I wanted to see how far he would take this act. The man was exhibiting big round balls here. No matter how much I want to kill a man, I can't help sitting back and admiring a pair of big round balls when they're put on display.

Tommy nonchalantly picked his liver up, took a loud slurping sip, put the liver back down, and wiped his lips with the back of a manicured hand. "I don't like you," he went on, his gaze crawling up my face and planting itself on my eyes, "but I understand you. So I'm going to humor you. I'm going to pretend that when you said you were going to kill me, you meant it. I didn't want this stupid drink you bought me, but you did buy it for me. In return I'm going to treat you like somebody who tells the truth and means what he says."

"Nobody tells the truth and means what they say," I interjected. "They might think they do, but they don't. Everything that comes out of everybody's mouth is a lie."

"Then you admit that you're nothing more than a shit talker."

"I admit nothing but the truth. The truth is, I don't lie."

"You're lying."

"If you say so."

Shaking his head, Tommy removed a pack of American Spirits from the inside of his coat and offered me one. "I'm afraid I don't smoke," I said. Tommy clicked open a zippo, lit up, clicked the zippo shut.

I removed a cigarillo from the inside of my coat and lit it with a zippo.

Tommy smirked. "I thought you didn't smoke."

I returned the smirk. "I thought I was a shit talker."

"You are, you are. But let's pretend you're not. I want to know why you would want to kill me. Far as I can tell, I've done nothing to you and you have no motive. Did I nail your old lady or something? Maybe that's it."

"That's not it. I don't have an old lady. I don't know you. I've never seen you before tonight. I have no connection with you whatsoever."

"Then why kill me?"

"I'll tell you if you buy me a drink. Think I'll just have a scotch this time. Chivas, straight up. I have to take a piss. Stay here." I placed my cigarillo in an ash tray that was a petrified lung, stood up and walked to the restroom. Along the way I was solicited by a number of porn stars. One of them was the gal I backhanded into the jukebox. I guess she'd forgiven me. Or forgotten me. At any rate, I said no to all of them, but I made sure to squeeze each of their full-figured ass cheeks and then assure them, in a deep-seated whisper, that I would indulge them at a later date.

I'm the guy that urinates all over the toilet seats in public restrooms. I make sure that every square inch of every public toilet seat I loom over is doused. The restroom in this place was small. It was flesh-walled like the bar itself and consisted of a sink, mirror, and toilet. The sink was the pelvis of a wide-bodied female and its faucet was a lumbar spine. The toilet was a kind of assemblage of rib cages and its seat was a large intestine curled into a horseshoe shape. I peed all over it, washed my hands, adjusted my tie, checked my face in the mirror for discolorations and ingrown follicles, checked my teeth to remind myself how goddamn white they were, fixed my hair, washed my hands again, and returned to my seat at the bar.

Tommy Thingdoer had bought me the Chivas I had requested. Weird. I hadn't expected him to. I had planned on bitching at him for being so inconsiderate.

I sat down. "Thanks for the drink."

Tommy nodded. The nod seemed to have some sort of hidden meaning behind it but I didn't say anything: whatever it was, it didn't matter. I polished off my godfather and slid it aside. I retrieved my cigarillo from the ash tray. It had gone out. I re-lit it and took a mean drag. I took a sip of scotch.

"There's ice in this shit," I remarked accusatorily. "I said straight up."

"I know. I told the bartender you wanted it straight up. But for some reason I don't think he likes you."

Since I sat back down Tommy's eyes had been smack on my eyes and they had yet to stray from them. More than that, he didn't seem uncomfortable with it. Before it had been a chore, a virtually impossible feat for him to eyeball me. Now he did it with ease. It was maddening, repulsive, excruciating. True, I had told Tommy to look me in the eyes just a few minutes ago. But I didn't expect him to be able to do it—that's why I told him to do it. Maybe he wasn't exhibiting confidence at all. Was I in the presence of fearlessness? I couldn't decide if I was angrier at Tommy for acting like a real man or at the bartender for putting ice in my drink.

I decided I was equally angry at both of them, so I flipped a mental coin. The bartender won.

"Hey dipshit. Hey assface," I blurted. "Hey you crummy bastard. Get your ass down here and fix my drink you satantic fag."

The bartender was down at the other end of the bar again. Just as he had done before, he looked in my direction, flipped up his chin, snapped his fingers and winked at me. Then he went back to caressing and fondling the bulging breasts of the porn star that was sitting in front of him. It was not his "wife". It was Lucy Whitetrash a.k.a. Katrina Kunt. She was a pasty-skinned Caucasoid and had a long, frizzy, glistening schlerm (short on top and long in the back with a perm) hairdo. Her physique was athletic but in a low-grade sort of way, as if she worked out in a barn instead of a gym. The only parts of her body that were not covered in Harley Davidson logos and theater faces were her breasts—which the bartender, the moment after I called out to him, immediately began sucking on. And the porn star immediately discharged a series of loud, fake moans.

107

"That sonuvabitch," I growled, hitting my drink in spite of the rocks. "I guess he got a divorce." I had a mind to go down there and get the bartender's attention the same way I had gotten it the last time, but I was starting to get weary. At this point I just wanted to kill my man and go home to bed. Sighing, I picked up my cigarillo and puffed on it, then put it out and addressed Tommy.

"I'm going to kill you because you're better-looking than me," I said squarely. "It's as simple as that. You're a threat to me. Your looks are stealing the eyes of all of these porn stars from my looks. I'm not afraid to admit that I'm jealous of you. And I'm not afraid to destroy you on the grounds of jealousy alone."

The expression that overtook Tommy's face was the same one that overtakes a face blindsided by the silent, reeking fart of a nearby stranger. "What? That's the dumbest thing anybody's ever said to me. Are you serious?"

"As serious as an erection. Your good looks are crouching my style. How do expect me to get a date with you hanging around."

"Get a date? Do you know where you are?"

"The center of the universe, of course. But that's beside the point. The point is, you're making it difficult for me to hit on the women in this place."

"You're not even hitting on any women. You're sitting up here at the bar sticking bugs up my ass. You really are a douche bag. The women here don't even have to be hit on. All you have to do is walk up to them, let them know your pockets are full of cash, and that's that."

I sighed in disappointment. "What else does hitting on a woman involve? You've just articulated the definition of hitting on a woman, Thingdoer. Are you living on this planet? I think it's you that doesn't know where you are. I think it's you that's the douche bag. Listen, what's going on here is simple Freudian economics. On a purely sexual level, your existence is a threat to my existence. So I'm going to terminate your existence. There's nothing you can do about it. Look me in the eyes all you want. Be as standoffish and as seemingly cool and composed as you want to be. The thing is, if I was a woman looking for some action and I had to make a purely material choice between you and me, I'd choose you. Physically you're not that much more attractive than I am, but you've clearly got the edge. Any dumbass can see that."

"You're an alien," spat Tommy. He was noticeably upset, and his eyes had moved back down to my mouth. Good. "By alien I don't mean an isolated or estranged person. I mean a bug-eyed fucking monster. You think women give a shit about looks? You think these porn stars care whether or not you're an Adonis or a goblin as long as you're packing enough green? You're an imbecile if you do. You're an imbecile anyway. A man with money is all a woman wants. Good looks are nothing more than a perk."

"That's one reading of the social dynamic that binds us," I said. "Another reading is that there are plenty of women that don't care about a man's money or his looks—they just want somebody with a quote-unquote good personality. But I don't care for either of those readings. I like my mine better. It's truer. It's more real. It's something I can wrap my head around and understand. I believe in it."

Tommy threw up his hands. "What a stupid thing to say. You're a total shitbrain. Just because you want to believe in something doesn't mean it works that way."

"That's your opinion."

"That's not an opinion. That's an objective fact."

"Says you."

"That's your response? Says you?"

"I'm really going to enjoy killing you."

Tommy paused. He stared into my eyes.

I returned the stare.

Tommy said, "I'm not talking to you anymore. I can't

109

believe I've talked to you at all. I feel stupider for having this conversation. I'm leaving. Don't try to stop me or I'll scream my fucking head off. Goodbye, idiot. I hate you."

Without another word, without another sip of his godfather, Tommy Thingdoer blustered to his feet and stormed out of the bar.

It took me about half a minute to down the rest of my scotch and bid farewell to the bartender by throwing a few loudmouthed obscenities in his direction. Then I left, too.

Tommy was nowhere to be seen. I didn't mind: I never had any intention of killing him. I never have any intention of killing any of the men I approach. But I like to tell them I'm going to kill them.

Tired and little grouchy, I went straight home that night. I lived just a few blocks away. The streets of Pseudofolliculitis City were loud and crowded but the air was cool and refreshing, and the walk lifted up my spirits. By the time I reached my block, my spirits were so uplifted that I veered into an alleyway. In it was a man and a porn star having sex. The man was not better-looking than me, but I killed him anyway. Splayed against a brick wall, the porn star was cooing and talking dirty as the man penetrated her from the rear. I snuck up behind them, grabbed the man's head. With a quick twist and a yank, I snapped his neck and tossed his limp body aside.

Then I squeezed the porn star's ass cheeks, told her I'd see her later, and went home to bed.

ELEPHANT INVASION

The elephants came on a Sunday morning when almost every-body was in the city shopping for wigs. The night before there had been a neighborhood meeting, and it had been decided that everybody's hairdos were too ugly and needed to be con-cealed by attractive (albeit ersatz) hairdos on a regular basis. So the next morning at oh-eight-hundred hours the residents of Sycophant Suburb opened their garage doors and piled into their station wagons and drove off towards bigger and better things.

Two of Sycophant Suburb's residents, a Mrs. Honda Gonnagitcha and a Mrs. Sicamore Vanderlick, didn't make the trip. Both firmly believed their heads of hair were in good shape, if not pleasing to the eye, despite the protests of their family members and peers. They both had brunette bobs with bangs.

"You bunch of diseased goofballs," Mrs. Gonnagitcha had blurted out at the meeting, unable to bear the absurd go-ings-on for another moment. "Don't you dumbasses have any-thing better to do with yourselves on a Sunday morning?"

"Yeah," Mrs. Vanderlick had added in a meek voice—but not so meek that her defense of and concordance with Mrs. Gonnagitcha's sentiment was not made perfectly clear.

And so the next day the two ladies stood on their front porches and watched their husbands and children pull out of their driveways and putter away. Donning big plastic grins on their tilted wide-eyed heads, they waved goodbye and wished their families a safe journey. (At the same time, they used the filthiest language imaginable to curse their families' idiocy un-der their breath.)

When everybody was gone, Mrs. Vanderlick came over

to Mrs. Gonnagitcha's house to brag about her newly renovated kitchen. This pleased Mrs. Gonnagitcha: she had just had her kitchen renovated, too, and was interested in dishing out a little braggadocio of her own.

"I have a Corian countertop," said Mrs. Vanderlick, not bothering to say hello as she ambled up to where Mrs. Gonnagitcha was standing on her front lawn.

Mrs. Gonnagitcha considered telling her neighbor that it was rude and bitchy not to say hello like that. Instead she said, "Me too. I also have a stainless steel refrigerator."

Mrs. Vanderlick shrugged. "Me too. I also have a stainless steel dishwasher and range."

Mrs. Gonnagitcha shrugged back. "So do I. I also have marble floor tiles and maple wood cabinets. And my ceiling is twenty feet high."

"Same here. Only my ceilings are twenty-five feet high."

"Did I say twenty feet high? I meant to say twenty-eight. That's what I meant to say."

"Do you have a skylight?"

"Three."

"I have six."

Mrs. Gonnagitcha scowled. "What do you have six skylights for? You don't need six skylights."

"I'd expect you to say that. After all, you only know what it's like to have skylight falling down on you from three different directions."

Mrs. Gonnagitcha didn't reply to this accusation. She intended to reply. In fact, the electrical signals had been sent from her brain to her mouth to say the words, "Too much skylight can lead to a crappy disposition." Just as she was about to open her mouth, however, she was distracted by the manhole in the street. Its heavy steel lid blew up into the air as if a bomb had exploded underground. But there had been no boom noise. The lid of the manhole seemed to have leapt out of the street all by itself.

"Did you see that?" said Mrs. Gonnagitcha.

Mrs. Vanderlick's face tensed up into a sphincter. "I'm not stupid. I see things when they happen."

Mrs. Gonnagitcha was offended by the sphincter-face and the snotty attitude as much as by the accusation that she was inadequate because of the lack of skylights in her kitchen. She jabbed a mad finger at Mrs. Vanderlick's chest and spat, "Why are you acting like such an asshole? You have no reason to act that way. All we're doing here is trying to one-up each other in a sophisticated manner. There's no reason to get all pissy about it. Hey. Are you listening to me?"

She wasn't. Entranced, she was staring at the open manhole in the street. It was a good-sized, good-looking manhole, almost three feet in diameter and perfectly circular, nothing oblong about it. For some people, it was a source of pride. Knowing that such a fine, shapely thing was embedded in the street of their suburb delighted them.

But there was nothing delightful about the manhole now. Not only was it missing its lid, a furious stream of elephants was flowing out of it like lava from a volcano. The elephants were diminutive, no bigger than well-fed chickens, and their hind legs were miniature human legs with feet. They emerged from the manhole four or five at a time. Discharging a high-pitched human scream out of each of their little trunks, they ran in every direction, galloping on all fours in a maddog frenzy.

Mrs. Gonnagitcha and Mrs. Vanderlick observed the spectacle with eyes that were golf balls, with open mouths that were the size and shape of ripe avocados . . .

The spectacle didn't last long. As quickly as it had begun, the flow of elephants out of the manhole stopped, as if a faucet had been turned off. They also stopped running and screaming and adopted attitudes that were in complete opposition to the attitudes they had exhibited up to this point. Now the elephants stood and grazed on the front lawns of the suburb like civilized beasts. Each lawn contained anywhere from ten to twenty elephants, all of which used their lazy trunks to pull out clumps of grass and delicately feed the grass to their mouths. Every now and then, while an elephant was lethargically chewing its food, it would stand up on its hind, human legs and glance around the neighborhood, its expression dumb, passive, hollow.

None of the elephants' sexual organs were visible. Their groins were small, smooth pastures of nothingness.

The last two elephants to exit the manhole made a point of returning the manhole's lid to its rightful place. It took some effort on their part—the lid weighed twice as much as their combined body weights—but eventually they managed to drag it back to where it belonged. Then they joined the other elephants on Mrs. Gonnagitcha's lawn.

"Holy Christ," whispered Mrs. Gonnagitcha, her head immobile, her eyes fixed on the mole on her neighbor's overlip. The overlip, she noticed, was all peachfuzzy and needed to be waxed. "How long do you think they'll stay?"

Mrs. Vanderlick stared down at the wrinkled grey back of an elephant that was grazing right next to one of her feet. She whispered, "I'm not sure. But I think I'm going to have a heart attack. I'm scared shitless. If we move, who knows what they'll do. I don't want to die like this. I want to die like a normal person, under normal circumstances."

"You're not going to die."

"You don't know that. What do you know? Not a damn thing."

Mrs. Gonnagitcha shook her head. "Calm down. God, you're so affected. Look. These things are nice and peaceful. A second ago they weren't so nice and peaceful, but they are now. They're harmless. I think you should pet one of them. Pet that one right there."

Mrs. Vanderlick winced as if slapped across the face. "I'm not petting that goddamn monster!"

The elephant slowly turned its head up to Mrs.

115

Vanderlick and blinked at her. It continued to chew its food.

"Lower your voice," said Mrs. Gonnagitcha, "especially if you're going to insult these things. I don't know if they have feelings, but they might, so don't be a bitch. Now bend down and pet that elephant. Do it."

"No."

"Yes."

"*You* do it. It's your yard."

"What's that got to do with anything?"

"I don't know. But I'm not touching that maniac."

Mrs. Gonnagitcha huffed. "You're such a slut. Fine. I'll do it. Get out of the way."

"I told you, I'm afraid to move."

"Don't be such a baby. You called it a monster and it didn't do anything. What's it going to care if you move or not? Here, I'll move. I'll move all over the place." She took a bow and started to riverdance, pulling the skirt of her starched Billingsly dress up to her breasts so that everybody present could see her long athletic legs flutter and stomp in fasttime. "See what I mean?"

"Exhibitionist," grumbled Mrs. Vanderlick.

Mrs. Gonnagitcha stopped dancing and dropped her dress. She eyeballed her neighbor. She took a step forward and laid into her neighbor's upper chest with the butt of her elbow.

Stunned, Mrs. Vanderlick went "Ahh!" and stumbled backwards, swinging her arms and trying to regain her balance, but she couldn't, and finally she tripped over an elephant and fell smack onto her rear. The annoyed elephant stood up on its two feet. It angrily blew its trunk. With a calm yet resolute stride, it walked across the street to another front yard where it could graze without any distractions.

Mrs. Gonnagitcha pushed out her lips and nodded at Mrs. Vanderlick. "There's more where that came from, if you want some more," she said. "All you have to do is get up. Otherwise stay down and shut up."

116

Mrs. Vanderlick sat there like a ventriloquist doll with grass stains all over her white skintight jeans. She was too dazed to answer. But she did manage to hurl a few nauseating curse words at her antagonist before keeling over and passing out.

Mrs. Gonnagitcha approached the elephant closest to her and squatted down. It didn't acknowledge her sudden proximity. She took this as a good sign and reached out and patted the animal on the lower back, just where its thick elephant skin threaded into the smoother human skin of its bottom. She moved her hand down to its bottom and patted it. The elephant giggled and moaned as its trunk stiffened and pointed at the sky. "Oops," said Mrs. Gonnagitcha. She removed her hand from the elephant's behind and placed it on its tiny head. The trunk immediately went limp and snatched up a bundle of grass.

Continuing to stroke its head, Mrs. Gonnagitcha leaned closer to the elephant's ear. "Excuse me," she said. "How much longer do you think you and your friends are going to be here? I only ask because when everybody gets back from the city, they might get upset. By everybody I mean the people that live in Sycophant Suburb. You really shouldn't be eating grass that doesn't belong to you, do you know that? It's not very polite. No, it's not a very polite thing to do. I don't really mind since I'm not really concerned with how my yard looks, but my husband is, and when he sees what you're doing, he's not going to like it, I can tell you that much. Well. I wonder if you'll all go away now. I think that would be a nice gesture on your part. I'll even help you take the lid of the manhole off so you can crawl back inside. One nice gesture deserves another."

The elephant didn't respond. It ignored what had been said to it and continued to consume the bright green grass of the Gonnagitcha's front yard.

Overhead a cotton field of clouds silently crept across the bright blue sky.

Frowning, Mrs. Gonnagitcha stood up and crossed her

117

arms over her chest. She evil-eyed the elephants that were grazing in her line of vision, trying not to lose her temper.

She lost her temper.

"Buncha goddamn hellions!" she hollered, shaking her fists. "Leave! Go! Shoo! Quit being here! I want you all to quit being here right now! Do you hear me?"

Except for the pair of elephants across the street who stopped grazing, stood up, turned their butts in Mrs. Gonnagitcha's direction, bent over and mooned her, none of the elephants acted like they had heard her.

Mrs. Vanderlick squeaked, "Evil bitch." She was still spread-eagle on the grass, but consciousness had leaked back into her. "How dare you kick my ass."

Paying the woman no mind, Mrs. Gonnagitcha flexed her jowls and angrily spat over her shoulder. She calmly smoothed out the wrinkles in her dress, primped the black bob of her hairdo with a cupped palm, walked into her garage, swore and gesticulated while rummaging through various piles of pack rat detritus, and walked back out into the front yard, a shotgun tucked beneath her arm.

"Stop!" said Mrs. Vanderlick as her neighbor moved towards her and cocked the shotgun with her strong thin arms. "I was just kidding! You can kick my ass all you like! Please, don't hurt me."

Mrs. Gonnagitcha scowled. "This isn't for you, you turd. It's for them. Get up and stop acting like a retard."

Mrs. Vanderlick obediently sprung to her feet. The head rush that resulted from moving so quickly, however, sent her onto her ass again.

Reality slipped into slow motion as Mrs. Gonnagitcha, a fearsome grin on her deranged face, which seemed to be trying to turn itself inside out, aimed the shotgun at an elephant and pulled the trigger.

The elephant exploded. While it was exploding, reality slipped back into realtime. The starfish spray of blood and bits of body parts accelerated, disseminated . . .

The sound of the shotgun prompted a number of the elephants to perk their ears up, but it didn't induce hysterics. Not even remotely. Mrs. Gonnagitcha had expected the murder of one of the elephants to inspire the rest of them to counterattack or, better yet, to retreat back into the manhole. But they barely even budged. Either they were purposely concealing their emotions, or they had lost the capacity to express their emotions. Or they were practitioners of the cult of apathy and had no desire to express their emotions. Whatever the case, it was frustrating.

Mrs. Gonnagitcha shouted, "You passive-aggressive assholes! Fine. I'll just continue to pick you off at my leisure. I'll just do that and see what you think about it." She marched back into the garage and filled a burlap sack full of shotgun shells. In the meantime, Mrs. Vanderlick, who suddenly felt sick to her stomach, puked on her jeans, called her neighbor a few more names and gimped home, sorry she had ever taken Mrs. Gonnagitcha's side at the neighborhood meeting, wishing she had gone to the city with her family to buy a new, fake hairdo.

Mrs. Gonnagitcha amassed a good three or four hundred shells, then marched back outside and, one by one, annihilated every single elephant on her property. She took her time, hoping that each murder she committed would spark some kind of reaction. There was no reaction. Save the few elephants that mooned her, the havoc she reeked went unanswered. When she was finished, her front yard was a wasteland of gore; mutilated bits and pieces of flesh and bones were scattered across the pools of blood that covered the lawn. It was a disgusting sight, and it didn't smell very good either. But Mrs. Gonnagitcha was too full of hate and fury to give a shit about it. All she gave a shit about at this point was ridding the rest of Sycophant Suburb of the strange creatures that were either refusing to respond to her aggression or incapable of responding to it.

By oh-one-hundred hours she had accomplished her goal. Every single front yard in Sycophant Suburb resembled the chopping floor of a slaughterhouse. Of all the elephants that had invaded the suburb that morning, not one of them remained alive and intact.

Mrs. Gonnagitcha nodded, and pumped the shotgun. There was a deep-seated clicking noise. An empty shell popped out of the gun in slow motion . . .

She proceeded up her driveway, her Billingsly dress torn and grisly, her face a finger painting of blood, her bob hairdo a tangled, sticky mess . . .

And the other Gonnagitchas returned from the city.

The station wagon peeled up the driveway, veered around Mrs. Gonnagitcha, and eased into the garage.

Mr. Gonnagitcha turned the car off. He got out and assertively slammed the door. The Gonnagitcha children crawled out an open window. The children were eight-year-old identical twins named Gonna and Gitcha. Both of them looked nothing like their mother and everything like their father, now more than ever since they were all wearing the same jet black pompadour wigs. On top of that, each child was wearing the same style of Beaumont suit as their father, although their suits were of course much tinier and cuter.

Gonna and Gitcha sidled up next to Mr. Gonnagitcha and followed him out of the garage. They stopped at the top of the driveway and vigilantly stared at their lawn . . . and at their neighbor's lawns . . . and finally, at Mrs. Gonnagitcha. Shotgun in hand, she stared back at them from halfway up the driveway with a blasé expression. This staring contest went on for a good half a minute before Mr. Gonnagitcha broke down. Pointing at his wife's head, he said, "You call that thing a good-looking hairdo?"

Mrs. Gonnagitcha tilted her head and grinned her plastic grin as the members of her family each used a stiff, flat hand to shield their giggling mouths.

TEN FLÂNEURS

A group of ten flâneurs liked to pretend that they were bowling pins. Dressed in skintight bourgeois three-piece suits, mustaches of various colors and crops, and derby hats fabricated from the hides of baby penguins, the flâneurs would set themselves up on the sidewalk in a big triangle and make their bodies as straight and rigid as possible, like statues, with tilted up chins, pursed purple lips and eyes wide with confidence. They were daring the city-goers to bowl them over, to run into them at top speed and scatter their stiff bodies all over the metropolitan concrete. "I dare you bastards to smash us!" one of them would cry out every now and then. But nobody took the dare. Nobody even noticed the flâneurs, except for the odd pack of children, usually spoiled brats whose parents neglected them and let them run hogwild, and these little hellions would stomp on the flâneurs' feet and punch them in their nuts until they couldn't bear it any longer and were forced to relocate, find somewhere else to set up shop.

One day the ten flâneurs had the good fortune to set up shop on a sidewalk where an entity who liked to pretend he was a bowling ball happened to be hanging out. The entity was old, thin and naked, albeit somebody had painted a suit not unlike the ten flâneurs' onto his skin so that you had to concentrate to see his nakedness. He was positioned there on the sidewalk next to a fire hydrant stained with dog piss, his legs and arms tightly wrapped around his body, his face pointing towards the sky. On his face were three orifices waiting to be penetrated by the wanton fingers of a bowler: an open mouth and two gouged-out eye sockets . . .

The flâneurs became excited when they spotted the entity. One of them threw his hands over his head and shook them like hell. Another started to do the chicken dance. Another chirped the chirp of a sexed-up monkey. And almost all of the flâneurs' faces were ravished by uncontrollable rictus grins. It was the first time they had ever engaged in such hilarity, and they made a pact with one another to engage in hilarity on a regular basis in the future. Then they got down to business. Composing themselves, they scrambled down the sidewalk a ways, lined up in their usual formation, and waited for the entity to bowl them over.

He didn't bowl them over. He stayed where he was, balled up, static, silent. The black breeze of the city washed over his face and poured into his three wide-open orifices, stinging the inside of his head like the taste of battery prongs.

"Hey fella," blurted the six-pin flâneur. "How about getting yourself in gear and nailing us like a bunch of dirty whores?"

. . . The entity quivered, twitched. He rocked back and forth on the small of his back, slowly at first, then faster, faster . . . Two of the flâneurs grew so excited, stiff hard-ons formed sturdy bulges in the fabric of their dress pants.

. . . The entity stopped rocking. He lay still.

The flâneurs with the erections glanced down at their crotches and sadly watched their bulges disappear. "Do not go gently into that good night," whispered one of them.

Losing his patience, the five-pin flâneur barked, "What's going on here? Why is that entity loafing over there like a sack of worthless bricks? Knock us down, sir! Break our bones, brother! Fracture our souls, pig! Blah blah blah, fiend!"

Intensifying the rigidity of his stance, the flâneur on the five-pin's immediate right used the corner of his mouth to tell his agitated colleague to calm down and stop embarrassing everybody.

A few more flâneurs expressed their discontent with the

entity's apparent unwillingness to set himself in motion. The three-pin stomped his foot on the ground and said, "Oh!" The eight-pin gave the entity the finger. The two-pin ran a fantasy across his mind's screen in which he knelt down next to the entity and screamed obscenity after obscenity after obscenity into one of his ear holes. The four-pin gnashed his teeth with the passion and fortitude of a man under the thumb of the Biblical God's apocalyptic wrath.

The one-pin flâneur glanced over his shoulder and evil-eyed everybody. "Cut that racket out, people!" Being the one-pin, his voice was the voice of authority and reason. "Don't you see that he can't roll himself? He needs somebody to pick him up and roll him."

The other nine flâneurs froze. A profound sense of doom swept over them. Their thin white faces flared up like torches.

The one-pin turned his evil-eye from his colleagues to the city-goers that were passing he and his colleagues by. It was nearing lunchtime and the sidewalk was becoming more and more crowded with bodies. Long, sharp, machinic strides, these bodies took, and the way they swung their arms was no less assertive and purposeful. Clearly they had somewhere important to go, somebody special to see, something serious to do . . . unlike the flâneurs, who had nowhere important to go, nobody special to see, nothing serious to do. But that didn't mean they didn't have *needs*.

"Hey!" announced the one-pin to nobody in particular. "I know all of you are very busy, but could somebody take a moment to pick that sonuvabitch over there up and roll him at us please! We'd appreciate it, we'd appreciate it! We may be idle flâneurs, but we have feelings, too! Is there a bowler in the house! I say, is there a bowler in the house!"

Of course, there was no response, verbal or physical. And soon a pack of ill-reared children entered the scene and began going to town on the flâneurs' private parts with their angry little fists, forcing them to move on. The ten men fell out

123

of formation and stumbled away, cursing, hunched over, clutching their bruised genitals as a stray dog moseyed over to the entity and mistook him for the fire hydrant he was positioned next to . . .

Despite the pact they had made with one another, the flâneurs never engaged in hilarity again.

THE OSTENSIBLY IMMORTAL PIECE OF BREAD

There is a piece of bread sitting on a shelf in my pantry. It's been sitting there for over four weeks now. Four weeks! I've been waiting patiently for it to grow mold on it.

It won't grown mold on it.

Usually when I buy a piece of bread I only have to wait a few days before it starts to go bad. The longest it's ever taken a piece of bread of mine to go bad is nine days. I've had this piece of bread for thirty-three days. It's still as fresh-smelling and fresh-looking as it was when I purchased it from the baker.

I even threw the bread in the darkest, dankest, dingiest corner of the darkest, dankest, dingiest closet in my flat and left it there for a week. When I retrieved it, the thing still looked good as new. I was distraught, bereft. Antagonized. I think I might have cried. The days continued to pass and I became more and more estranged as the piece of bread insisted on remaining pristine, unsullied, and good enough to eat.

And so I have decided to return to the baker who sold me this piece of bread and kill him.

In addition to being a violent or turbulent situation and a whirlpool of extraordinary size, a maelstrom is also an apparatus that, when it is not in use, resembles a dirty knee sock. It even smells like a dirty knee sock. Once you slip your arm into it, though, the smell disappears and the exterior of the maelstrom mirrors over as the delicate hairs that line its interior like a mink pelt slip themselves into your pores and metabolize with your nervous system. This is a little excruciating. A few seconds later the mercurial skin of the maelstrom fades and pales until the color of its skin is indistinguishable from your own. It's good camouflage, only now it looks like you shaved one of your arms. But who pays attention to arm hair these days.

The maelstrom is a highly effective and entertaining weapon, particularly for ultraviolence enthusiasts. Imagine your fist and forearm is a stick of boiling hot lava wrapped in razorwire. Then imagine the lava and the razorwire are physical manifestations of poststructuralist theory . . .

After I slipped the maelstrom on and waited for it to coalesce with me, I made sure it was functional by testing it out on an old stainless steel cappuccino maker that I never use. I simply held out my forearm and placed the machine on top of it.

Six seconds later the machine had been deconstructed and assimilated.

The bakery was only a few blocks from my building. On the way there I bumped into an old friend of mine. His name was Eddie Krapps and he didn't recognize me. This was understandable: not only had we not seen each other for years, I was disguised as a bag lady. But then Eddie snapped his fingers and said, "It's you!" He thrust his hand out for a shake. He was left-handed. So was I. On instinct, I grabbed his hand and began to pump it.

The inside of his hand became the outside and the outside melted into the maelstrom and was gone.

"Oops," I said.

Eddie lifted his arm to his face and stared incredulously at a grisly wrist, which looked like somebody had stuck a clump of burnt, bloody mincemeat onto the end of it. He began to convulse and foam at the mouth. White froth spilled all over his tie and business suit. Finally he collapsed onto the sidewalk. It all happened in a matter of seconds. Not knowing what to do, I apologized. With my free, maelstromless hand, I captured a passing stray dog, shook the dog until it passed out and placed it on top of him, to conceal him. The dog wasn't much bigger than a human head. But it would have to do.

I pushed the front door of the bakery open and stepped inside. Immediately I was accosted by the baker's major domo. His name was Mr. Dangletooth. He was a short man with a short man's complex who used to be the mayor of the city until his wife left him for a haberdasher. After his nervous breakdown, he was forced out of politics and into the baking industry, the only industry that tolerates (and in some cases caters to) unstable psyches. Mr. Dangletooth was wearing a pinstripe suit that was two sizes too big for him. The chichi dress shirt he had on was fairly tremendous, too; his beady-eyed pinhead was barely peeking out of its collar. He resembled a onetime tall fat man who had shrunk in his clothes.

I didn't like him.

"What do you want? What do you want?" he bleated. Mr. Dangletooth didn't like me either—partly because I was tall, partly because I made no effort to conceal the fact that I didn't like him. "Do you have business here today?"

I didn't reply to him, didn't even acknowledge his self-conscious existence. I looked over his head and scanned the bakery for the baker.

Crowded in here today. And loud. Sounded like the floor of the stock exchange during prime time, only the cruel buzz of voices and catcalls didn't rise and fall, it remained constant.

As usual, the customers all looked like bag ladies, although there were only a handful of actual bag ladies in the place. The baker's peculiar neuroses would only allow him to sell bread to that strain of people. Since everybody wanted and needed bread, and since the baker's bakery was the only reputable, reasonably priced bakery in the city, everybody who wasn't a bag lady, if they wanted a portion of decent bread, had to

127

disguise themselves in that fashion in order to purchase it. This policy was staunchly upheld yet inattentive to authenticity. In most cases it was easy to tell who was and who was not a bag lady. As long as the baker's customers made an effort to cater to his absurd demand, though, he would grant them the pleasure of their sour dough, their challah, their focaccia, their honey whole wheat . . .

The bag lady disguise I had on was decent but it was nothing special: a broomhead hat, loud rundown high heels, a moth-eaten skirt and shawl, torn fishnet stockings, some hastily applied rouge, some false buck teeth, a fake wart on my nose, a crappy bag slung over my shoulder—the standard ensemble. Had I wanted to impress the baker and make his day, I would have jumped into a garbage bin and rolled around for an hour or two, maybe even slept there for a night. But I didn't want to stand out and draw attention to myself.

The baker was nowhere in sight. All I saw above and across the ragamuffin heads of the customers were one, two, three, four, five order-takers behind the counter trying to nego-tiate the orders that were being spit at them and the fistfuls of cash that were being waved and thrust in their faces.

Where was the baker?

Usually he was standing on an elevated podium artfully situated in the far corner of the bakery. With eyes wide and alert, with chin held high, with arms folded across his hogshead chest, the baker, who only baked at night when the bakery was closed so that he could maintain this panoptic position during the day, kept one vigilant, intimidating eye on his staff and the other on his customers, ensuring that nobody in his jurisdiction stepped out of line in any way.

Nobody ever stepped out of line.

He was a powerful man, the baker. He stood almost seven feet in the air and had the bulging, ripped up physique of a bodybuilder. Everybody was afraid of him. Not so afraid that people didn't push and shove and carp and curse one another under their breath, but nobody pushed and shoved too hard or carped and cursed one another under their breath too loudly, even in the baker's absence. The absence of the baker, which is a rare occurrence during business hours, is almost as declarative as his presence in that his absence ordains that his presence may be reinstated without warning at any given time. Personally I had never been here in the baker's absence, but I had heard about it. It felt weird.

I looked down at Mr. Dangletooth. I blinked and cocked my head as if I had just noticed him. His shrill, wet eyes and the crooked sequence of lines on his forehead told me he was well aware that I'd been well aware of his company from the moment I stepped in the door. I was trying to get his goat and he knew it. What he didn't know was that my primary motive for coming here was to kill the baker. Having the opportunity to irritate the baker's major domo in the process was just a convenient diversion.

I continued to irritate Mr. Dangletooth by playing dumb. In a halfass bag lady voice, I said, "Oh. Hello. Do you know where I might find the baker?"

Mr. Dangletooth wound up and fastballed a dirty look at my face—I could almost feel its impact. I expected him to start hollering at me. He didn't. Maintaining his dirty look, he reached inside of his outfit, fished around for a second, and pulled out a long, crumpled sheet of paper with patches of chicken scratch all over it. He gave it a cursory glance and said to me, "I'm sorry. You're not on the list, sir. You'll have to leave. Please leave now."

The restraint with which my maelstrom-cloaked arm was kept from lashing out and hammering Mr. Dangletooth in the face—it was immense, that restraint. It would have given me so much pleasure to nail that little stuck-up peon and put an end to his uppity sass once and for all. But I had to keep things in perspective. I was here for the baker, not the baker's major domo. Just put up with the man, I told myself, and don't make a scene.

I leaned closer to Mr. Dangletooth. "You're telling me everybody in this bakery is on that piece of paper? Let me see it." I reached out and tried to take it from him.

He mashed it up and stuffed it back inside of his suit. "I'm not telling you anything," he replied, "other than to get out. Will you or will you not get out of here?"

"On what grounds? What is this, a country club? Look at me." I dipped to one side and then the other, showing off my bag ladyness. "I'm doing my part. Knock this crap off and let me by."

"Pardon me," croaked two bag ladies. One was walking in the door. The other was walking out with three slices of what looked like plum bread in hand. (Full loaves weren't for sale in the bakery. Bread was only sold by the slice, and there was a three slice limit per customer. But you could come back as many times a day as you liked.) Both bag ladies bumped into me as they passed. I snarled at them. Then I snarled at Mr. Dangletooth. He was standing in front of me, barring my way like a fire hydrant. I got rid of my bag lady voice and said, "Well? I don't see you giving that one"—pointing at the bag lady that had just entered, an imposter like me whose outfit was far less convincing than mine—"a hard time. I don't even know why I'm wasting my breath talking to you. Back off. Back off or else, little man."

"Or else what?" Mr. Dangletooth huffed.

I bent over, placed my chin in front of his nose and drilled a high heel into the floor. "Or else you'll make me hate you," I seethed. A tent of fear pitched itself on his face. Good. Now we were getting somewhere. "Move aside, you," I ordered.

Mr. Dangletooth held his ground for a second or two before complying. As I made my way past him, however, he grabbed me by the elbow. I froze, rigid with fury, and peered down at him with round rabid eyes.

In his hand was the crumpled up slip of paper again. "If

I could just get you to sign your name on this document here," he said in a pleasant but assertive voice, as if we had not just had an altercation, "and then if you could do me the favor of undergoing a retinal scan, well, there's a very good possibility you might be able to carry on with your business. A very good possibility indeed."

Suddenly the maelstrom seemed to develop a personality of its own. I felt it tense, shudder and cock itself, and I had to grab it on the wrist with my free hand to keep it from flinging out. It had no effect on my hand. The maelstrom's roots were snug in my flesh and synapsed to my nerves: it knew who was and who wasn't part of the family.

I closed my eyes and took a deep breath. Mr. Dangletooth had ceased to be a convenient diversion. He had quickly evolved into a raging menace.

I opened my eyes and surveyed the bakery again.

Still no baker. Still a hoard of customers trying and failing to be served in a timely fashion by overworked, more or less incompetent order-takers.

Three more bag ladies entered the bakery and whisked by me. I flexed my jaw, I shook my head. I turned and faced Mr. Dangletooth.

He shoved the paper and a ballpoint pen towards me. Ignoring the gesture, I unzipped my bag and removed the piece of bread that wouldn't grow mold on it. I presented the bread to Mr. Dangletooth in an open palm.

"Do you see this piece of bread?"

"Yes. Yes I see it."

"It's over a month old."

"Uh-huh."

"Uh-huh? That's all you have to say?"

Mr. Dangletooth's arms flopped to his side. "What do you want me to say?"

"I don't know," I griped. "How about swearing in disbelief?"

"Holy shit," he monotoned.

I stuck a mad finger in his face. "You little creep. Why don't you and I just cut out the bullshit and talk straight, okay?"

"I'd prefer not to," he retaliated with an air of superiority. "Without bullshit I really wouldn't have a great deal to say. I'd prefer to have something to say."

"Shut up," I said. Mr. Dangletooth blinked. I blinked back. "Listen to me. This bread in my hand, this piece of bread I'm holding underneath your crummy nose—any idea where I bought it? Don't bother answering because I'm going to tell you where I bought it in the next sentence that comes out of my mouth. I bought it *here*, right *here* in this bakery. And do you know what else? This piece of bread is thirty-three days old and there's not even a spec of mold on it! Are you beginning to understand? Are you beginning to catch my drift? I certainly hope so. Now then. I demand to see the baker at once."

The major domo frowned at the bread. He sniffed its underside, touched its outer ridge with a pinky finger. At last he pensively ran his tongue back and forth across his teeth. "It doesn't look like a thirty-three day old piece of bread to me," he shrugged. "For all I know you could have bought it yesterday. Do you have a receipt?"

"You *know* the baker doesn't believe in receipts."

Mr. Dangletooth smirked. "So he doesn't. Well, I don't know what to tell you. There's simply no way that piece of bread is thirty-three days old. If it was, it wouldn't look so youthful and rosy. I don't understand what you're trying to do. Do you hope to get a free slice of bread out of this, is that it? You have a slice of bread, sir. A perfectly healthy, perfectly good-looking slice of bread. Go home and enjoy it."

I returned the bread to my bag. Not caring if I made a scene anymore, I used my free hand to grab Mr. Dangletooth by his too-long, atrociously patterned tie. I yanked his hobbit-like face up to within an inch or two of my own. "Hey! I put a lot of effort into watching that thing not grow mold on it over the last few weeks. Who are you to say that I haven't?"

Seemingly unaffected by my powerful grip, which I intensified, and which then clearly affected him, Mr. Dangletooth squelched, "Why do you care if mold grows on your bread or not? Most people would rejoice in a piece of bread that refuses to be devastated by time."

The hint of halitosis I tasted on his breath crippled my fury. I was ready to strangle him, or even better, to hold him out in front of me like a rag doll and slap him back and forth across the cheeks with my maelstrom, which would rip off and assimilate his cheeks (and most of the facial features attached to them) as if they were made of cotton candy instead of flesh. But once my nose got a whiff of his hideous breath I found myself as tame as a sedated ape in a cage. I let go of the man's tie and took a step back, giving him some room to reorganize himself. As he picked up the paper and pen he had dropped and adjusted his tie and collar, I said, "That's not the point, whether or not I or anybody else might rejoice in this ostensibly immortal piece of bread. The point is—this piece of bread is *ostensibly immortal*. Now get out of my way!"

At my exclamation, the loudest and most resonant exclamation to leap out of my mouth since my arrival, every single bag lady in the bakery stopped grunting and throwing elbows at one another and looked over their shoulders at me. Even the order-takers paused. Everything was absolutely still, absolutely silent. At least fifty foreboding eyes were staring at me. Did I care? No. No I didn't. Under different circumstances I might have cared—I don't like it when one person stares at me, let alone a whole goat herd—but not today. I stared back at them with eyes that said, "I could care less if you're staring at me. Stare at me all day and night, if you like. It won't matter. No, it won't matter to me."

The population of the bakery read this message in my gaze and, all at once, returned to their affairs.

The baker's persistent absence was beginning to make me paranoid. At first I was just irked by it. Now I began to think that the baker's absence was a result of my presence. I wondered if he was watching me through the video cameras in the ceiling corners. I wondered if he was peering up at me through a knothole in the bakery's weathered hardwood floor. I wondered if he was watching me through the disguise of a bag lady. Finally I forgot about the baker and wondered if everything that happens in the world is in reference to *me* . . .

Mr. Dangletooth drew me out of my reverie. He reached up and snapped his fingers in front of each of my ear holes and then in front of my face, just a millimeter or two beyond the tip of my nose. My eyes fluttered . . . and I calmly told the major domo to go to hell.

"You go to hell," he replied.

"I'm in hell. But that's as obvious as a kidney punch, isn't it. Just don't snap your fingers at me is all I'm saying. I hope you're listening to me."

He wasn't listening to me. He wasn't even looking at me. His brow a rumpled mass of flesh, he was scratching his chin and staring at my arm, the one with the maelstrom on it. The shawl on my back was a ratty piece of crud and only concealed the upper portion of my body. My bare arms (one hairy, one seemingly not hairy) had been exposed to the major domo's eyes all along. Why had he chosen this moment to recognize the incongruity? Why had he noticed the incongruity at all? Most people don't take note of these kinds of things.

Then again, Mr. Dangletooth wasn't most people.

"Why have you shaven one of your arms?" he smirked. "You shave one arm but you don't shave the other one? Ha! That's the most ridiculous thing I've ever seen in my life. Or were you born with a hairless arm? Whatever the case, you're a nincompoop. Why won't you just go away and never come back again?" Before I had a chance to respond, he turned around and announced to the entire room, "This stupid nincompoop has shaved one of his arms and left the other one hairy. Can you believe it? I mean, can you people believe it?"

They couldn't. Everybody paused and looked at me again, with twice the intensity that they had looked at me just a moment ago. Some of them began to point at my arm, shake their heads, and whisper belittling remarks in each others ears. I caught a few people grabbing hold of their mouths to keep them from exploding into hysterics.

Mr. Dangletooth didn't bother grabbing his mouth. He threw back his puny bald head and his mouth opened and yakked out a choppy stream of laughter. "Ha-ha-ha-ha-ha-ha-ha-ha-ha-ha-ha-ha-ha-ha-ha-ha-ha-ha-ha-ha-ha-ha," he said.

Well. That was the last draw. Of course it was the last draw.

I backhanded Mr. Dangletooth across his laughing face with the maelstrom.

His face came off and left behind what looked like the aftermath of a bite-sized grenade nailing him between the eyes. His skull was clearly visible. My quick but dire blow had dismembered his jawbone, which hung there like a lynched thing. It had also ripped out an eyeball. I watched the eyeball, along with the rest of his facial flesh, disappear into my bubbling, fizzing, gruesome forearm. Five short seconds later, though, my forearm smoothed over; except for the hairlessness it looked like a normal forearm again.

Everybody gaped and gasped as the living remains of Mr. Dangletooth, who didn't know what hit him, and who would never know what hit him, dropped to the floor like a pillar of bowling balls that abruptly and collectively decide they would prefer not to be stacked upon one another anymore. He gurgled. He gesticulated. He lost control of his bodily functions.

He curled up into a ball like a potato bug and lay still.

I turned to my audience and shrugged my shoulders, once, powerfully. My shawl flew off my back. I was naked from the waist up now, my lower half concealed only by my skirt, stockings and heels. My muscular, hairy chest was in full view, and I flexed my pectorals one at a time. Then I tipped my head and shook off my hat, unleashing enviable flaxen locks, and I spit out my buck teeth onto the floor. "Gross," said a bag lady impersonator's six-year-old child. Like her mother, she was accordingly decorated. I pointed at the child with a finger that said, "Keep your disgust to yourself, young fiend, or I'm going to give you something to be truly disgusted about." The frightened child's mouth became a hole. I nodded. The child dove underneath her mother's cruddy burlap skirt, never to be seen again.

My bag slipped from my shoulder when I shrugged off my shawl. I had been very careful not to touch the bag, or any other garnish or article of clothing I had on, with the maelstrom, which would suck anything it touched that wasn't my own flesh and bone into oblivion. I had not been so careful with Eddie Krapps hand. In any case, there was adrenaline squirting through my tubes now. Naturally I was a little on edge, and I almost picked up the bag with the maelstrom. That would have been the end of my campaign here. Had I picked it up with the maelstrom, the bag and the piece of bread inside of it would have been history. That bread was proof—proof that the baker wasn't holding up his end of the bargain. What was his end of the bargain? To produce and peddle bread that submits to the laws of human physics! But I caught and tamed my maelstrom before it had a chance to do any dirty work, so in that respect all was well.

I retrieved the piece of bread from the bag. I spread my legs apart, gently gripped the bread by its crust with the fingertips and thumbtip of my free hand, and brandished the bread over my head for all eyes to see.

"This piece of bread you see in my hand is ostensibly immortal," I said in a commanding, echoing voice. "I purchased it from this bakery thirty-three days ago and it has yet to grow mold on it. In effect, I have returned to this bakery to kill the baker. Killing the baker's major domo was not my intent, but the man was antagonizing me. Don't get the wrong impression. I feel no remorse for killing him. I didn't like him. Why would I want something that I don't like to continue to exist? Still, his death was not premeditated. Not in a formal sense anyway. I fantasized about his death on a number of occasions, true, true, but I never anticipated the realization of my fantasies. Do you understand? It doesn't matter if you do or you don't. Just show me the baker. Show him to me at once. I don't know where he is but I have a feeling somebody in this room does. I kindly ask you to produce him for me. Mark my use of the word *kindly*, people. If my desires are not fulfilled right now, right away, I may have to exercise the word's polar opposite."

Frozen, unable to speak, awe-struck, totally helpless—my audience could do nothing but glare at me with trembling chins. I heard the door jangle open behind me and sniffed the stench of rotten banana peels and Vienna sausages. "Beat it," I snapped without turning around. There was a gasp as the potential bread buyer no doubt caught sight of Mr. Dangletooth's corpse. And the corpse's steaming head.

The door jangled closed.

"I'm asking you sunzabitches a question and I want an answer," I said. I was on the brink of losing the shred of temper that remained in me. *"Where is the baker?"*

My paralyzed audience didn't budge. I flexed my jaw, took a step forward.

One of the bag ladies took a step forward. At last, a bag lady with a pair of balls.

I could distinguish neither the gender nor the authenticity of this aggressor. But whether the person had actual balls and was actually a homeless weirdo didn't mean a thing to me. What meant something to me was this . . . fortitude. This willingness to step into the ring and face me like a real man in drag.

S/he lifted a hand and stabbed a crooked, bony finger at me. I waited for the person to say something. S/he didn't, s/he just kept stabbing. I spat, "The baker! Where is he!"

Silence.

Silence!

. . . and then s/he opened her mouth. "The present whereabouts of the baker don't matter, so you can just forget about it," s/he said in a calm, creaky, genderless voice. "The matter at hand here is your inability—or rather, your *disability*—to come to terms with that ostensibly immortal piece of bread. That is not the baker's fault. Nor is it my fault, or any of my brothers-and-sisters-in-arms' fault. That is *your* fault. The shocking thing about it is that you lack the sense to draw this conclusion on your own! Or maybe you do have the sense to draw that conclusion and chose not to use it. Or maybe you actually drew the conclusion and chose to ignore it. I don't care what your impetus was. I only care that you acknowledge your idiocy to yourself and go about your business." That said, s/he lowered her finger, turned around and made her way to the counter. The rest of the bag ladies, after a short pause during which they nodded at me disparagingly, followed in her wake. The bustle of consumerism revived and carried on as if it had never been interrupted.

"Nice invective," I said, mostly to myself. "First class, really. I'm not just saying that."

I was ignored.

It would have cost me a certain amount of sweat, but I was confident that I could accomplish a massacre without too much trouble. I stood there and considered doing it for a long time, my eyes fixed on the smooth ersatz flesh of the maelstrom . . . I imagined myself at the center of a tremendous coliseum swarming with lunatic bag ladies that I gruesomely deconstructed one after another, the deafening cheer-roar of the faceless spectators in the grandstands making me stronger, happier, full of so much joy I was intensely saddened at the prospect of losing so much joy, so I killed faster and with more flair until nothing remained on the main floor of the coliseum except for a few monstrous, trashy piles of body parts and me, the grinning bare-chested gladiator in high heels who stood tall and godlike and whose existence nobody would ever think to burden with an ostensibly immortal piece of bread again, not in a million years . . .

This fantasy sequence ran across my mind's screen for almost a minute. Then another bag lady entered the bakery. Her bag accidentally smacked into me and I snapped back into reality.

One last time I scanned the bakery for the baker.

There was no baker.

I swore out loud so everybody could hear me.

Nobody heard me.

I swore again, louder . . . and left. Like some bimbo preparing to make the Walk of Shame, I gathered up my shawl and my hat and my buck teeth and my bag . . . and went home. When I got there, I realized I had not eaten breakfast yet. I hadn't eaten breakfast in over a month. So I dropped the ostensibly immortal piece of bread into a toaster and waited for it to turn into an ostensibly immortal piece of toast, wondering what it was going to feel like to have the taste of God in my mouth . . .

STRANGER ON THE LOOSE

A recurrent scene that runs across my mind's screen: I pick up a thin-stemmed glass of wine, I take a sip, I bite off a chunk of the glass and chew it like a piece of filet mignon, tasting it, savoring it, relishing the bits and pieces of my mouth in my mouth . . .

The stranger and I were standing in the middle of a freshly rototilled expanse of granite. We had nothing to say to one another. We stood there with our heads bent, frowning at our toes. The heavy rays of the sun baked the backs of our necks.

Eventually ennui overpowered the stranger. He flicked a seed onto the ground, urinated on it, and a metropolis sprouted into the sky like a legion of screaming beanstalks growing in fasttime. The baroque verticality of the superstructure that suddenly loomed over us stretched out to the horizon and beyond.

Urban thunder rang in our ears. "Wer sorgen hat, hat auch likör," the stranger shouted over the blather of car horns, the mania of street urchins, the dire speed of commerce, the roar of white noise, the passive ecstasy of interactive multidimensionality . . . He leapt into the maelstrom and disappeared in a flash of video light.

I don't speak German so I didn't know what the stranger said to me. I had a sneaking suspicion that, in so many words, he told me: "You are the root of all ego." But I couldn't be sure. For all I knew he could have told me: "There's toothpaste resin on your lips." Or: "It ain't nuthin' but a G thang." Or: "My soul is a monster that lives in a body without organs."

At a loss, I leapt into the metropolis in pursuit of the stranger. In pursuit of the clarity he owed me.

The metropolis was a haystack, the stranger was a needle.

Chances were I'd never find him. But I had to try, I had to try.

Actually I didn't have to try. If I wanted I could have just turned my back on the city, sat down, relaxed, breathed, blinked, pretended I'd never met the stranger. But that would be a little boring, sitting there with nothing to do. And I have difficulty pretending to do things.

The street I landed on was a virtual cirque de soleil, an orgy of colors and smells and commotion. Graphite gargoyles wearing mirrorshades crouched on the rooftops of every building, and the walls of every building were plated with either movie screens or mirrors reflecting movie screens. People wearing mercurial facemasks and silver jetpacks passed over me. People wearing black business suits and bowlers passed by me. So did a legion of stilt-walkers. Steam hissed out of manholes. Neon signs shaped liked sexual organs fluttered and fizzed. Colossal LED and Big Ben clock faces stared down on me from every direction. Each of the clock faces told me it was a different time.

I began asking people at random about the stranger.

I tapped a pedestrian on the shoulder. "Have you by chance bumped into a stranger today?"

The pedestrian made a face and told me to get a job.

I walked into a pawn shop. "Any strangers come in here today?" I said to the proprietor. "I lost one and I need to find him."

The proprietor smirked at me. "Nope. No strangers. Sorry."

I thanked the man and walked back out onto the street. Strode over to a taxi cab, knocked on the window. "Picked up any strangers today?" I asked the driver. He blinked up at me. I repeated the question. He barked, "I don't give rides to strangers and they don't ask for rides from me. Now if you'll excuse me." He went back to reading the front page of the city newspaper. The headline, I noticed, read:

STRANGER ON THE LOOSE!!!

"Hmm," I said . . . and hurried over to a kiosk. I bought a paper, hurried into a café. Along the way I tapped a few people on the shoulders and asked them if they had happened to see a stranger today. They all grinned bright white grins and shook their wide-eyed heads at me.

In the café I bought a black coffee and sat at the only open table in the place. The rest of the tables were occupied by stiff-backed men in pince-nez and skintight white outfits chainsmoking cigarettes and staring at each other in silence. Before I sat down, I asked one of the men if I could bum a cigarette. He swore, fished one out of a pack, and flicked it at me without looking at me.

The cigarette was stale and the coffee was bitter, but I smoked and drank them anyway as I read the paper. The headline story was all about the stranger. I soon discovered that every single article in the newspaper was about the stranger.

The headline story read:

STRANGER SEEN LOITERING

A stranger was spotted loitering on the corner of Simulacra Street and Lampoon Boulevard this morning at 9:37 a.m., sources say. He was described by onlookers as an average-sized, average-looking male of indefinite ethnicity. Apparently his actions at the time of the sighting were entirely innocuous. He did nothing but loiter and mind his own business. When approached by a city-goer and asked what he thought he was doing, he replied, "I'm doing what I'm doing."

Authorities are baffled by the sudden emergence of the stranger into the social sphere. "We're not sure if we should arrest the man," said Chief of Police Dorian Knotbottom, "or leave him alone. At this very moment there is an entire think-tank of law enforcement administrators trying to decide which option to choose."

In the meantime, city-goers are encouraged to be on guard. Anybody that finds themselves confronted by the presence of the stranger is advised by the psychiatric division of the police department to pretend that the stranger doesn't exist.

The basic thematic structure of the other articles I read was the same as the structure of this one: first the stranger was said to be sighted at this or that location doing this or that thing; then the authorities were said to be in a quandary as a result of the stranger's materialization; finally city-goers were warned to disregard the stranger's existence. I must have read thirty articles that followed this schematic. It wasn't particularly enjoyable, reading the same thing over and over. But I had nothing better to do.

The speed with which the stranger moved from place to place was impossible. One minute he was on the east end of the city, the next he was on the west end. Not only was there no way the stranger could move so fast, there was no way reporters could find him and write and print stories about him so fast. It was ludicrous. Every now and then I would glance up at the man sitting at the table next to mine, point at the newspaper and shake my head in disbelief. The man never acknowledged me. His face was pointing in my general direction and I knew he could see me gesturing at him. At last I said, "Hey you. I'm gesturing at you and I know you see me. How about a little feedback?"

The man cleared a lump of phlegm out of his throat and robotically sipped his coffee.

I blew my nose into a napkin. The napkin was as coarse as sandpaper. I cut my septum on it and yelled, "Ouch!"

Everybody looked at me.

While I was in the restroom cleaning out the wound with soap and water, I skimmed a page of the newspaper that had been cut out and pasted onto the wall over a urinal. It was

143

a clipping from The Cowshit Telegram. Like the newspaper I had been reading, The Rabbit Pellet Press, the subject of every article was the stranger.

One article in particular caught my attention. It said that the stranger had been seen purchasing a tall cappuccino with skim milk in The Café Plastique at 12:36 p.m.

Was that the name of the café I was in?

I looked at my watch. 12:37 p.m.

"Hmm," I said . . . and exited the restroom.

Outside I found the café overrun by a blizzard of angry bodies. The bodies belonged to photographers, cameramen and good-looking, well-dressed short people with microphones who were all yelling and desperately struggling to climb over one another as if they might have been a litter of piglets fighting for their mother's teats. Flashbulbs were going off like machine guns. And nearly all of the silent, staring, smoking customers in the place had been trampled to death.

I stayed in the corridor that led to the restroom to ensure that I didn't get trampled to death, too.

If I stood on my tiptoes I could see the stranger. Reporters and newscasters were spitting questions at him. "Why are you who you are?" was one question. Some others were: "What is your motive for existing?" and "Who is the energy source of your belief system?" and "Do you consider yourself an individual?" and "How many individuals does it take to screw in a light bulb?"

The stranger ignored all of the questions posed to him. He calmly paid the cashier for his coffee, snapped a lid on top of it, and pardoned himself as he made his way towards the front door. Before opening the door, however, he turned to his audience, smiled and said, "Wer sorgen hat, hat auch likör!"

"Stop!" I heard myself blurt over the stormy buzz of the mob. "I want to know what that means!" I pointed an avaricious finger at the stranger when I asked the question.

Silence landed on the mob like napalm. Suddenly the

café was absolutely quiet and everybody's head was turned in my direction. Nobody moved, nobody breathed.

If I was the sort of person that went limp whenever the public eye decided to fix itself on me, I would have been in trouble. But I'm not that sort of person. Fact is, I crave the public eye. There's nothing more invigorating than making an ass out of yourself while a bunch of people are watching and judging you. And the bigger ass you make out of yourself, the better.

Unlike everybody else, who looked at me with idle yet curious expressions, the stranger regarded me with a surprised expression, his eyes two big white circles, his mouth a big black circle. "Remember me?" I said. My finger was still pointing at the stranger. I wiggled it accusatorially. "Didn't think you'd see me again, eh? Well here I am. What are you prepared to do about it?"

The stranger shrugged.

Then, just like old times, he bent his head and frowned at his toes.

Half of the cameramen and photographers pointed their machines at me. I said, "Still the same old disinterested jackass, I see. Even now that you're a celebrity. But that's to be expected. After all, you're a stranger." I paused. Cameras began to roll, flashbulbs began to pop. A few reporters and newscasters began to ask me what my ontological connection to the stranger was.

I ignored their questions. "Tell me what that German phrase means," I said. "Tell me, and I'll leave you alone. You'll never see me again, I promise. What does it mean? Answer the question."

The stranger slowly lifted his head and looked across the café into my eyes. A dirty tear rolled down his cheek, traced his jawline and disappeared into the cleft of his chin.

I nodded resolutely.

The stranger screamed like an old lady who's kitchen is

145

suddenly ransacked by giant rats. He ran out the door.

I ran after him.

The media ran after me.

A mutant pigeon with two shrunken human heads swooped down out of the sky and made a loud shotgun noise. The noise was made by the bird because it was constipated, but it functioned as a signifier for the beginning of the chase.

I chased the stranger all the way across the city. We must have ran three, four miles. The media was on our asses the whole time. Whereas the stranger and I speedweaved through passersby as we made headway, trying not to bump into and knock over anybody, the media trampled passersby into blood and guts. It was like the bulls running through the streets of Pamplona on a day nobody expected them to be running; by the time pedestrians heard the pandemonium behind them and turned around to see what was going on, the stranger and I were in front of them and they were being hammered into the concrete by spitshined wingtips and penny loafers.

Virtually all of the purveyors of the news were preoccupied with the chase. And yet news traveled fast. Apparently the news no longer needed the medium of human consciousness to disseminate itself—somehow it could disseminate itself on its own. By the time the stranger and I were closing on the outer limits of the metropolis, city-goers had caught word of the chase. The streets had more or less cleared and people were hanging out the mirrored windows of the city's skyscrapers cheering and booing and swearing and hollering and laughing and spitting and hogcalling and warcrying. There was also a bee swarm of jetpackers buzzing overhead. Most of them were FBI agents disguised as mimes and drug-addicted homeless people. They watched and documented our every move.

We continued down Pseudo Street, Kwazi Street, Imitation Avenue. Then down Ditto Avenue, Bogus Boulevard . . . Finally the stranger veered onto a nameless street. At the end of the street was a brick wall that had the words EXIT HERE

146

slopped across it. The graffiti was the color of mercury.

Without hesitating, the stranger accelerated and leapt over the wall. He didn't leap high enough to clear it, but that didn't matter: the wall was a hologram . . . for the stranger. For me, I painfully discovered, it was a wall. The moment I leapt into the air the hologram solidified. My screaming face tasted cold, hard brick . . .

As I seeped into a sponge bath of dreams, I heard the echo of the stranger's voice sounding off his favorite sequence of words. I slowly lifted my hand into the air and tried to grasp the echo, to catch it, to reel it in . . .

In my dreams my skin metamorphosed into the pages of a newspaper. I was a walking papier-mâché, and the articles on my body were all about how I was a walking papier-mâché. And the headline emblazoned across my chest read:

PAPIER-MÂCHÉ SEEN WALKING . . .

SHRIEK

A man woke up to the sound of a shriek outside his door! He leapt out of bed and opened the door to see who had emitted the shriek. Nobody was there. So he attributed the shriek to the bite-sized version of himself that had taken refuge in his refrigerator. When he opened the refrigerator, however, he discovered that he had drowned in a pitcher of fresh milk. So he decided to drink his coffee black.

EVOLUTION AND
ITS VICISSITUDES

It was a glorious day, the day that stage of evolution came to fruition. It happened around two in the afternoon. Suddenly, spontaneously, for no biologically determinable reason, the male genitalia developed a method of constant self-cleaning that allowed men, once they had finished urinating in public restrooms, to forego the tedious business of washing their hands. The development was especially beneficial to men with SBS (Small Bladder Syndrome) who had to wash their hands so frequently the skin of their fingers and palms had begun to wear away like house paint. A beautiful thing had happened. Inspired like Romantic poets under the influence of the Muse, virtually every man alive, ranging from Wall Street suits to third-world pygmies, made a break for the nearest public toilet. Most of them didn't even have to urinate, but this communal bum rush was of course not about urination. It was about freedom.

The enthusiasm with which the penises of the world were removed from their housings and handled by excited hands! The joy with which men returned their penises to their housings and paraded out of the restrooms without so much as glancing at the restroom sinks and soap dispensers! By six o'clock men stopped washing their hands altogether. If their hands got dirty, all they had to do was shove them down their pants for a few seconds. Some even opted to eat their dinners off of their genitalia, but these men were all poseurs—the utilitarian value of a cock and balls, after all, doesn't compare to that of a porcelain plate when the consumption of food is involved. Despite this piece of unpleasantness, however, things were running very smoothly. For the first time in their lives, men were admitting to themselves that life was worth living, unlike that morning, and all of the days preceding that morning, when men had been intensely, if not pathologically suspicious about the merit of life. But that period of doubt and trepidation, it seemed, was over . . .

. . . until the next morning, around 2:35 a.m., when a mass movement of horny, shitfaced men stumbled home from the restaurants and bars and lizard lounges they had been celebrating in and crawled into bed with their women. They took their women by their shoulders, shook them like rag dolls until they woke up, and began to have sex with them. The women, in turn, began hollering. Not because they were still half-asleep and weren't in the mood to have sex. It was because of their men's penises.

"Your member is too clean!" shouted the women. "I like your member dirty and filthy! It feels like I'm being violated by a bottle of Formula 409! What happened to your nasty old member! This cleanliness is disgusting!" In response to these exclamations, the men frowned and cursed. What had been, in the blink of an eye, communally perceived to be a joyous occasion was, in the blink of another eye, communally perceived to be a nauseating occasion as women angrily shoved their men off of them and told them to go to hell. The men, then, still frowning and cursing, retired to the bathroom toilets to relieve themselves. And while they were relieving themselves, they each employed their own individual variants of drunken logic to figure out a way to reverse the socially liberating yet sexually estranging process of evolution . . .

DISNEY REANIMATED

"God is not dead. He has become hyperreal."
—Jean Baudrillard, *Simulacra & Simulation*

Eventually Badass worked. Named after the self-proclaimed disposition of the biochemist who created it, the drug was administered by means of a simple, single injection.

More baboons were killed than soldiers in the Civil War before Badass was perfected. Then one day a dead monkey opened its eyes, cursed in its native language as if waking into the embittered bear hug of a hangover, rolled onto its feet, squatted, and took an angry shit all over the clean white floor of the laboratory. The scientists present broke out into song and lit long, expensive cigars. Between songs and cigar puffs, they talked about what (or rather, *who*) to do next. Clearly the baboon was functioning normally. And if it continued to function normally for a sufficient duration and passed all of the requisite tests, it was only logical that Badass be tried out on a human subject. But who?

That night at the bar the scientists came to a quick unanimous decision. In the not-too-distant future they packed their bags, divorced their wives (moral support no longer needed from those Suzie-homemakers) and flew to Disneyland. They spent a few days entertaining themselves on the park's rides and dining on sauerkraut and sausage links in the restaurants of a simulacrum of Germany. Then they got bored and decided it was time to exhume Walt Disney's body. The body was located underneath the Pirates of the Caribbean attraction in a cryogenic sepulcher. Prior to his death by cancer, Disney had requested that his dead body be preserved in deep-freeze until the technology to reanimate him was developed. So the scientists ferried him to a simulacrum of a German hospital, thawed him out and gave him a shot of Badass.

Disney cursed in the voice of Mickey Mouse after he opened his eyes. As he rolled onto his feet, squatted and took a shit on the clean white floor of the operating room, the scientists once again resorted to singing and smoking, and subsequently a group of slapdash orderlies wearing synthetic moose antlers rolled a few trash cans full of grain alcohol into the room and everybody started to get drunk.

"Can I have some toilet paper?" Disney asked. This time he employed the ornery voice of Donald Duck. "I could use a pair of pants and a shirt, too."

Nobody paid attention to him: too busy partying and talking on their cellphones, making dinner plans with full-figured, five-large-a-night hookers.

Disney sighed.

He drank a few handfuls of grain alcohol, stole a dirty surgeon's outfit from a locker in the closet, and snuck away.

In addition to the hypodermic full of Badass, Disney had been injected with a little geriatric cocktail that made him look a little younger and a little more handsome than when he had died at the age of 65. Not that it mattered to him. He had never cared much about his own image unless he was making a television appearance. But he looked pretty good right now, despite his outfit, which was crinkled up and stained in places with blood. Out in the streets of Disneyland people recognized him as a Walt Disney lookalike dressed in a mad scientist's costume.

"I'm not a lookalike," he kept telling the children that came up to him and kicked him in the kneecaps for playing what they considered to be a bad joke on them. "I'm the real thing. They just reanimated me a few minutes ago. Seriously."

Nobody took him seriously. Finally an indignant group

153

of parents, thinking he was a liar, told him he ought to be ashamed of himself for filling their children's heads with nonsense. He wanted to tell them that he had spent his lifetime filling children's heads with nonsense and nobody had ever complained until now, but he refrained, suddenly realizing that the children and parents were not children and parents. They were lookalikes of children and parents. The park was filled with children and parent lookalikes. It occurred to him when a young, innocent boy unzipped his chest and face and a midget in a pinstripe suit shrugged out of his skin. A number of other people, he noticed, did likewise, and for no apparent reason. A security guard unzipped himself and out came a groundskeeper. An ugly pigeon-toed woman with no tits and no sense of style unzipped herself and out came a busty porn star in a lavish ballroom gown. A wiry blond-haired Aryan in a scuba-diving outfit emerged from the fleshy shell of a fat black woman with an afro. Another well-dressed midget relinquished itself from the guise of child. There was one person, a mustachioed gentleman wearing an origami uniform, that looked the exact same on the inside as he did on the outside; that is, the face, body and outfit that constituted his outer layer was a replica of the face, body and outfit that constituted his inner layer. Everywhere Disney looked, people were randomly shedding their bodies like snakes. He wasn't the fraud here, they were. What right did they have to assume he was an imposter? But no matter what he said he knew he would not be able to convince them otherwise. In a sense they were right. If the world is constituted mainly by representations of the real, who's to say the representations aren't themselves the real? Majority rules, after all.

Depressed, Walt Disney decided to leave Disneyland. He didn't know where he would go. For now, getting out was enough. The only problem was, every exit door he encountered was only a lookalike exit door. And when he tried to open them, it only *looked* like he was trying to open them . . .

"Shit," said Disney, "I can't get outta here." As he spoke

154

the words a giant Goofy approached him.

"Nice outfit," it said.

Disney's mustache twitched in distress. "It's not an outfit."

"Think so?" replied the Goofy, and unzipped itself. Beneath was Pluto. The Pluto unzipped itself and revealed a real dog, a St. Bernard with a tiny barrel of booze hanging from its neck. The St. Bernard proceeded to unzip itself as well.

"Have you ever tried to take yourself off?" asked a girl that resembled a broken-down version of Judy Garland as Dorothy in *The Wizard of Oz*. Her voice was the deep-seated rasp of an actor who had drank and smoked his way through life. "Maybe if you tried to step out of yourself, you'd think differently."

Disney spit on the Dorothy's glittery red shoes. "Beat it, geek," he snarled. The Dorothy made a face, shrugged, turned and skipped away, leaving pixie dust in her wake, and leaving Disney in a state of high anxiety.

Maybe she's right, he thought. Maybe I'm not who I think I am. Jesus Christ! Is there a zipper on my body?

He was afraid to feel himself up. But he did it anyway. Sure enough, there was a zipper. A tiny, almost imperceptible plastic tab was sticking out of the nape of his clavicle bone.

"Holy cow!" he screamed. He dashed back to the simulacrum hospital to interrogate the scientists that had reanimated him. Clearly those bastards were responsible for all this. Back in his day people didn't make a habit out of taking their bodies off, and he certainly didn't used to have a zipper on his own body, which, presumably, could be taken off, too. Somebody had some goddamn explaining to do.

When Disney returned to the operating room in which the injection of Badass had been administered, he found the room teeming with baboons. The skins of the scientists littered the floor and the baboons, all of them piss-drunk, were gibbering and farting and belching and drooling oceans of saliva and making all kinds of obscene gestures. A few of them were having sex with long-legged prostitutes.

Disney blinked at the spectacle. He was irked, but he wasn't freaked out. Part of him had almost expected it.

"I'm back," he said.

No response.

"Hey you people. Hey you sunzabitches."

No response.

Annoyed, Disney dealt the monkeys a long, lewd invective. Not surprisingly, he was ignored.

He blustered into a storeroom circumscribed by shelves packed with medical supplies. Standing there alone in the darkness, he meditatively tapped his foot against the floor and filled and refilled his cheeks with air.

He hit the light switch. He flexed his jaw and pinched the tab of his zipper . . .

Inside Walt Disney was another Walt Disney. He was an exact replica of the recently shed Walt Disney, and was also equipped with a zipper.

Walt Disney unzipped and squirmed out of himself and exposed another Walt Disney.

Inside this Walt Disney was another Walt Disney.

Inside that Walt Disney was another Walt Disney.

Inside that Walt Disney was yet another Walt Disney.

Inside that Walt Disney was still another Walt Disney.

He wanted to stop taking himself off, but he was obsessed now. There was no going back. He would keep taking himself off until he could no longer take himself off—until he found out what lay at the core of his body, his being, his identity . . .

Every time Disney disposed of another layer of himself, the replica that emerged was a little bit smaller. Eventually he was so small even a microscope would have had to squint to see him clearly.

At this point of diminution, he removed his last layer.

. . . There was a flickering neon sign. Rectangular in shape, the sign was no bigger than an electron. Written on it in a humdrum font was an anagram for the real name of God.

"Ah-ha!" Disney yawped.

But he didn't yawp anything. He had no mouth with which to speak. And by degrees the sign stopped flickering and faded out to black.

"FIE," SAID HER KNIGHT
IN SHINING ARMOR

For years Betty Lomax had been praying for her knight in shining armor to come knocking on her door. Every night she asked God to deliver him to her, but every morning, when she lay her ear against the front door, all she heard was the sound of the postman tearing open her mail and reading it to the neighborhood children. She wished she could see how the expressions on the children's faces fluctuated as they consumed and processed all of her personal information, but the door didn't have a peephole. She kept forgetting to have one installed.

One morning the postman was reading a love letter that Betty had sent to herself. The love letter contained a poem that the sender of the letter—Betty used the alias Lord Bartholomew de Lacan—claimed was his own. "She walks in beauty, like the night," the postman proclaimed, wowing the crowd of children that had gathered on her lawn with broad theatrical gestures. "Of cloudless climes and starry skies, and all that's best of dark and bright meet in her aspect and her eyes: thus mellowed to that tender light which heaven to gaudy day denies . . . Hey, wait a second. This poem isn't de Lacan's, it's Byron's! You know, Lord Byron? He was this protobeatnik with a club foot who wrote all kinds of grabass poems and slept with all kinds of dirty whores. That's right, children. The key to a dirty whore's heart is a grabass poem. Boy oh boy. Wait till that Lomax gets a load of this bullcrap! I better write her a note on this letter and tell her her lover's a big fraud."

The postman knelt down on one knee, placed the letter on his thigh and began scribbling on it with a red pen. As he

158

scribbled the children complained about how bored they were getting standing there on Mz. Lomax's lawn with nothing to listen to. A few of them threatened to run home and tell their moms that the postman was invading Mz. Lomax's privacy. The postman didn't care. He was sleeping with all of their moms and knew that if they ran home and told on him, he would be able to convince the moms that their children were pathological liars without too much trouble.

Unlike the children, Betty waited patiently for the postman to finish his note to her. She kept her ear against the door, trying to divine what was being written by listening to the sound each letter made when it was put down on paper. Betty had an abnormally acute sense of hearing. The postman was writing very softly, however, and she could only make out a few words: *gullible*, *doppelgänger* and *exungulate*. She didn't know what exungulate[1] meant and wanted to retreat to her library and look it up in the dictionary. But by the time she got her ear back to the front door, the postman might be talking to the children again, and she didn't want to miss anything. She held her ground.

As the postman was about to sign his name at the bottom of his note, a commotion erupted from the crowd of children. The commotion startled him and caused his hand to spasm, and the pen that the hand was holding ripped across the note and left a lightning bolt of ink in its wake. It looked as if the note had been crossed out. Crossed out! That Lomax probably won't even read it now, the postman told himself. She'll see the note but she'll think whoever wrote it crossed it out because he thought it was inadequate in some way and didn't want her to read it. So she won't read it. Now I have to write it again! But not before I shout at and maybe even spank the person responsible for making my life monotonous . . .

---

[1] From *The Superior Person's Book of Words*: "EXUNGULATE *v.* To trim or cut the nails or hoofs. "Mom, it really is too much! I wish you could do something about it; it makes me sick. Richard is in the bathroom, exungulating himself again."

Contrary to the postman's presumptions, the responsible person was not a child. It was Betty Lomax's knight in shining armor. He had finally come. But he had come straight from a battle during which he had been bludgeoned in the face. His eyesight, not to mention his mental stability, was sufficiently marred, and he mistook one of the more corpulent, nerdy-looking children, Douglass McQueen, for an ogre. He beheaded the child. That was the commotion that startled the postman and induced the spasm in his writing hand.

"Damn ye ta thy hellfyre!" bawled the knight, gloatstanding over the lower portion of his conquest. The upper portion had rolled into the street and gotten run over by a passing ice cream truck.

The neighborhood children grabbed hold of their mouths in surprise. The postman double-taked the spectacle. Four times. Then he realized that, no matter how many times he did a double-take, he would be no wiser than if he had never done a double-take in the first place. The gory death of Douglass and the presence of the war-beaten knight was simply too peculiar and out-of-context to be reckoned with.

The postman stood up. "What's going on over there?" he asked.

"Ah miht ax ye the saym thinge!" The knight thrust a powerful metal finger at Lord Bartholomew de Lacan's letter.

The postman glanced down at the letter in his hand. He frowned at it as if the letter had landed there like a horsefly that knows a thing or two about what it means to be stealthy. Shit, thought the postman. I wonder what'll happen if I just pretend the letter is a horsefly. What if I just slap it and let it fall to the ground dead? Will this bloody, bearded, glinting person go away? I doubt it. He looks pretty upset. Gonna have to reason with him, I guess. But what kind of reason will this person find reasonable?

The postman had no idea. But he had to say something in his defense, especially in that now the knight was not only

160

pointing at the letter with his finger, but with his sword, which was dripping with the blood of the neighborhood dork and stained with the blood of all of those supernatural creatures he had killed in battle just under an hour or two ago. The knight didn't know that the letter was written by a love-professing Lord Bartholomew de Lacan. Nor, for that matter, did he know that Lord Bartholomew de Lacan was, on paper at least, Betty Lomax in disguise. He didn't know that the postman was a postman either. His confused state of mind prompted him to assume that the postman was a gentleman caller and that the letter he was holding was a love letter to Betty that he himself had written. So the postman was his enemy. Granted, the knight had taken a long time to answer Betty's prayers. But he was here now. The postman would have to pay for his reckless impertinence. He would have to be maimed and destroyed and sent to hell like everything and everyone that had ever obstructed the yellow brick road that was the knight's love life, even if he was a good, God-fearing person. The postman was neither good nor God-fearing, but the knight was ignorant of this character flaw. It would have been nice to know that the postman was an evil God-hater. But in the end it didn't matter: good and God-fearing or evil and God-hating (or, incidentally, good and God-hating or evil and God-fearing)—the postman was going to die.

And the postman knew it. He could see it in the knight's cherry red eyes. Then again, the knight wasn't a monster, he was a human. A human like him. There had to be a way to talk himself out of this mess. The postman just had to talk fast. He had to respond to the knight's accusation with speed and intelligence and a little wit wouldn't hurt either. It wouldn't be the first time he had sweet-talked his way out of a bind. On how many occasions had he suddenly found himself face to face with one of the neighborhood's incensed husbands, who walked in on the postman and his wife in mid-hump? But somehow he had always managed to talk himself out of it. He would do the same thing here and now. It was just a matter of opening his

161

mouth and giving his tongue the run of the house . . .

Before the postman had a chance to open his mouth, however, the neighborhood bully, Rogan the Kish, who had picked on and beat up Douglass McQueen every day for the last five years, but who had secretly been in love him, broke in. "You big ungainly hayseed!" said the ten-year-old Rogan, impressing the postman and confusing his peers (and the knight) with his use of the word ungainly. "I'm not afraid of you, you smelly lump a cowshit. I'll kick your ass!" All five feet of Rogan leapt at all seven feet of the knight, his long scraggly hair flapping in the wind, his fists swinging like rototillers, a cavity-ridden sneer that seemed carved into his jaw fizzing with furious mucus.

The knight lowered his sword and smacked Rogan the Kish in the face with a steel backhand. Rogan's head didn't come off, but his neck snapped. And when his body landed in the street the ice cream truck sped by again and ran over it.

The sound of the truck's dreamy, tinkling music dopplered away . . .

The rest of the neighborhood children looked on in absolute awe . . . Then one of them screamed "Mooooom!" and they scattered like road runners.

Betty had been listening to these goings-on intensely. This was all very exciting for her—not a single sound escaped her vigilant ear. Her knight in shining armor had come for her! Not only that, he was fighting for her! True, he was fighting children, but still, fighting is fighting, and most of those children were disrespectful little brats anyway. She couldn't remember a happier moment in her life. She wanted to yank open the door and throw herself into the knight's mighty arms. But no, no, she had to wait for the knight to knock on her door. If she didn't, if she opened the door herself, the knight would take offense, he would mistake her forwardness for the forwardness of a harlot, and then, with a long sad sigh, he would bid her farewell . . . forever. No, she couldn't be so hasty. Regardless of what happened, she could not open the door before the knight knocked on it. Biting the insides of her mouth, she ordered herself to be patient. Patient, and *strong* . . .

The knight turned and fixed his flaming eyes on the postman. He growled.

The postman cowered. He tried to say something. Nothing came out of his mouth. The knight swung his long sword around his body a few times with the velocity and agility of a numchuck-wielding ninja. The postman squeezed shut his eyes and told himself he was dreaming.

When he opened his eyes, the knight's sword was bearing down on him.

The postman's consciousness persisted for a few seconds after his head was severed from his body. He was able to see the toes of his black government-issue boots rush up at his face and nail him in the nose, and he even managed to swear a few times as his body slumped into a pile of limbs and his head bounced out into Betty's front yard like an abandoned basketball.

The knight huffed in triumph and, as always, gloat-stood over his conquest. But he soon cooled off and commended the postman, in spite of his utter lack of combat skills, for being such a worthy opponent.

The body of the postman lay in front of Betty's door. The knight sheathed his sword and kicked the body out of the way. It landed in a nearby rosebed, crushing and killing a number of flowers. The knight didn't mean to do that. He felt badly. In his medieval opinion, things like roses were a gift from God. Their beauty was evidence of His existence, and he felt like he had just punched Him in the kidney.

The knight walked over to the rosebed and carefully removed the postman's body from it. Kneeling down, he tried to straighten out and fluff up the flowers that had been mangled.

It was an unfortunate turn of events for Betty Lomax. When the knight walked over to the rosebed, Betty thought he was walking away from her without knocking on her door. In an outburst of recklessness, she grabbed hold of her doorknob and yanked open the door and threw herself out into her front yard, pulling out her hair, crying a rainstorm of tears, begging the knight to come back, come back, come back . . .

Betty saw where the knight was and what he was doing. And the knight saw where Betty was and what she was doing.

"I love you," said Betty.

"Fie," said her knight in shining armor.

Later, as Betty got drunk on stale gin and read and re-read the letter that Lord Bartholomew de Lacan had written to her, she wondered if the knight had left her because she told him she loved him or because she opened her door before he had knocked on it. She also wondered about the etymology of the word "Fie".

ON FILMNOIRMAKING

"Cut!" shouted the filmnoirmaker and stomped across the set in a gesticulating fury. The cameraman had fucked up again and he wanted to curse, beat, strangle and humiliate him. But he was a filmnoirmaker, a rare breed of human being, and he mustered up the strength to contain his rage before it got out of control.

The filmnoirmaker placed his chin on the cameraman's shoulder. He smacked his lips and whispered in his ear with the tonal cache of a true gentleman. "I need you to capture the aura of that shadow," he said. "Do you understand what I mean by aura?"

The cameraman frowned, as if he knew the answer to the question but had forgotten it. The frown was an act—he knew the answer to the question all right. The filmnoirmaker knew he knew the answer, but he didn't admit to having that knowledge in his possession. He pretended the frown had never materialized in the first place.

"According to the cultural critic Walter Benjamin," the filmnoirmaker continued, "an aura is the inner glow that gives an object, namely a work of art, its character and singularity."

"I know what an aura is," interjected the cameraman in a snotty, offended voice. He stared straight ahead as he spoke, refusing to turn and face the face that was perched on his shoulder like a parrot.

"Do you? I don't know about that. I really don't. The thing is, you're not capturing the aura of that shadow. No, you're not capturing its aura at all." The filmnoirmaker paused and waited for the cameraman to make an excuse. No excuse was made; the cameraman stared on in silence. Irritated, the filmnoirmaker jabbed the cameraman's cheek with his pointy nose. "Are you listening to me?" he asked. His lips were no more than a centimeter or two from the cameraman's ear hole now. "Look, I realize that the act of filmnoirmaking itself is an aura killer. I realize that. The shadow that will be viewed on screen will of course not be the real shadow and so, to a degree, the screen shadow will lack the character and singularity that the real shadow possesses. That's obvious. That's as obvious as the connotation of an up-angle shot on a stormy sky passing over a city in fast time. Nevertheless, you can and you will record the shadow's aura, despite the fact that you yourself, as the cameraman, are the agent that facilitates the act of aura killing. Do you understand me? I hope so. Please do your job or get out of here. Please do that, you bastard. There are plenty of out-of-work cameramen that would die to be in your blue suede shoes."

The filmnoirmaker smacked his lips again. He removed his chin from the cameraman's shoulder and skipped back towards his high chair with an elastic tread.

The cameraman angrily threw his fists onto his hips and threw an evil eye at his employer. "How can you tell if I'm capturing the shadow's aura or not?" he said. The filmnoirmaker froze in mid-stride as if he was an actor in a movie that somebody had just paused. "You're way over there. I'm the one behind the camera. From where you're sitting you're in no position to pass judgement on my cinematographic proficiency. And anyway, even if I'm not capturing the shadow's aura, you can always go back and pencil it in during the editing process. Jesus Christ."

"*Pencil in* the shadow's aura?" the bemused filmnoirmaker murmured to himself. The expression on his ashen, aquiline face described a wild incredulousness enforced by an even wilder wrath.

The crew members on the set were mostly stunt men,

grips and extras. All of them recognized the filmnoirmaker's expression and braced themselves for an onslaught of verbal pyrotechnics. The shadow, in contrast, sighed, shook its dark head, leaned against the shadow of the street corner's lamppost and lit the shadow of a cigarette. It was the only character featured in the scene being shot right now and this was already the twenty-sixth take. The contours of the shadow, which was being cast by a tall thin man wearing a trench coat and fedora, delineated a short fat man wearing a zoot suit and a tando, the lights from above being arranged just so. The tall thin man who the shadow belonged to was not a character in the noir film that the filmnoirmaker was shooting. His shadow, however, was the main character. Sometimes his shadow made him jealous. After all, he had to do all the work, to stand or walk or run in this or that position under this or that light source while his shadow took all of the credit for his pains. Then again, he was the one who got paid at the end of the day. But he still couldn't help hating his shadow now and then. "It would be another story," he often told his closest friends, "if the shadow was the one casting me. Then I wouldn't get so mad."

But the tall thin man wasn't mad now. Not at his shadow anyway. His shadow was the farthest thing from his mind. This shoot had been going on for eleven hours. His feet were sore. He had a headache. And his patience was running thin.

The frozen-in-his-tracks filmnoirmaker's back was turned to the cameraman. Instead of about-facing and bitching the cameraman out at the top of his lungs, as everybody expected him to do, the filmnoirmaker, always wary of his *uberman*-empowered temperament, kept his cool. He walked backwards until his back ran into the cameraman's chest. He turned his head and glanced over his shoulder. Observing one half of the cameraman's face with an eye corner, he said, "Before I fire you, I want you to know that you're a total ass. I want you to know that. First of all, you moron, I am a filmnoirmaker and filmnoirmakers enjoy, among other things, an innate ability to discern whether or not a cameraman is capturing the aura of an object by way of observing and interpreting the angle at which the cameraman has positioned his camera, and especially by way of observing and interpreting the depth of the hunch of the cameraman behind his camera. Your camera was improperly angled. Not only that, you were standing almost straight up!

"Second of all, you dumbass, an aura cannot be instilled after the fact. Have you ever seen a film in which an aura was instilled in an object after the fact? It's impossible! No matter how sophisticated a special effects team a filmnoirmaker has under his command, an inner glow, once lost, cannot simply be *penciled back in*, as you so crudely put it. Why? Because it's an inner glow! That is to say, it's on the *inside*. True, plenty of filmnoirmakers have suited objects with an *outer* glow and called it an aura. But not this filmnoirmaker. This filmnoirmaker happens to take pride in his work. I think you may be the biggest pinhead I've ever met in this business."

"Leave him alone," said the tall thin man, smoke chugging out of his nostrils in fitful streams. "He's trying his best. Just go back to your chair and let the man do his thing. Come on already. I am *so* bored."

"*Bored?*" the flabbergasted filmnoirmaker repeated . . . then shot a furious stare at the tall thin man. "Who are you and how did you get in here?" he cried. "Somebody tell me who this motherscratcher is, subjecting my authority to inquiry."

"He belongs to the shadow," chirped a grip.

The filmnoirmaker gave the tall thin man a once over. His lips condensed. "Oh yeah," he said.

"Wrong," the tall thin man snapped at the grip. "The shadow belongs to *me*."

"I don't see the camera being aimed at you, buddy," the grip retorted.

"I don't see me asking you to tell me what you don't see."

"Well I'm telling you what I don't see anyway. I don't

see you being of any consequence whatsoever. You're nothing."

"Without me my shadow wouldn't exist. That makes me something. Well, maybe not something. But not nothing. I'm more than nothing."

"If you're more than nothing you have no choice but to be something. But don't worry: you're nothing. Trust me."

"I don't know you. But I hate you."

"I don't hate anybody, even you. But I don't like you. I don't like you at all."

"Enough!" shouted the filmnoirmaker, and made a wild cutting motion across his throat with the butt of his hand. The grip and the tall thin man obeyed the gesture, but not before calling each other a few ugly names.

Sighing, the filmnoirmaker placed an index finger on each of his temples. He applied pressure and moved the fingers in slow circles. "Can you believe the magnitude of the bullshit I have to put up with?" As he asked this question he was regarding a gaggle of cigar-smoking stunt men, their burly arms folded across their barrel-chests. They looked at each other and shrugged. The filmnoirmaker stopped rubbing his temples and made a pissed-off face, pissed-off because the stunt men had clearly not, in light of their communal shrug, which was a response to his question, identified the conspicuously rhetorical nature of his question.

In response to the filmnoirmaker's pissed-offedness, the stunt men looked at each other and shrugged again.

This must be some kind of test, mused the filmnoirmaker. *A test of my ability to negotiate buffoonery. I'll not break. No, these buffoons won't break me . . .*

The filmnoirmaker's expression resembled that which would result from somebody forcing open his mouth and popping a rotten grape into it as he walked back to his high chair. "Mind you," he said to the tall thin man, "I'm not going back to my chair because you told me to. I'm going back there because I'm going to smash it." Sure enough, twenty seconds later the

170

pulverized chair lay on the ground in a pile of woodchips. The filmnoirmaker nodded in satisfaction, assuring his audience that what he had done was an effect of choice, not impulse. He turned to the tall thin man, pointed a finger at him. "In the future I advise you to keep your comments to yourself. From now on, just be quiet and cast your shadow. It's not like there aren't entire goat herds of tall thin men banging on my door all day and night looking for work!" Then, to the cameraman: "And you, I haven't forgotten about you! You get the hell outta my sight! I'm shooting this scene myself. And tomorrow I'm replacing you with somebody that knows a thing or two about capturing an aura!"

The cameraman frowned again. This time the frown was genuine, although it didn't signify confusion. It signified that he was on the brink of tears.

"Are you going to cry?" asked the filmnoirmaker, astounded. A number of grips, also astounded, cupped their mouths and began juggling wide-eyed glances between one another. "Oh my God. Don't cry. I don't like it when people cry; it makes me uncomfortable. I don't want you to stay, but I don't want you to cry either. But I'd rather have you cry than stay. At any rate, let's not make a spectacle out of ourselves. Let's not make a scene. Scenes should only be made when the camera is rolling! You should know that."

The cameraman did know that. But he still made a scene. Wielding the melodramatic, exaggerated gestures of a silent film actor, he staggered all over the set, groping, grave, intent, then sobbing, moaning, gnashing his teeth, clawing invisible enemies, wrenching fistfuls of hair from his head, sucking in his breath so that his round red eyeballs nearly bugged right out of his skull . . .

It was an effective move on the cameraman's part. He had no idea the move was effective. He didn't even know the move was a move. But it worked.

The filmnoirmaker had a soft spot for silent film histrionics. His childhood dream was to become a silentfilmmaker, but this dream was shattered one horrible day when his father not only told him that Santa Claus, the Easter Bunny and the Tooth Fairy didn't exist, but that he wouldn't make any money being a silentfilmmaker because nobody pays to watch silent films anymore. He revealed these atrocities to his son in that order. The nine-year-old filmnoirmaker locked himself in his room for weeks thereafter, and it was during this period of isolation and introspection that he developed his passion for film noir. Nonetheless he maintained his passion for silent films. To this day he watched them voraciously, wishing with increasing emotion that life itself was a silent film. It would be a much more pleasant world, he thought, if people gesticulated at instead of talked to one another. It would also be nice if there was corny background music playing nonstop, all day and all night, from some giant unseen speaker in the sky. A world cast in black and white instead of color appealed to him, too. Colors gave him a migraine if he paid an inordinate amount of attention to them, and in his view things looked much more mysterious and captivating when they were not color-coated. In any case, the filmnoirmaker took a great interest in the cameraman's mute anguish. The cameraman had no idea he was evoking the filmnoirmaker's interest: his manner of conduct was merely a reaction to being fired and suddenly lacking the means to buy groceries and pay rent.

The filmnoirmaker's curious, entertained smirk magnified as the cameraman's performance continued. A loitering extra standing a few feet away from the filmnoirmaker's high chair adorned his face with the exact same curious, entertained smirk, hoping to capture the attention of the filmnoirmaker and gain his approval through this act of mimicry. The act was ignored, and the extra's smirk slumped into a sad, defeated grimace.

"I can't believe this is happening to me!" the cameraman suddenly exclaimed. "Why can't I keep my fat mouth shut!"

"No talking!" hollered the filmnoirmaker. "You're ruining it for me!"

The cameraman didn't hear him. He was too overwhelmed by melancholia. He continued to exclaim things.

The filmnoirmaker warned him once more to shut up. "Stop that," he said, and shifted into director mode. He proceeded to inform him how to not speak. "You must pretend that your tongue doesn't work. You must pretend you never learned to speak as a child. You must pretend a great pigeon has swooped down off of a high ledge and snatched your mouth away with its powerful beak!"

None of his directions worked. The cameraman pursued his vocal antics pellmell.

Shaking his head in disappointment, the filmnoirmaker signaled a stunt man, one that had not pissed him off earlier. The stunt man nodded gravely. He snuck up behind the maniacal cameraman, hammered him on the top of the head with a fist, dragged him over to a nearby manhole, slid the top off of the manhole, emptied him into it, and slid the top back onto the manhole.

And that was that. For now, that was that. No more bull. The play is the thing—time to get back to it . . .

"Right," said the filmnoirmaker, thanking the stunt man with a deep nod. "Places everybody. Places." Nobody had any places to take except the tall thin man, who was required to stand in a certain position underneath the lamppost and perform a certain series of motions. The camera, then, would record these motions through the vehicle of the star of the filmnoirmaker's film, the tall thin man's shadow.

The filmnoirmaker abandoned his high chair. He approached the camera and positioned himself behind it. As he leaned his face into the camera lens, he made sure that his back was sufficiently hunched and the camera was angled just so.

"There's that aura," he said, pausing to admire it, to relish it, to marvel at his ability to capture it with such purity

173

before shouting out "Action!" for the twenty-seventh time . . .

THE BACK OF THE MAN'S HAND

The man was scrutinizing the back of his hand with eyeballs that seemed to want to worm their way out of the sockets that bound them. He was trying to memorize it. The idea was, if somebody asked the man whether or not he was familiar with a place that he happened to be familiar with, he could say, "I know that place like the back of my hand!"

But no, the back of his hand was too complicated. There were too many veins on it, too many tufts of hair, too many oddly shaped freckles, too many oddly positioned pores, and all of these features were too disproportionate to one another to keep in any kind of mnemonic order. There was also a little birth mark that resembled a little Rorschach ink blot near one of his knuckles. One minute it looked like a fly; the next, like Lyndon Johnson; the next, like his ex-wife being sodomized by an egg plant . . . It would take him forever to memorize the back of that hand! He would be better off trying to memorize the back of his ass. There weren't that many veins on his ass, after all, and there were no freckles either, albeit the hair tufts that covered it were so profuse, people might have gotten the impression that the ass was a miniature plot of artichoke plants if they were to catch a glimpse of it. And there was also the problem of not being able to look at and study his ass up close, unless he became a contortionist, and he wasn't a very flexible person. In addition, if he said, "I know that place like the back of my ass!" people would think he didn't know that place from, well, his ass. He didn't like people not thinking he didn't know things from his ass. It was much more socially acceptable to use the back of his hand as the locus of his knowledge of the place in question. On top of that, he didn't even really have to memorize the back of his hand in order to equate his familiarity with said place to the familiarity of said hand. He could just lie about it. Nobody would know if he actually knew his hand down to the last insignificant detail. Even if he never looked at the back of his hand his whole life, nobody would know, because nobody would ask him, because nobody was curious about things like that, because everybody always assumes that everything everybody says is the truth. Yes, it was going to be all right. The back of the man's hand, strange and complex creature that it was, would nevertheless serve him well, given the right circumstances. Now it was only a matter of those right circumstances manifesting themselves . . . which was highly unlikely. Who would have the nerve to approach the man and ask him if he was familiar with a certain place? At heart, the man was, despite a few quirks, kindly and good-intentioned; but he looked like an evil-doer with his beady black eyes and his sharp crowlike face and body, and the way he was always gesticulating and swearing underneath his breath whenever he ventured out into the public sphere weren't the most inviting qualities either. But let's say he looked and acted like a game show host. What were the chances that somebody would ask him if he was familiar with some place? Maybe they would just want to know what time it was, or where the nearest hat store or hot dog stand was. Maybe they would just want to tell him his ears stuck too far out of his head (and they stuck too far out, yes, they stuck too far out). Even if they did ask him if he was familiar with some place, though, what were the chances that he would actually be familiar with some place? What if he was asked where, say, Cleveland, Ohio, was? He didn't know where Cleveland was. He suspected it didn't even exist. At any rate, he couldn't say, "Cleveland? I know that place like the back of my hand!" unless he was telling the truth. It's one thing to lie about the knowledge of the back of your hand, but it's quite another to lie about your knowledge of a certain place that a certain somebody is interested in. Do that, and there may or may not be consequences. He didn't like consequences. Consequences had a tendency to be very unpleasant things, and he preferred to avoid very unpleasant things at all costs. Best forget about expressing himself through the medium of the back of his hand. Best focus his attention on other matters . . . like expressing himself through another medium. If somebody came up to him and asked him how he was doing, for instance, he could say, "I'm as happy as a clam!"

But no, that medium would only produce more lies. He wasn't happy, after all, he was miserable. And clams are just a bunch of brainless softbodies. They might look like they're smiling, they might look like they're happy, but the truth is, they're mollusks, and they don't have any feelings . . .

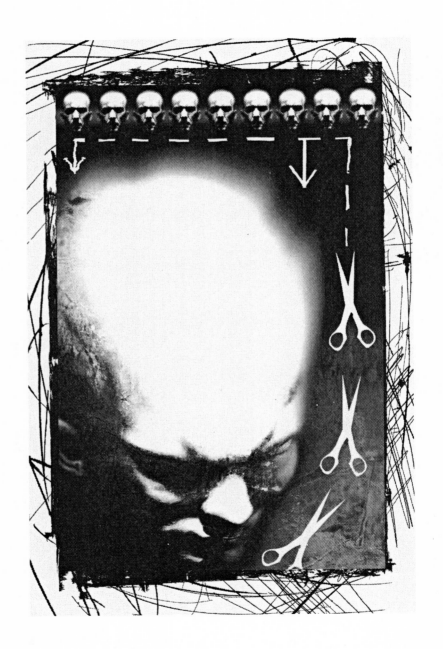

A BARBER'S TALE

One day a barber's customers decided to start shaving their heads on a regular basis so that they could put him out of business. The barber was a good man. He always treated his customers with respect, and while he was cutting their hair, he always made sure that the jokes he told were sufficiently dirty. He couldn't understand why they had forsaken him. Bereft, he closed his barbershop and headed to the nearest whorehouse. To drown his sorrow in pussy.

Hanging over the front door of the whorehouse was a neon sign. The sign said, "No children, pets or barbers."

The barber cursed under his breath. He cursed out loud.

He glanced over his shoulders one of a time, pulled a bowler and a fake handlebar mustache out of his briefcase, and applied them to his head.

"What's your pleasure?" asked a whore as he walked inside. She was wearing just what the barber liked: red high heels and stockings and a Persian garter belt. He also liked her pointy yardsale breasts and the live (albeit drugged up and lethargic) fox that was draped around her shoulders (he had a fetish for sedated, conniving animals). But the whore had a shaved head. All of the whores in the whorehouse, he realized, had shaved heads.

"Why doesn't anybody have any hair?" said the barber in a disguised voice, as if the voice of a barber might be as recognizable as the scream of an anteater.

The whore batted her mascara-soaked eyelashes. She ran her fingers across her skull. "Because hair is for poseurs. Real people don't need hair to establish a sense of their own

179

selfhood. Now give me fifty dollars and eat me." She adopted the posture of a soldier at ease and pointed at her sex with the determinacy of a soldier at attention.

Admiring her sex with tender, understanding eyes, the barber said, "No thank you." Then he tipped his hat and left. He no longer needed the solace, the psychotherapy that came from nailing a good whore. Clearly his customers had begun shaving their heads for personal reasons, for the purpose of asserting themselves as powerful social subjects, not for the purpose of skidrowing him. He returned to his barbershop, determined to maintain a more positive outlook on life, determined to shave his own head. But when he got there he was greeted by his customers. "Surprise!" they yelled . . . and ripped the bald masks off of their heads. Beneath the masks were a bunch of hairdos. Each of the hairdos were full-bodied, lopsided, shaggy— just crying out for a nice trim.

Blank-faced, the barber excused himself and headed to the nearest whorehouse. To drown his sorrow in pussy . . .

AVALANCHE OF MY SELF

The Generator is a machine disguised as a drunk man. He's standing in the limelight. Cross-eyed and pigeon-toed, his smooth pink body is teetering from side to side.

Suddenly The Generator opens his mouth and burps. The burp manifests itself as a blast of booze that shatters The Crystal Movie Screen and leaps out into the cold black vacuum of space. The booze spills everywhere, forming a sea in the nothingness that rears back its whitehead and tidalwaves everything in its path. It is the avalanche of my Self.

When The Generator sobers up, he arbitrarily decides to disguise himself as me. He puts the disguise on over the one he is already wearing.

Like my burp before me, I leap out into space . . . fall . . . scream and curse . . . pass out . . . wake up . . . scream and curse . . . and land on a rickety wooden raft adrift in the winedark sea. In the distance I see a sixteenth century French sailboat on which a band of pirates dressed in drag perform strange rituals. In my hand I discover an over-the-counter antidepressant pill that, when I pop it into my mouth and swallow it, not only evens out my bipolar disposition, it cures my face of ugliness, too. I make a mental note to myself. The note reads: "Obtain patent."

A female movie star is on the raft with me. She's standing on the edge of the raft, shielding her eyes from the green light of the sun as she peers at the island we are approaching. Did she crawl out of the sea? Or has she been here all along? More importantly—is she in character or out of character? I ask her. She rolls her eyes and gives me the pestered look female

181

movie stars give to men that hit on them. "My name is Sandra Bullock," she yaps.

I nod at her. "That's not what I asked you."

"But that's what I'm telling you."

"Fine. You're name's Sandra Bullock. What's your real name?"

The movie star frowns. Her lips pinch together as if a mouse trap has snapped down on them. "My real name? Audrey Hepburn. I'm dead, you see."

"So you're in character?"

"I never said that. All I said is that I'm dead."

"Technically that's the same thing as saying you're in character."

"Whatever. Anyway I'm trying to film a movie here. Please stop talking to me. Go bother somebody else."

"Okay," I say . . . and punch the movie star in the stomach. She doubles over in open-mouthed pain. I squint at the island. The island is using building-sized mechanical insect legs to lift itself out of the water and move closer to us. It's impatient and can't wait for the raft to get there. The sky is a rainbow of unknown colors.

"Nice special effects," I say . . . and shove the movie star into the sea. She struggles to get back on the raft. I don't let her. Every time she grabs onto the raft I kick her in the forehead. She curses me, threatens me, spits at me. She tells me she's sleeping with the director of this film. "You're in deep shit when he finds out what's going on here," she assures me.

I shrug. "I've been in deep shit before. I'm not afraid to be in it again."

A purple wavelet washes over the movie star's head and the sea consumes her.

The island sets itself down in front of me with a groaning noise, like an old man with a bad back sitting down on a toilet. The island is man-made. On it is a graphite mountain and a crescent beach defined by grey grains of salt. On the beach is an unkempt, whitetrashy house that is just a step above a trailer home. The house has been painted the same purple color as the sea by a man wearing a black bowler and an expensive skintight black suit with broad, pointy shoulders. He's standing on the porch of the house. A lazy, unlit cigarette is hanging out of his mouth and circular mirrorshades are covering his eyes. I near the porch. He tosses me a spring line. I tie the raft off.

"There's a storm coming," I say.

The stranger removes the mirrorshades from his eyes and the cigarette from his mouth. He blinks at me. His eyes are the color of radio waves. His face is an airy, obfuscated cross. "No there isn't. You're mistaken. Why should I believe a murderer anyway?"

"I'm not a murderer."

"I just saw you drown that girl back there. You're a murderer."

"No I'm not. For your information that girl was a movie star. It's not called murder when people kill movie stars. It's called mercy. Unfortunately movie stars are nearly impossible to kill." I point over my shoulder. The movie star is climbing out of the water onto the raft. "See what I mean?"

The stranger's face turns the color of white noise. "Oh . . . well, I'm just happy to be part of the film. Even if I don't have any more lines after this next one. Come on inside." He takes off his hat and wedges it under an armpit, then leads us through an upside-down door.

Inside the house is a racquetball court. That is, the inside of the house is a racquetball court. In one corner of the court is a kitchenette complete with refrigerator, dishwasher, microwave, stove and even a chef with a hearty double-chin and a tall white hat.

"My wife used to be a whore before she evolved into a person with values," is the chef's greeting. "I want the whore back."

In the opposite corner of the racquetball court is a young

183

lady. She has flaxen hair tied up into two bushy pigtails. Fake freckles have been painted onto her cheeks with stale ketchup. She's sitting cross-legged. Her eyes are closed and she's whispering to herself in Pentecostal tongues.

"What's her problem?" I ask the stranger, forgetting he has run out of lines. I ask the cook.

"She's a little bitch. That's her problem."

The movie star takes offense at this accusation. She threatens to sic the director on the cook's ass, too.

"Don't worry about her," I say. "Her sense of her Self is problematic to say the least. She thinks she's the world's primary referent. She thinks everybody wants something from her."

"I don't think I'm the world's primary referent."

"But you do think everybody wants something from you. Same damn thing."

"Not it's not. To think you're the world's primary referent is to think that everything in the world happens because of you. I don't think that at all. I just think everybody wants to fuck me."

I raise an eyebrow and glance at the cook. He raises an eyebrow and pulls three small onions out of his pocket. He begins to juggle them.

I look at the movie star and say, "I don't want to fuck you."

"Bull," she responds. "You tried to kill me. Thousands of people have tried to kill me before. The reason? They wanted to get in my pants and I wouldn't let them."

"I never wanted to get in your pants. Did I ever make a move on you? No."

The movie star makes a disgusted face. "You are so full of shit. What was all that conversation about whether I was in or out of character, huh? Just idle chit-chat? I don't think so. I think you're the one with the problematic sense of Self here. I think *you* think *you're* the world's primary referent."

"I don't think I'm the world's primary referent." Pause.

"I know it."

The movie star shakes her head at me. The cook, in contrast, ignores me and begins to dice up vegetables on a cutting board, mumbling about how his life has been socially constructed by a "bitch ethic." I get the feeling he has suddenly become deathly afraid of me. I want to ask him if that's true, but I decide to leave him alone. I point at the movie star and say, "And since I am what I know, everybody wants something from *me*. What do they want? They want me to go on existing. If I don't go on existing, nobody else does. Get it? It doesn't matter if you do or not. I just think it's funny that you think you're hanging out on the same ontological plane as me. You're a moron. If you don't mind I'm going to pretend you're not here now. After all, you don't have any more lines."

With great difficulty the movie star tries to fling a slew of obscenities at me. Nothing comes out of her mouth, of course, so she storms out of the house. I follow her, try to catch her, but she gets away from me. She dives into the sea and swims about a hundred feet before she is gored and tossed around and butchered and finally eaten up by a great white shark. The eyes of the shark are miniature television screens on which the film *Jaws 3-D* is running.

"Nice special effects," I say, admiring the view. Dark storm clouds are visible now and they're moving in fasttime across the iridescent sky. The camera focuses on the clouds for three beats, then cuts to a long down-angle shot on me. I'm standing alone on the porch of the house on the crescent beach. By degrees the camera moves in to an extreme close-up on my face, which is exhibiting the vexed expression of a soap opera star just before the scene cuts to a commercial. But I'm not vexed. I'm trying to remember my next line . . .

IGSNAY BÜRDD THE
ANIMAL TRAINER

1

Igsnay Bürdd was the most distinguished and sought after animal trainer in the Biz. Everybody wanted to work with him, although few did—the man wasn't cheap. On average he charged $13,000,000 per film and anywhere from $1,000,000 to $100,000,000 per animal. During an interview today on The Red Sky At Morning Show, he was asked how he differentiated the cost of animals. "Size? Sort? Smell?" smiled the interviewer, Kalypso Shadrach, delighting in her alliterative manner of inquiry. Igsnay Bürdd stared at her with an alarmingly expressionless face until her delight dissolved. Maintaining his expressionlessness, he told her how much he charged for certain animals without explaining why. "Dogs cost four million. Bats cost twenty million. Whales, uh, seventeen million. Beavers and aardvarks, twenty-eight million. Goats, seven million. Insects . . . what're insects again? Fifty-something million, except for cockroaches, horseflies and praying mantises, all of which I despise and refuse to work with. Snails I charge eighty million. The most expensive animal I ever trained was the Loch Ness monster: a hundred million for that big bastard. Can I go now?"

Kalypso turned to the camera and smiled a fake, uncomfortable smile. "Isn't Mr. Bürdd eccentric, folks? Everybody loves a good eccentric." She turned to Igsnay. "How does it feel to be loved by everybody, Mr. Bürdd?"

The animal trainer stared intently at the morning show host. Her face began to twitch.

187

"Your face is twitching," he said. Kalypso blushed, and her face twitched harder.

Igsnay called her a diseased freak. He stood up and strode off the set, a long blood-red cape whisping and fluttering in his wake . . .

Two days later Igsnay Bürdd was lounging in his June home. He owned a home for each month of the year, and this one was located in Ez, France, an exquisite little town just down the street from Monte Carlo that overlooked the blazing blue waters of the Mediterranean. It was good to be back. It was good to be sunbathing next to one of the pools on one of his rooftops. It was good to be sipping pina colada (with a splash of lime juice) after vodka and tonic (with a splash of orange juice) after martini (with a splash of saki instead of dry vermouth, plus a twist of kiwi). He never worked during the summer months and he planned to do exactly what he was doing right now for the next three months. Sit on his ass all day and get punch drunk under the sun, and in the evening, maybe do the same under the moon and stars, or play some Beethoven or Wagner on his grand piano, or make himself a long, tall sandwich, or stick a needle between his toes and stare at a wall, or invite a few handfuls of call girls and go-go guys over and throw an orgy— anything that didn't require an immoderate use of his intellect, which had been compared to a number of philosophers, physicists and filmmakers by a number of pop as well as scholarly critics. In fact, he preferred not to use his intellect at all during the summer, insofar as it was possible. "The less I think, the less I am," he told his butler Hancock on a daily basis, "and the less I am—the more I have the potential to become."

"Yes, sir," Hancock would always reply, placing Igsnay's drink in the most accessible position imaginable. Usually Hancock would bow, retreat to the nearest bar and begin concocting Igsnay's next drink. Today, however, he bowed and placed a silver platter with a cellphone sitting in the middle of it

188

underneath Igsnay's face.

Igsnay looked at the cellphone as if it was a pile of rotten minnows. His eyes fluttered in consternation and his cheeks sunk into his teeth. "What the hell is this?" he snarled.

"Telephone, sir. I believe it is Mr. MacForager. I assured him that the master would prefer not to communicate with him, or with anybody affiliated with him, or with anybody affiliated with anybody for that matter, until September. But Mr. MacForager was fairly insistent. Would you like to take the call, sir? Or shall I politely tell him to go to hell?"

MacForager was Igsnay's agent. He was an annoying, oily sonuvabitch and Igsnay hated his guts, but he was good at his job. He had given MacForager specific instructions to *not* contact him during the summer, not under any circumstances. But here he was on the phone. Igsany threw his martini in the pool. "That reneging moron!" He grabbed the cellphone and ordered Hancock to retrieve the martini glass and empty out and refill the now sullied pool water. The martini glass quickly sank to the bottom of the pool, so after saying, "Yes, sir," Hancock set the empty platter down on a nearby table, rolled up the sleeves on his tuxedo, took three graceful strides and swan dove into the water. Hancock was almost ninety years old and it took him a few tries to retrieve the glass, which was at the very bottom of the deep end. Twice he almost drowned. But eventually the thin stem of the martini glass found itself pinched between his bony, liver-spotted fingers, and then Hancock found himself vomiting chlorine-soaked water (and Earl Grey tea, and a few halfway chewed-up pieces of cake) all over the poolside.

"Pardon me, sir," burped Hancock.

Igsnay didn't hear him. Too busy bitching out MacForager for calling and interrupting what he referred to as The Festival of Nothingness. He continued to bitch him out for a long time before allowing MacForager to explain why he had called. MacForager didn't mind. He had been bitched out by Igsnay thousands of times and knew exactly how long Igsnay would bitch before expending the vast number of curse words and word combinations he had stored in his lexicon. As Igsnay's demonic-sounding voice surged out of MacForager's cellphone, which lay on the kitchen counter of his June-July house[1] in Wagga Wagga, Australia, MacForager went hunting for Koala bears with a tribe of aborigines that lived in his back yard. He returned an hour or so later with one Koala bear slung over each shoulder. After he skinned the bears, took a shower, and drank half a cup of coffee, he glanced at his watch, counted to ten, and picked up his cellphone.

"I said, do you understand me you slimy turd?"

"Yes, Mr. Bürdd," replied MacForager. "Yes I do."

"Fine fine fine . . . Well? What is it then?"

"Something's come up. Something involving Harry Xi."

"Harry Xi? What does that idiot want?"

"He wants you, Mr. Bürdd. He's been calling me all morning begging me to hook you two up. I kept pretending he was a long distance telephone service salesman and hanging up on him, but he kept calling back. He's very insistent."

Igsnay pounded on his thigh so hard he gave himself a charley horse. "Insistent?" he said, wincing. "Everybody's insistent! Jesus. For once why can't somebody take fuck off for an answer? People just don't give up like they used to. It's very depressing. Depressing, I'm telling you! . . . Look, I don't want my name affiliated with that crummy goat herder's movies. You know that! Hell, even he knows that. I once told him with my own mouth how much I detested his work and how I would rather spend an afternoon yanking the tails off of cows than work with him, let alone talk to him. What makes him think I want to work with or talk to him now? I'd rather choke to death on peanut butter. I'd rather tie a string around one of my

---

[1] Unlike Mr. Bürdd, Mr. MacForager can only afford one home for every two months of the year.

toes and wait for the toe to fall off. I'd rather—"

"He's willing to pay top dollar. I believe the words 'half' and 'billion' were used. In that order."

A pause . . .

Another pause . . .

During the first pause, MacForager had stayed on the phone. During the second pause he lay the phone down on the kitchen counter again and, this time, raided the refrigerator. He couldn't find anything worth eating, so he removed a slip of paper from a drawer and with a fountain pen wrote down his grocery list. When he was finished he folded the piece of paper in half, put it in his back pocket, and picked his cellphone back up.

"Well, Mr. Bürdd? What should I do? Should I call Mr. Xi back and give him good or bad news?"

Igsnay was shaking his head. He had been shaking his head nonstop since the beginning of the first pause. He was shaking it mostly at Harry Xi, but part of him was shaking it at Hancock, who, having suffered minor brain damage while retrieving the martini glass from the pool, was now emptying the water out of the pool with his mouth. Kneeling there on the poolside, he would bob into the pool, gather a mouthful of water, bob up, turn his head to one side and spit the water over his shoulder. Igsnay told him to snap out of it and go to the hospital. Then, to MacForager: "Half a billion dollars? Where does that dumbass get all his money? Not from his movies. That fucking creep. What, does he want me to train an entire goddamn jungle?"

"No. Not at all. Matter of fact, he only wants you to train one animal."

"One animal?" Igsnay's head-shaking accelerated. "Half a billion dollars for one animal? What the hell is it?"

"He wouldn't tell me."

"He wouldn't tell you! Who does he think he is? Who do you think *you* are?"

191

"I don't know, Mr. Bürdd."

An irate Igsnay assaulted MacForager with a fusillade of questions: "Am I awake? Is this happening? Are you my agent or one of my ex-wives in disguise? Eva? Zelda? Am I dreaming? Should I pretend this isn't happening and hope it goes away? Why is my life little more than a repository full of bullshit artists?"

"I don't know, Mr. Bürdd," repeated MacForager. Igsnay replied with another, lengthier fusillade of questions. MacForager repeated himself again. This dialogue persisted for another fifteen minutes, at which point Igsnay, his throat sore and his mouth dry, finally agreed to take on the job.

"Just make sure Xi Switzerlands me my money and builds me a training arena before I so much as step on the same land mass he's stepping on," Igsnay added. As he hung up his cellphone and dialed the hospital,[2] he wondered which land mass he would purchase, and what he would rename it, with his impending paycheck.

2

Harry Xi was a household name in the Biz. He had emerged onto the scene only five years ago with *I, Spacetime Worm*. The film contained a host of well-known movie stars, cutting edge special effects, a descendant of one of the pinheads from Tod Browning's 1932 iconoclastic film *Freaks*, and three long orgies, one in zero gravity. Critics hated it with extreme prejudice,[3] but the general public loved it. In the next five years Xi directed four more movies: *Rictus*, a spoof of the film *Grinning in the*

---

[2] At this point in the narrative, Mr. Hancock is obviously in need of medical attention. He has ripped off his tuxedo and undergarments and is now stomping on them, claiming they are "swamp creatures!" and "hideous insects!" and "little miniature versions of my father!"

[3] When Ronald P. Hogcall reviewed it on The Red Sky At Morning Show, for instance, spittle flew out of his mouth and a pumped up purple vein cut his red-as-a-radish forehead in two.

Dark; *The Fleeting-Improvised Man*, another adaptation of Daniel Paul Schreber's book *Memoirs of My Nervous Illness*; *Egg Raid on Mojo*, a filmic rendering of the Beastie Boys song of the same name; and *Voorhees Unbound*, a remake of *Friday the 13th, Part VI: Jason Lives*. All of these features met with the same critical damnation and mass appeal. Xi's next project was a film called *The Inscribing Socius*, a science fictional documentary about the making of the film *Noname Film*, itself a nonfictional documentary about the fictional life of a homunculus named Noname Cake. Shooting would begin at the end of the year in Helsinki, but Igsnay's services were required at once. The training of whatever it was that needed to be trained would take place in Hong Kong. A long way from Ez, France, but at least Igsnay had a home right across the water in Kowloon—a home that was, of the twelve he owned, one of his top five favorites.

During the flight to Hong Kong, Igsnay drank grass-hoppers from a brandy snifter while watching a video that was a montage of himself in action. He always videotaped himself when he worked and had pieced together this montage with his own eight fingers.[4] The montage's background score was, of course, Beethoven's ninth symphony. During the fourth movement Igsnay experienced something like a multiple orgasm, only without the wet mess. He just kept on shuddering . . .

Harry Xi met him at the airport. Xi was a portly, pug-nosed little roundbody with a jet black pompadour. Physically he was the antithesis of the tall, sinewy, stately-looking Igsnay Bürdd with his aquiline nose and slicked-back platinum hair. Their fashion senses, however, were on the same wavelength: both men wore dark Derridian bodysuits and long flowing capes, as well as an excess of silver jewelry.

---

[4] Two of Mr. Bürdd's fingers were bitten off and eaten by two of his trainees. He lost his right middle finger to a crocodile and his right pinky finger to a baboon. Sometimes it's dispiriting for the animal trainer, being deformed, but at least he's left-handed, and at least the crocodile and the baboon both won Academy awards for their performances.

"Welcome, Mr. Bürdd! Welcome!" exclaimed Xi and reached out his hand for a shake. Igsnay looked at the hand for a few seconds before gripping and pumping the thing. It felt like a fish that's been out of the water for too long. This displeased Igsnay. He strengthened his grip, hoping Xi would do the same. He didn't; he made a confused, constipated face. So Igsnay strengthened his grip until he heard one of Xi's knuckles snap out of place. Xi passed out. Igsnay shrugged, then stepped over his body and into the open door of the director's stretch limo. He watched a Jacques Cousteau rerun and made himself a Gibson with a supersized onion garnish while the limo driver bent over and applied smelling salts to Xi's coin-sized nostrils.

Once Xi had been roused and snapped his knuckle back into place, and smoked two joints, slammed two velvet hammers and swallowed three tablets of Vicodin, Igsnay said, "Take me directly to the subject. I realize I have at least three months to train it, but I'd like to begin right away if it's all the same to you."

"Right away?" replied Xi, a numbed-out flesh heap slouching there on the limo's soft leather upholstery. His tone of voice was halfway between a question and a test to determine whether or not he could mimic Igsnay's tone of voice.

Igsnay detected the dual nature of Xi's tone. He gave him a dirty look. "Yes, *right away*. We can start here and now with you telling me what kind of subject I'll be dealing with. The fact that you've told me nothing about the subject so far is as inconceivable to me as it is obnoxious and distasteful. You've also neglected to tell me what exactly you'd like me to train this thing to do. This isn't a joke of some sort is it? I abhor jokes, even if they aren't being played on me. My response to every joke I have ever seen or heard has always been a flexing jaw."

Xi sat up as straight as he could in his seat. He held the position for three seconds, then slumped back down. Sitting up straight was just too hard for him to do right now. "Well," he hiccuped, "I can tell you this. You'll be training this subject to do three things: smoke a cigarette, walk on its hind legs, and speak the line, 'May I have a glass of ice water please?'"

Igsnay choked on his drink. "That's *it?*" he coughed in astonishment. He couldn't believe it. Now he really thought a joke was being played on him. All he had to do was train one animal to smoke one cigarette, walk on its hind legs and speak one line? He had trained countless animals to smoke cigarettes. His last assignment, in fact, required that he train a giraffe and a Gila monster to chainsmoke. Likewise he had trained any number of animals not only to stand on their hind legs, but to walk and run races and do the tango and the mamba on their hind legs.[5] As for training animals to speak, that was his speciality. His proudest moment as an artist—yes, Igsnay Bürdd considered himself an artist above everything else, even a capitalist—was when he previewed a film directed and produced by his half-brother Tarantula Videoflesh called *Beyond the Quantum.* Starring in this film was a racoon who Igsnay had trained to recite The Declaration of Independence (by rote, mind you) with a flawlessly articulated Scouser accent, this while he stood in front of a podium on his hind legs and chainsmoked cigarettes, no less. To train that racoon had itself only taken Igsnay three and a half weeks, and he had been paid considerably less to do it than Xi had paid him to do this job. There had to be some kind of caveat here. Something smelled fishy. What was Xi hiding up his ass?

Igsnay asked him. "What are you hiding up your ass?"
"Whaddya mean?"
"You know what I mean."
"No I don't."
"Yes you do."
"No I don't. I'm stoned. Kinda drunk, too."
"That doesn't mean you don't know what I mean."

---

[5] One of these animals, a zebra who now goes by the stage name Winym, became a professional ballerina as a direct result of Igsnay's tutelage.

"That's true." Xi reached under his seat and pulled out an eight-ball of cocaine. He laid some of it out onto a mirrored table and began dicing it up with a razor blade.

Igsnay bit his lip and growled, "If you don't tell me what kind of animal I will be training *this instant* I'm going to open the door of this goddamn limousine and hurl my body out onto the goddamn highway. And that'll be the end of your goddamn movie."

Xi shoved a rolled up dollar bill into his nostril, leaned over and snorted a fat, six inch line of coke. He shoved the dollar bill into his other nostril and snorted another line, then took a pinch of coke and flicked it all over his shit-eating grin. Suddenly Xi was having no trouble sitting up straight in his seat. "Relax," he said cool-headedly. "You'll see what's what soon enough. Better if you see in person anyway. Sure, I could tell you now . . . but I think half a billion dollars is enough to buy me a little attitude. Don't you?"

3

During the short yacht ride from Kowloon to Hong Kong, Igsnay reclined on a lounge chair on the roof of the yacht and stared at the sprawl of sharp, mirror-plated skyscrapers that rose out of the island's dark mountains. In his hand was a champagne glass containing a banshee. On his mind was Harry Xi and how much he hated him, and how he would like to tie an anvil to his ankle and throw him in the water. This fantasy number ran and reran across his mind's screen and so did a few others involving the demise of Xi. Soon Igsnay got bored and decided to think about nothing. But he couldn't think about nothing while staring at Hong Kong's skyline; he had seen too many of those Godzilla films and kept visualizing the giant lizard climbing over it. He closed his eyes and tried to think about nothing. No dice. Behind his eyelids was an obsessive urge impelling him to visualize what kind of animal awaited him on the other side of

196

the bay. If he thought about that, he knew he would just get madder and madder, and eventually he might tie an anvil to his own ankle and thrown himself in the water. He opened his eyes and stared up at the sun, hoping the pain would put an end to this little fit of compulsive thinking. It didn't. His eyes had developed an immunity to the sun and he could stare at it for hours on end without injury. That gave him two more things to think about. One: how have my eyes developed this super-human characteristic? Two: how could I have forgotten that my eyes had developed this superhuman characteristic and turned them to the sun in order to negate these thoughts in my head by means of the pain that I hoped the sun would, via my eyes, invoke in me? Which led to a third thing for Igsnay to think about: Isn't pain itself a thought? When one experiences pain, isn't that experience, the mere awareness of that experience, a thought? Of course it was. And this affirmation led Igsnay to believe that, in the conscious order of the world, and arguably in the unconscious order of the world as well, there was no es-caping thought, and to think about escaping thought was only to perpetuate thought's ruthless grip on the human psyche. So he forced himself to stop thinking about thinking about think-ing things and thought, I think I would like a crock of iced saki.

"Hancoooooock!" he cried.

But Hancock wasn't there. He usually went everywhere with Igsnay, but not this time. This time Hancock lay snoring on a hospital bed in Nice with his skull sawed open and a hand-ful of French surgeons sniffing at his brain like so many con-fused puppies, trying to figure out what was wrong with it. Igsnay was on his own.

4

A flourish of synthesizers and electric violins swept over the train-ing arena as the feature presentation began and the animal trainer emerged onto the scene. He grinned a glow-in-the-dark grin despite the bright white rays of the floodlights that were pouring all over him.

Applause, cheers, cries of alleluia, fedoras and bowlers flying up in the air . . .

The training arena was the usual reconstruction of the Roman Colosseum in its pristine form. It was well-known in the Biz that, in order to secure the services of Igsnay Bürdd, a filmmaker was required to build him a Roman Colosseum according to his specifications, unless the filmmaker wanted Igsnay to train in a city or region where he had worked before and where a Colosseum already stood. There were fifty-three Colosseum's with Igsnay's name on them in the world. The one in Hong Kong was the fifty-third. At first the dire congestion of Hong Kong's cityscape made it difficult for Xi to procure a site on which to build. But once he offered the Chinese mafia enough money, a site was immediately made available and a full-fledged Colosseum was erected in a matter of days.

Igsnay's training arenas all resembled the Colosseum as it stood over 2000 years ago in Rome, brandspankingnew-looking, its monumental walls strong, sturdy, whitewashed. Unlike the original, however, Igsnay's training arenas had roofs. Dangling from the underside of these roofs were gigantic spinning crystal disco balls that contained the holographic image of Igsnay Bürdd striking various poses.

The training arena seated 50,000 spectators. Today it was nearly full. The majority of the spectators were Asiatic, but Igsnay noticed the odd ruff of blonde hair and pair of blue eyes.

Approximately half of the audience consisted of camerapeople. Some of the camerapeople crouched behind immense old-fashioned machines on tripods, others positioned hand-held minicams in front of their faces, others simply stared on with eyes that had VR implants in them. Igsnay stopped in mid-strut and posed for them all . . .

He always wore the same ensemble when he trained: a mirrorcape and a mask. The mirrorcape had the texture of warm

198

mercury; when he stood in the middle of the arena, which, unlike the elliptical Roman Colosseum, was perfectly round, the
cape reflected the image of virtually every spectator, even the
nosebleeders. The mask varied depending upon Igsnay's mood.
In good moods he liked to wear a giant yak skull. In bad moods
he preferred the hollowed-out head of a freshly slaughtered pig.
In funny moods[6] he wore the faces of movie stars. These faces
were fantastically lifelike, more real than real, and he never wore
less than three faces at a time.

Right now he was wearing five faces. The hair above
and beyond these faces was his own, but instead of going with
the slicked-back look, Igsnay had had his platinum locks done
up into a little tornado that actually twirled, hissed and even
howled now and then, as if it might be on the verge of collaps-
ing on a small farm community.

The topmost face on Igsnay's face was Vodka Razorlake's,
the highest paid actor in the Biz and one of Igsnay's favorites.
Beneath this face was Fang Fadora's, also a high-paid actor, albeit not a very competent one, but his paycheck per film was
nowhere near the size of Vodka Razorlake's. Nobody's was. Still,
Fang refused to make any film that wasn't a *Zapfentraum*,[7] and
Igsnay couldn't help respecting and admiring that little scruple.

Beneath Fang's face was Landomere Sax's, and beneath
Landomere Sax's face was Q.Q. Tangent's. Both actors demanded
no less than sixty million per film, both exhibited enough ec-
centricities on and off screen to capture Igsnay's esteem and enthusiasm.

Beneath Landomere Sax's face, the fifth and last facemask

---

[6] Mr. Bürdd considers a mood "funny" when he feels neither good nor bad
nor anywhere in between the two—precisely how he feels at this very
moment.

[7] A porno with extreme special effects. To this date, four of the highest
grossing films ever made are *Zapfentraums*, and three of them (*Indigo
Squirrel Bait*, *Cum Get Soma This* and *Whatsa Wigga Gonna Do?*) star
Fang Fadora.

Igsnay Bürdd was wearing, was the face of Igsnay Bürdd. Whenever he trained in this kind of getup, his own face was always
the bottommost face he wore on his face. Beneath this face was
of course his own face, that is, his real, fleshy face. Nobody in
the audience could distinguish between the two. But Igsnay
could tell the difference, and that was enough.

At this point, of course, the spectators could only see
Vodka Razorlake's face. They wouldn't be able to see Fang
Fadora's face until Igsnay ripped Vodka Razorlake's face off, and
they wouldn't be able to see Landomere Sax's face until Fang
Fadora's was ripped off, and so on. But chances were they would
only see Vodka Razorlake and possibly Fang Fadora's face anyway. The only reason Igsnay ever ripped a facemask off was if
some aspect of a training session wasn't going his way. Usually
this never happened. Usually his training sessions went smoothly
and, when he was in a funny mood and wearing X layers of
facemasks, he made it through entire sessions, from start to finish, with the topmost facemask intact. There was the occasional
incorrigible trainee, however, that necessitated he remove a face
or two, although he had never encountered a trainee that had
compelled him to remove all of the faces he had affixed to his
head. In other words, of the five faces that Igsnay was wearing
right now, most were backup materials, plan Bs he would turn
to if things got hairy out there today. Everybody loves a good
mask, after all. And the more masks you wear, and the more
masks you take off, the better. At any rate, considering that he
had yet to be introduced to the thing he was supposed to train,
let alone told what the thing was, the pessimist in him ensured
him that bad weather was on the horizon.

The pessimist was right.

But the optimist in him was strong enough to persuade
him, for the time being at least, that the pessimist was an idiot.
He continued to parade around the training arena, saluting the
spitfire audience with sharp thrusts of his long sinewy arm, un-

til a hole in the arena wall irised open and out popped Harry Xi.

The director staggered over to greet the animal trainer.

Given the vitality of Xi's stagger, Igsnay assumed the man was less than sober and more than tipsy. That he was wearing a milkman uniform reinforced his assumption. Igsnay stood there, shielding the lower half of his face with his mirrorcape like Lugosi's Dracula, and watched this roly-poly little man approach him with growing curiosity. In that bright white outfit he looked like a giant snowball.

The chubby, stubby fingers of one of Xi's hands were wrapped around a milk bottle. As he staggered closer and closer to Igsnay, the babble-buzz of the audience grew louder and louder.

When the two mogul's hands clasped, the babble-buzz detonated like a bomb in the basement of the tower of Babel. A flashbulb tsunami ensued. Xi and Igsnay bore cheesy grins and continued to shake hands in the tsunami's midst.

"Why are you dressed up like a milkman?" Igsnay ventriloquized through his rictus grin. The sight of the director's ludicrous outfit reaffirmed his enmity for him.

Xi shrugged. He looked the animal trainer up and down. "I don't know. Why are you dressed up like Igsnay Bürdd?"

5

It took a while, but eventually the fanfare mellowed out and Xi and Igsnay stopped shaking hands. Xi unscrewed the cap from the milk bottle he had been holding in his free hand and took a big gulp. "Ahhhh." He wiped the frothy mustache off of his upper lip with the back of a chunky forearm. "White Russian. Want a sip?"

"No. No I don't." Invisible rays of hate beamed out of Igsnay's lime green eyes and landed on Xi's bland brown eyes. "Look, you," he said, "knock this shit off. Introduce me to these people and bring out the goddamn subject already. Otherwise I'm getting out of here. I don't care how much you're paying me. *Verstehen Sie?*"

Xi said, "Ja," and nodded reluctantly. Before he turned away, Igsnay grabbed the milk bottle, wrapped his lips around its mouth, threw back his head and chugged the whole thing in five gulps. Then he whipped the bottle at the arena floor with all his might.

The bottle exploded.

Igsnay threw out his arms.

The audience exploded.

A thin black worm squirmed out of Harry Xi's left ear. It traced his jawline down to his mouth, and stiffened. "Good afternoon, Hong Kong!" Xi blurted into the sharp tip of the worm, "and welcome to the house of Igsnay Bürdd!" More hysteria. While Xi waited for the hysteria to settle, he tried not to succumb to the drug overdose that was, he abruptly realized, about to sweep him off of his feet and possibly disable or even kill him. For a moment he actually thought he was dead. Then he realized nobody was clapping or screaming anymore and came to his senses.

The introduction lasted thirty minutes. Every twenty or so seconds there was a minute or so long ovation during which Xi tried, successfully for the most part, to convince himself that he had mentally overpowered drug overdoses before, he would do it again. Igsnay was impatient for him to finish. But his relaxed yet poised posture, coupled with the easy expression on Vodka Razorlake's face, described the epitome of patience. And the spectators knew it. The facial expressions of their reflections on Igsnay's mirrorcape, when they weren't frenzied, clearly stated: "*There* is a patient man."

After the introduction ended, Harry Xi allowed himself to collapse. A vintage Volkswagen beetle overflowing with bodybuilders in G-strings swerved out onto the arena floor and screeched to a halt next to his body. The trunk popped open. Three bronze bodybuilders and a bony rapper with his pants clumped around his ankles popped out of it. Each of the bodybuilders had an electric instrument and played an off-key beat as the rapper rapped about what it was like to be a rapper rapping to an off-key beat being produced by three bodybuilders playing electric instruments. When the rapper ran out of words, the four entertainers picked up Harry Xi. They used bungee cords to strap him to the roof of the Volkswagen, and the bodybuilders began posing. The rapper rapped about what it was like to be a rapper rapping in the presence of three posing bodybuilders. This time the rapper didn't run out of words. Instead the bodybuilders got tired of posing and stopped, so the rapper rapped about what it was like to be a rapper rapping in the presence of three posing bodybuilders who decide to quit posing in an ostensible (and absolutely ineffectual) attempt to foil the rapper's rap. Finally the rapper and the bodybuilders climbed back in the trunk and shut it, and the Volkswagen beetle swerved away to the stormy clamor of applause.

6

The barn-sized disco ball hanging overhead had been spinning since Igsnay entered the training arena, but the intense white beams of the many floodlights that circumscribed the arena's upper walls had overshadowed (or rather, overilluminated) the multicolored flecks and specs that the disco ball had been throwing all over the place. Now the floodlights dimmed. The disco ball could be appreciated for its hypnotic beauty and especially for the image of Igsnay it contained, which burned brighter. To express their appreciation, a number of spectators—all of them Asiatic, noted the animal trainer—leapt to their feet and began disco dancing in place. A select few even ripped off their faces to reveal the dimple-chinned puss of a young, thin John Travolta. The synthesizers and electric violins responded to this spectacle with the backbeat of *Stayin' Alive*.

A hole in the arena wall irised open.

Igsnay Bürdd's trainee crawled out of the hole.

Sound of a needle screech-scratching across a record . . . then crickets chirping . . . then silence. Except for the steady purr of the disco ball and the swoosh of the platinum minitornado that was Igsnay's hair . . . silence.

Igsnay maintained his position on the arena floor's centerpoint. He turned and faced the animal.

From this position he couldn't make out what it was. Too far away, this thing, and the pieces of light cast by the disco ball, while bright, moved too quickly over its body. He was tempted to run closer and get a better look, but that would never happen. He would wait for the animal to come to him. Soon the floodlights would be turned back on anyway, and no matter how close or faraway it was, it would be seen.

It had four legs, no tail and was the size of a man—despite himself, a squinting Igsnay could ascertain that much. It wasn't until an insignificant functionary[8] threw a heavy metal switch and re-illuminated the floodlights that a suddenly bug-eyed Igsnay recognized the animal not only had four legs, no tail and was the size of a man . . . it *was* a man. Granted, the man had a thick bristly mat of unattractive hair all over his back, and he was making his way towards Igsnay on all fours. But he was a man all right. A man!

At a total loss of words and feelings, Igsnay did the only thing he could do: grabbed the flap of skin underneath his ear and, with a quick yank, ripped Vodka Razorlake's face off. The sound of a piece of paper being torn in half thunder-echoed in the training arena.

The audience roared.

---

[8] This functionary possesses the wild white hair of Albert Einstein and is standing behind a hidden green curtain underneath the bleachers of the training arena. He is of no particular importance to the grand scheme of this narrative. Hence the use of the adjective "insignificant" to modify him.

Oblivious to the audience, Igsnay, now veiled by the long flat face of Fang Fadora, which had been surgically tailored to look like an Easter Island face by the actor, forced his bug-eyes to retreat back into his skull by means of a stern frown he used to inspect every inch of the specimen that was approaching him. He kept telling himself that the man was an animal in a bodymask. Every time he told himself this, however, the next thing he told himself was: Bullshit, you *know* that's a man. The only real question in Igsnay's mind was whether or not the man was as dysfunctional as he looked or if he was merely an actor acting dysfunctional. If the latter was true, the actor was talented—assuming he was trying to act like an animal. His gait was the lumbering sway of a dazed alligator. The noises coming out of his mouth were the half-hearted snorts and oinks of a hog. The black carpet on his back belonged to a gorilla, the genitals dangling between his legs belonged to a horse.[9] And the way he paused, glanced sheepishly over his shoulder, elevated his hind leg and urinated and crapped all over the arena floor . . .

At the sight Igsnay ripped off Fang Fadora's face. Now he was sporting the visage of Landomere Sax, star of countless anti-antimainstream films, owner of countless tropical homes, father of countless unknown bastards. He tilted Sax's visage to the sky and tightened up his muscles, reestablishing his strong, tall stance. Psychologically he was Humpty Dumpty teetering back and forth on the narrow crest of a brick wall. But physically, physiognomically, he was all the king's horses and all the king's men. He just hoped that his body didn't all of a sudden decide to get psychosomatic on him.

The crowd roared again when Igsnay defaced himself but the roar was not as deafening and grandiose as before. People knew something was up. As of yet nobody appeared to have

---

[9] Here Mr. Bürdd realizes that these two features, the back hair and the cock and balls, might in fact be props. But if so they're the most lifelike props he has ever seen.

noticed that the animal lumbering towards Igsnay Bürdd was not an animal but either a man acting like an animal or a man that had the unfortunate dispositions of a number of animals, this because everybody had been enraptured by the presence of the notorious animal trainer.

Then a little boy in the first row named Robby Dinkle sprung to his feet. He pointed at Igsnay's trainee and screamed the following scream with the potency and volume that only little boys in the heat of epiphany can shore up: "Hey you guys! It's—Merlin Version!"

In one fluid motion all mouths closed and all eyes turned and fell on Robby Dinkle. The eyes ran the length of his pointing arm, then ran the length of the space that lay between the tip of his index finger and Igsnay's trainee.

A communal gasp erupted like a hurricane taking a breath.

Not a bad eye for a ten-year-old punk whose idea of a fun-filled afternoon was using a magnifying glass to set fire to ants and tree frogs, especially in that Merlin Version had been out of the Biz for most of Robby Dinkle's short but obviously well-informed life. Ten years ago Version had been the hottest commodity on the Bigscreen, hotter than Vodka Razorlake was now, and certainly hotter than the other people whose faces Igsnay was wearing. By the age of twenty-nine Version had starred in over twenty-five films, half of which were the highest grossing films ever produced and consumed. Like most actors, he wasn't particularly talented. But, also like most actors, he had razor-sharp cheekbones, steel grey eyes, a blinding white grin that couldn't be stared at for more than a few seconds at a time without hurting your eyes, and a suit of swarthy skin shrink-wrapped around a lithe rockhard musculature. In addition—and this is what made Merlin Version unique—he knew how to fly. That is, he was born with the power to fly from any given point A to any given point B. He didn't have wings on his back or broad flaps underneath his arms or anything. Rather, he had an exaggerated case of telekinesis that allowed him to elevate and maneuver his body with remarkable precision and coordination. He wasn't the first person to go public with this power. But he was the first to become an actor.

Directors and producers, especially producers, *loved* Merlin Version. The time and money saved on wire specialists, special effects crews and green screen manufacturers was enough to buy them houses with roofs containing no less than two and a half pools. So when Version went bad, there was an understandable slumping of the shoulders amongst certain homeowners. Most films featured protagonists that could fly. With Version out of commission, the obscene price of technology and simulation would have to be paid by everybody.

For his sixth birthday Version's father and mother, descendants of the Whitebait dynasty, presented him with his first syringe of heroine. By the time his twenty-ninth birthday rolled around, he had imbibed in every upper, downer and inbetweener on and off the market, and his body, every inch of it an intimate acquaintance of more than a few souped-up needles, looked something like a sprinkler head. Nothing a little bit of makeup couldn't take care of, though.

One day Version had a meltdown on the set of *Superman vs. The Freud Thing*. He was in the middle of a shoot, weaving through the dark, empty, foreboding buildings of downtown Detroit, when all of a sudden his body decided it was time to acknowledge the lifetime of drug abuse that had been inflicted upon it. He had a seizure in mid air. "Keep rolling!" said Jordache Noble, the director of the film and at the time Version's lover. The camerperson followed the actor as, like a bright red kite that's been struck by lightning, he freefell to the concrete sidewalk with a wince-inducing thud. *Superman vs. The Freud Thing* was never completed. But Noble did make a bundle off of the clip of Version's "fall from grace."

Merlin Version spent the next four years in a coma. He woke up to find that he had virtually no motor skills. His tongue was paralyzed, too. Surprisingly, three years and dozens of rehab facilities later, his motor skills had barely improved and his tongue was still a dead eel in his mouth. He gave up rehab and went to live in the forest that surrounded Walden pond, where he had once frolicked as a carefree child, his parents having owned a mansion in Concord. Unlike Thoreau, however, who had built himself a little house and lived more or less like a man during his illustrious two year stint as a social outcast, Version lived like an animal. He foraged for nuts, roots and berries like an animal, he scurried around nude like an animal, he made animal sounds like an animal, he beat up and killed animals smaller than him like an animal . . . Sometimes Walden's visitors had the good fortune to see him emerge from the woods, crawl over to the edge of the pond full of candy wrappers and cigarette butts, and satiate his thirst. Children tended to yelp and bury their faces between their mother's breasts. But Version liked the attention, even if it did make him realize how much he missed being a movie star, not to mention a walking, talking person who could fly.

Igsnay read the tabloids on a regular basis so he was familiar with the degradation of Merlin Version, which the tabloids had been reconfirming at least once a month since his move to Walden. But did Harry Xi expect him to treat and train Version like an animal?

Apparently so.

Igsnay spent half a minute insisting to himself that Zeno's third paradox was true. "Merlin Version can never cover the difference that separates him from me," the animal trainer whispered through firmly clenched teeth, "because to cover that distance means he has to cover half that distance, and to cover half that distance means he has to cover a quarter of it, and to cover a quarter of it, that means an eighth, and an eighth means a sixteenth, and a sixteenth means a thirty-secondth, and so on, and so on, ad infinitum, we can never meet, the two of us, his approach will last forever and ever and I'll never, *never* have to confront him . . ."

It wasn't long before Igsnay admitted to himself that Zeno's paradox was sound in theory and bullshit in reality. Defeated, he ripped off Landomere Sax's face.

7

Q.Q. Tangent has a cardinal-red monobrow shaped like a handlebar mustache and a supertrim upside-down isosceles triangle of cardinal-red hair arrowheading from his thin lower lip down to the tip of his long strong chin. His anemic skin accentuates the cardinal redness of these two features and makes him look like something of a clown, albeit a demonic-looking clown.[10]

The blustering wind of Igsnay's tornado hairdo grabbed hold of the handlebars of Q.Q. Tangent's monobrow and made them writhe like furious snakes. Good thing the tornado wasn't wired to his mood. It would have ripped the monobrow right off.

Merlin Version paused again to defecate.[11] He was only about ten meters away from Igsnay now and his force-to-be-reckoned-with stench drifted into his nostrils. Version smelled worse than most of the animals he had trained. Not so bad that

---

[10] It should be noted that the syntactical appendage "albeit a demonic-looking clown" is unnessesary. What the appendage presupposes is that, at some point in history, there existed at least one clown who was not demonic-looking. Which is impossible.

[11] As a result of this act of defecation, the following meaningless dialogue took place: "Looks like somebody's heading for a case of diarrhea," remarked a few of the more vigilant and forward-thinking spectators. The more intellectual spectators, in contrast, leaned over to the spouse or child or friend or stranger at their side and said, "The abject's a bitch, ain't it? Just keeps on comin' back." One of these intellectuals went on to quote the psychologist Jacques Lacan in English with the faintest hint of a French accent. "I give myself to you," he bleated, "but this gift of my person is changed inexplicably to a gift of shit!" The intellectual threw back his head and laughed out loud. The people sitting near him ignored the laughter, hoping their inattentiveness would shut him up. It didn't.

Igsnay broke down and flinched—it would take a lot more than that to make him flinch—but he did raise an eyebrow (well, he raised one flailing handlebar), and when Version dropped his leg and started towards him again . . . off came the face of Q.Q. Tangent.

The facemask of Igsnay Bürdd plastered on the face of Igsnay Bürdd exhibited an arrangement of facial features so fine a flurry of flashbulbs attacked it and a few thousand spectators began gnashing their teeth in awe and deference. Of course, none of these people had any idea he was wearing a facemask. They thought it was his real face.

Which was what filled Igsnay such glee . . . or, what was supposed to fill him with glee.

It was a power-knowledge trip for him. He knew the face on his face was not his "real" face, but nobody else knew, and that epistemological lack in the Other should have incited a superiority complex in him, a superiority complex so crystalline and megalomaniacal that no animal could help but submit to the gaze, the words, the gestures of this ineffable figure of domination. But Igsnay wasn't feeling very superior right now. He was feeling fairly inferior. Had he really just shed four facemasks in two minutes? He hadn't even begun training yet! Not formally, in any case—Igsnay's immediate presence itself is a kind of training instrument. That's why Merlin Version, immediately after he had been thrust onto the arena floor, had begun to approach him without being provoked: he couldn't help himself, he saw Igsnay standing there and realized he had no choice but to go to him. Had Version been an animal, Igsnay would have been pleased. But Version was not an animal. He was a goddamn man!

It would have been nice if he could about-face and run away. Such a display of fear, however, would no doubt malign his venerable name, if not destroy it. Not that he was afraid. Igsnay Bürdd, afraid of a trainee? Not in this life. Disgust was what he felt, not fear, and it was disgust that made him want to run away. But if he ran away in disgust it would be perceived as fear. What could he do?

He needed to talk to Xi immediately. Version was only a few meters from his toes now, and if he didn't do something fast . . .

"HALT, FIEND!" he suddenly heard himself shout. It was a mighty, resonant shout. Version obeyed and buried his face in the floor. The act of submission garnered a surge of "Oos" and "Ahs" and another flurry of flashbulbs.

An eerie hush fell over everybody as Igsnay removed his munificent mirrorcape and began swinging it around his body like a shadowboxing matador.

The audience was mesmerized by the mirrorcape. To see it flow through the air like that! They couldn't get enough of it. "Don't stop!" people could be heard yelling in all kinds of languages with the passion of lovers dancing on the threshold of orgasm. But it wasn't until Igsnay heard "Don't stop!" yelled in a Germanic language that he took the mirrorcape by its starch-stiff collar and began spinning it around like a pinwheel, slowly turning his body in place as he did so . . .

A minute and a half later his body accomplished a 360-degree turn. The audience was hypnotized. Males and females, adults and children, camerapeople and photographers, Asiatics and Aryans, drunks and soberites—they stood or sat in their seats dumbly, with lamppost backs and blank faces and drool flowing down their chins. For the moment their psyches belonged to Igsnay Bürdd. It wasn't the first time he had hypnotized an entire audience with his mirrorcape, but it was the first time he did it for something other than self-amusement. Usually he would order everybody to start acting like excited chickens and hogs.[12] But today he had nothing like that in mind.

Igsnay draped his mirrorcape back over himself and re-

---

[12] The sight and sound of 50,000 people clucking and oinking (among other things) at the same time rarely fails to make Mr. Bürdd smirk.

moved a finger-sized microphone from his mirrorsuit. He aladdin-rubbed the microphone three times. It sprouted into a megaphone bigger than his head. He placed the butt of the megaphone on his lips. "YOU DO NOT SEE ME," he intoned. "YOU *CANNOT* SEE ME. FOR YOU ARE ALL NOTHING BUT A LOT OF CACTI GRAZING IN THE DESERT SUN. STAND FIRM, CACTI, FIRM AND TALL, AND BE SILENT AS A MEADOW FULL OF SLEEPING FETUSES. IN DUE COURSE I SHALL CRACK MY WHIP AND YOU WILL AWAKEN, FEELING FINE, IF ONLY A LITTLE CONSTIPATED AND ORNERY." For good measure Igsnay reiterated the directive in six varieties of Chinese as well as in German, Czech-German, Fuehrer-German, French and Russian. When he was finished, he aimed the megaphone at Merlin Version, who, since his face had been flush against the arena floor, hadn't been hypnotized by the mirrorcape. He shook his head at the mop of hair on Version's back—like dreadlocks, that stuff—and said, "STAY WHERE YOU ARE, SCUM!" Version obeyed, although his body was noticeably wracked by a shudder of dread.

Igsnay tilted back his head a little and aimed the megaphone at the disco ball. He took a slow, deep breath. "HARRY XI!" he intoned. "HARRY XI! YOUR PRESENCE IS REQUESTED IN THE TRAINING ARENA—*NOW!!!*"

Igsnay impatiently taptaptaptapped the metal-plated sole of his mirrorboot against the hardwood floor as he waited for Xi to mind him.

8

Harry Xi was being pushed by a reindeer. The reindeer was walking on its hind legs. A cigarette dangled out one side of its long, lean mouth. Igsnay recognized the reindeer as one of the stars of Xi's first film, *I, Spacetime Worm*. Benjamin Slaughterboom had trained him. Slaughterboom was famous, but his annual income was nowhere near the size of Igsnay's, and at any rate Igsnay knew for a fact that he hardly did any of his own training; a large team of ghost animal trainers did most of the work and he took all of the credit. Naturally Igsnay despised him, but not with all of his heart. Slaughterboom had once had the opportunity to disparage him on a talk show and didn't do it. He didn't compliment him, but he didn't disparage him. In the Biz that's the highest praise there is.

Xi lay on a portable hospital bed with annoyingly squeaky wheels. He was hooked up to an IV dripper. His pompadour had been shaved off, and his skin was the color of Elmer's glue. The little man looked like a cancer patient . . . except for his double chin and his yawning mound of belly.

The reindeer rolled the bed next to Merlin Version, then used its front hoof to remove the cigarette from its mouth and flick it on the floor. Smoke coiling out of its moist black nose, it stared at Igsnay as if he was a pair of headlights. Or was it staring at the reflection of its immaculately groomed body on his chest? Igsnay nodded at it. The reindeer huffed. Igsnay huffed back at it. The reindeer scratched itself, turned and goosestepped away, kicking its hooves high in the air.

Dazed, Xi arched up his head and frowned. "Mr. Bürdd? Mr. Bürdd, is that you?"

"You know it is. And you know I know you know it is."

Xi's head fell back into his pillow. "So I do." He stared at the disco ball for a second, turned his head to one side and then the other. "Hey. What's going on here. Why's everybody drooling all over themselves?"

"Forget about them," said Igsnay. "We need to have a talk."

"We do?" Xi pulled an oxygen mask out from beneath his covers. He placed it on his mouth. It gripped the mouth like a hungry squid and began to feed it O2, making a loud, emphatic sucking noise. Xi's eyes rolled back into his head a few times before Igsnay tore the mask off and reprimanded him, then placed the mask on his own mouth[13] and began toking on the O2. He only allowed his eyes to roll back into his head once, however, before removing the mask and tossing it aside.

"Jesus, did that hit the spot," sighed Igsnay, and ripped off his face. He wouldn't be needing it anymore.

The bedridden Harry Xi and the crouching Merlin Version were circled by the embittered Igsnay Bürdd one, two, three times . . . The animal trainer came to an abrupt halt. He locked his knees, folded his arms across his chest. His chin rose like a flag.

"How dare you, you . . . you director!" he seethed. "I ought to bring you up on charges. I ought to have you thrown in jail. You, and that crummy MacForager, who as of this moment is officially fired!" He unfolded his arms and threw an index finger above his head when he said "fired!"

Xi pushed himself up onto his elbows. "What's the problem?" he asked, trying to keep his head straight. The head kept flopping over onto his shoulders.

Igsnay folded his arms again. "I'm not going to play this assheaded game with you."

"I understand." Xi's head flopped back between his shoulder blades. He gave up trying to keep it straight and left it there.

Igsnay bit into his lower lip. "Okay, okay . . . I'm going to assume that what's happening here isn't some kind of degenerate prank. That is to say, I'm going to assume that the reason I'm here isn't to play your joke's butt. Perhaps I'm assuming too much. But where would I be without my assumptions? Where would we all be. If we took everything at face value, *ennui* would quickly overpower and destroy us, wouldn't it."

"Uh-huh."

---

[13] Technically this mouth is not Mr. Bürdd's mouth. It is the mouth of the facemask of his face on his face.

"That was a rhetorical statement. In any case—I am an animal trainer. That means I train animals. That also means I *do not* train humans. I don't care how much of an animal a human might appear to be. Give me any old beast of the sea or land or air and I'll train it through and through. I'll train it to smoke, to play cards, to juggle, to drive a stick shift. I'll train it to dress itself up in women's underwear. I'll train it to be a politician, a lawyer, a haberdasher, whatever you want. But give me a human . . . I can't train humans. Who knows what makes those goddamn things tick! What prompts an animal to perform this or that task is fairly simple to decipher. What prompts a human to perform this or that task, on the other hand, is anybody's guess. Unless you're a halfway decent acting coach, of course. Merlin is a pathetic, stinking, creeping excuse for a human being, but he's still a human being, and what he needs is an acting coach—*not* an animal trainer."

"I've tried acting coaches," said Xi. "I've tried them all. And do you know what they all did? Failed."

"What about Olaf Action? What about Frank 'The Frank' Frank? What about Pickering Dymentcha? Did you try them?"

"Tried 'em all."

"And?"

"Nothing." Xi's elbows gave and he collapsed onto his back. Merlin Version, still face down and cowering, tilted up his head to see what was going on. He immediately wished he wouldn't have. Igsnay snapped his teeth at him and hollered, "DOWN, WRETCH, OR I SHALL BE INCLINED TO BEAT YOU TO DEATH!!!"

"Mr. Bürdd," Xi broke in, "I must be honest with you. I believe I'm going to die. My lungs have collapsed, my liver's collapsed, my pancreas has collapsed—everything inside of me's collapsed! I need a surgeon to come out here and perform surgery on me without delay. Is there a surgeon in the house!"

215

"Nobody can hear you."

"I need a surgeon!"

"You're really going to need a surgeon if you don't cut out this dumbass routine and start talking straight with me." Igsnay took hold of his chin. He stroked its sharp underside with his thumbnail. "Are you sure this isn't a joke?"

"I thought you already assumed it wasn't."

"I did. But what's that got to do with anything? Assumptions aspire for truth, they're not *the* truth. I'm searching for the truth."

"Happy trails."

Igsnay lips compressed into a thin white line. "You're a silly man, Harry Xi," he said. "You're a silly, silly man. This conspiracy of yours, this attempt to get me to train degradation's posterboy to smoke a cigarette, walk on his hind legs and say, 'May I have a glass of ice water please?' is altogether futile. I wouldn't know the first thing about teaching this idiot how to smoke."

"But—"

"But my ass! I know what you're trying to do. The goat herd would pay arms, legs and genitals to see Version back up there on the Bigscreen, even in a bit role. You'd have the 500 million you prepaid me back in a matter of weekends. Don't get me wrong. I can't stand you, and I can't stand the films you make. Your cinematographic eye is particularly disgusting. But the entrepreneur in me can respect your intentions here. *The Inscribing Socius* would in all likelihood turn into a classic overnight if Version appeared in it acting like a human instead of the dirtyrotten mongrel he clearly is." Igsnay stomped over to Merlin Version and kicked him in the ribs. The actor-cum-human-animal yelped in pain and urinated on his inner thigh, but he kept his face against the floor, deathly afraid of looking up into the eyes of his master and sovereign.

Xi said, "I need more nourishment." He climbed out of

216

bed, retrieved the oxygen mask and attached it to his face again. The milkman outfit he was wearing earlier had been replaced by a hospital gown that exposed his backside, which, to say the least, was not model material. Igsnay angrily spit over his shoulder when he saw it, then snatched the mask off Xi's face again and took another hit himself. Xi flung open the curtain hanging beneath his bed. Inside was a minibar. Igsnay told Xi he wasn't in the mood for a drink. "I'm not in the mood for any of this nonsense," he insisted. Xi made him a Harvey Wallbanger anyway. He didn't refuse it. He didn't refuse any of the drinks Xi made for him. Nor did Version. Granted, when Xi first slid that dog bowl of Tanqueray underneath Version's face, he shied away from it. But shortly thereafter he began to sniff and lick it, and finally he was lapping at it, full speed ahead.

Had the spectators been cognizant, they would have sounded off a lunatic cheer.

Igsnay, like Version, drank with enthusiasm. He didn't lap at his drinks, but the way he sipped them was highly frenetic. Xi was drinking Southern Comfort straight up and his manner of sipping was also frenetic, but he took loud sloppy sips with his lips whereas Igsnay's lips behaved with more finesse and sophistication. In the end, however, it didn't matter how anybody's lips were behaving: all three celebrities were drunk. Xi took the opportunity to try and convince Igsnay to train Version, who had passed out in a fetal position and was snoring like a warthog with bronchitis. Curiously enough, Xi was successful and Igsnay was eventually convinced, but he didn't allow himself to go down without yet again telling the director, in great detail and with a fair amount of wit, how disagreeable he was, as a person and as an artist and capitalist, and how much he loathed him. Also, he had two new conditions. The first was that, if he was going to train a human, it would have to be done in private; not a pair of eyes or a camera of any kind could be present. The second condition concerned the price for his pri-

217

vacy, which Xi was required to pay him on top of what he had already paid him. Xi protested and they began haggling over this price, but their words were slurring so much they couldn't understand each other, so they used a kind of primitive sign language to come to an agreement. Then they lifted Merlin Version onto the hospital bed and rolled him out of the training arena.

Before Igsnay Bürdd disappeared from sight, he reached into his mirrorsuit and pulled a long black whip out of it. He raised the whip over his head and cast it out in front of him . . .

The spectators yawned, blinked, wiped their chins, farted. Some of the them coughed and hacked up phlegm. Others grumbled for their breakfasts.

9

The room is a mirror. Its floor, walls and ceiling are all mirrors. There's also a little mirrored disco ball hanging from the ceiling. It spins at a rate of 35 kph, this disco ball, and contains the image of a mirror-coated Igsnay Bürdd wearing the hollowed-out head of a freshly slaughtered pig. There are no cameras, but there is a clap track wired to the animal trainer's mouth. All he has to do is click his tongue and the room, which is situated in the basement of his "Prufrock"[14] home, floods with applause.

It takes him a long time to train Merlin Version, almost five months of working, on average, six days a week, fourteen hours a day. At least once a week Igsnay gives up on Version. He will beat him in frustration and storm out of the mirror room, threatening to leave him there forever, by himself, at the mercy of his many reflections, which bear down on him infinitely, from every direction. "Or maybe I'll come back with a

---

[14] This is a special, secret home-without-a-month that lay two miles beneath the city of Prague. That Mr. Bürdd uses the word "Prufock" to refer to it has no relevence to T.S. Eliot's poem "The Love Song of J. Alfred Prufrock." Prufrock is simply the first name of the first transvestite Mr. Bürdd made love to.

pair of scissors and castrate you!" he often adds. Version cringes and trembles, too terrified to lick his wounds, but Igsnay always comes back, and never with a pair of scissors.

The day on which Version first manages to stand on his own two feet, light a cigarette and, while he is smoking the cigarette, say, "May I have a glass of ice water please," is perhaps the happiest day of Igsnay's life. He falls to his knees and clicks his tongue over and over until it is too sore to click anymore. And then he stands up and orders Version to "repeat the feat" 100 times in a row without the slightest error.

Two weeks later, Merlin Version is primed and ready to face the music of a rolling camera.

10

Igsnay Bürdd didn't train another subject for three full years after the "Version Occasion."[15] During those years he lived in his homes, lazed beside his pools and drank drinks that were made and served to him by the eternally faithful Hancock. Luckily his brain damage had not rendered him incapacitated. He couldn't really talk, and the left side of his face had no feeling in it and hung off of his skull like wet mud. But his arms and legs and mind worked fine.

The Inscribing Socius was a colossal hit. The film raked in billions of dollars at the box office. Harry Xi died of an aneurism shortly before its release, but he had the opportunity to preview it with an audience that gave him a standing ovation. And that year at the Academy Awards he posthumously received an award for best picture. The acceptance letter was written one clairvoyant night while he was taking a break from editing the final cut of *The Inscribing Socius*, the success and genius of which he was absolutely convinced, and it was presented at the Academy Awards by none other than Merlin Version, who, by

---

[15] A name devised by the Kalypso Shadrachs of the world to signify the incident.

then, had not only regained his ability to speak, he had regained his telekinetic powers and was a full-fledged drug addict again, too. The acceptance letter read:

> *Thank you very much for this great honor. Thank you God Almighty most of all. [Pause here and admire the ceiling.] I will always cherish this moment. Wow. Let me tell you, making a film, any film, is a difficult thing. How many sleepless nights I've spent pacing the hallways of my houses! But in the end it's well worth the effort—especially when the product of my sleeplessness is a film like* The Inscribing Socius. *Thank you, my friends. Thank you for your support, your praise, and, most importantly, your love. God be with and protect you all.*

When Merlin Version finished reading the letter, he said a prayer in Harry Xi's name and then flew off stage. The movie stars, directors, producers and other Biz affiliates that comprised the audience pointed at him as he passed overhead and whispered secrets in each other's ears.

ABOUT THE AUTHOR

D. Harlan Wilson is the author of the books *The Kafka Effekt* and *4 Ellipses*. Nearly 100 of his stories have been published in anthologies and magazines throughout the world. He lives in East Lansing, Michigan, where he teaches literature at Michigan State University.

ABOUT THE COVER ARTIST

Simon Duric lives in Nottingham, England. His artwork has appeared in a variety of magazines, including *The Third Alternative*, *Kimota*, *Roadworks*, *Hidden Corners* and *Redsine*. For more information on Duric and his work, refer to his official website at www.redsine.com/duric8/man.html

D. HARLAN WILSON'S
ONLINE CHAPBOOKS

4 Ellipses
available at www.bizarrEbooks.com

Enter a mansion in which every room is a foyer . . . Watch a young girl get strapped to the front of a monster truck and senselessly rammed into a brick wall . . . Experience the pain of a man who is attacked and persecuted by a malicious denim outfit . . . Make a face at the spectacle of a real-TV studio being overtaken by a horde of angry, murderous fictional characters . . . 4 Ellipses is a short collection of offbeat fiction that's sure to make at least one of your lip corners twitch on a regular basis. Rearrange the nub of your tie and nosedive into this irreal vortex.

Irrealities
available at www.pulpbits.com

Stories from 4 Ellipses, The Kafka Effekt, and Stranger on the Loose. The perfect D. Harlan Wilson sampler.

ERASERHEAD

PRESS

books of the surreal and bizarrre

www.eraserheadpress.com

Eraserhead Press is a collective publishing organization with a mission to create a new genre for "bizarre" literature. A genre that brings together the neo-surrealists, the post-postmodernists, the literary punks, the magical realists, the masters of grotesque fantasy, the bastards of offbeat horror, and all other rebels of the written word. Together, these authors fight to tear down convention, explode from the underground, and create a new era in alternative literature. All the elements that make independent films "cult" films are displayed twice as wildly in this fiction series. Eraserhead Press strives to be your major source for bizarre cult fiction.

HIDEOUS BEAUTIES

stories by Lance Olsen (images by Andi Olsen)
208 pages / $13.95 / ISBN 0-9729598-0-7

A collection of a dozen outrageous fictions, each based on a photograph, painting, sketch, collage, or assemblage by an equally outrageous artist (Hans Bellmer, Ed Kienholz, Joel-Peter Witkin, et alia), that explores the amphibious edge where language and image splice.

RAZOR WIRE PUBIC HAIR

an illustrated novel by Carlton Mellick III
176 pages / $10.95 / ISBN 0-9729598-1-5

A psycho-sexual fairy tale about a multi-gendered scewing toy purchased by a razor dominatrix and brought into her nightmarish lifestyle of surreal sex and mutilation.

MY DREAM DATE (RAPE) WITH KATHY ACKER

stories by Michael Hemmingson
176 pages / $10.95 / ISBN 0-9713572-9-3

Sex, drugs, Raymond Carver's ghost, Barbie dolls loving GI Joe dolls, the pure vaginas of French girls, the un-pure vagina of Kathy Acker, crack whores, nutty neighbors, scatological girlfriends, iniquitous fiends, Jesus freaks, pornographers, pushers, movers, shakers and winning lottery tickets.

SKIN PRAYER

fragments of abject memory by Doug Rice
232 pages / $14.95 / ISBN 0-9713572-7-7

"A series of mysterious and deeply evocative meditations: erotic, surreal, tender, grave, and profane."

- Carole Maso

STRANGEWOOD TALES

an anthology edited by Jack Fisher

176 pages / $10.95 / ISBN 0-9713572-0-X

Bizarre horror by Kurt Newton, Jeffrey Thomas, Richard Gavin, Charles Anders, Brady Allen, DF Lewis, Carlton Mellick III, Scott Thomas, GW Thomas, Carol MacAllister, Jeff Vandermeer, Monica J. O'Rourke. Gene Michael Higney, Scott Milder, Andy Miller, Forrest Aguirre, Jack Fisher, Eleanor Terese Lohse, Shane Ryan Staley, and Mark McLaughlin.

SHALL WE GATHER AT THE GARDEN?

a novel full of novels by Kevin L. Donihe

248 pages / $14.95 / ISBN 0-9713572-5-0

Have you ever felt dislocated within the world? Did you ever have "one of those days" when everything unravelling before you seems truly bizarre and you begin to question your own sanity? Meet Mark Anders, the #1 bestselling romance writer in America.

SATAN BURGER

an anti-novel by Carlton Mellick III

236 pages / $14.95 / ISBN 0-9713572-3-4

Six squatter punks get jobs at a fast food chain owned by the devil in an apocalyptic godless world.

"It's odd... very crass... vulgar... funny... and just all around easy and delightful to read." - *Nacho Cheese and Anarchy*

ELECTRIC JESUS CORPSE

an anti-novel in 12 parts by Carlton Mellick III

384 pages / $17.95 / ISBN 0-9713572-8-5

The story of the messiah, Jesus Christ, thrown into a surreal and zombie-plagued version of modern day Earth.

"This is one of the most odd, strange, weird books I have ever read, and enjoyed every minute of it." - *Top Site*

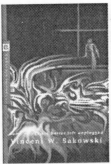

SOME THINGS ARE BETTER LEFT UNPLUGGED

a novel by Vincent Sakowski
156 pages / $9.95 / ISBN 0-9713572-2-6

A postmodern fantasy that satirizes many of our everyday obsessions. "Full of images and situations that stretch the imagination." - *PEEP SHOW*

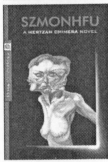

SZMONHFU

a novel by Hertzan Chimera
284 pages / $16.95 / ISBN 0-9713572-4-2

The story of Jane, a delicate young redhead on a blistering erotic adventure of discovery. "Sick! Sick! Sick! SZMONHFU is truly one of the most disgusting books I've ever had the misfortune of reading." - AAS REVIEWS

THE KAFKA EFFEKT

stories by D. Harlan Wilson
216 pages / $13.95 / ISBN 0-9713572-1-8

A manic depressive has a baby's bottom grafted onto his face; a hermaphrodite impregnates itself and gives birth to twins; a gaggle of professors find themselves trapped in a port-a-john and struggle to liberate their minds from the prison of reason—these are just a few of the precarious situations that the characters herein are forced to confront.

SKIMMING THE GUMBO NUCLEAR

a novel by M. F. Korn
292 pages / $16.95 / ISBN 0-9713572-6-9

The colorful denizens of the southern delta nether regions of the state of Louisiana are grappling for their very lives as pollution and nuclear waste transform this sportsman's paradise into a grand epic wasteland of surreal pandemic plague.

COMING SOON
FROM ERASERHEAD PRESS
watch www.eraserheadpress.com for new releases

ALL THE MUTANT TRASH IN ALL THE GALAXIES
by MF Korn

YELLOW #10
by Trevor Dodge

MY FLING WITH BETTY PAGE
by Michael Hemmingson

ANGEL SCENE
by Richard Kadrey

TEETH AND TONGUE LANDSCAPE
by Carlton Mellick III

THE DECADENT RETURN OF THE HI-FI QUEEN
AND HER EMBRYONIC REPTILE INFECTION
by Simon Logan

THE STEEL BREAKFAST ERA
by Carlton Mellick III

Printed in the United States
1295600001B/406-411